Disha Books
Abhimanyu

K.P. Balaji was tragically killed in Bombay in 1976. He left behind him forty and fifty years of a most extraordinary life.

In Kerala, where he was born, Balaji learnt Kathakali under Balakrishnan, a disciple of one of the greatest of teachers, Guru Chandu Panikker, and gave his first public performance at about the age of ten. Though he could not in later years continue to be a practising exponent of Kathakali, he characteristically enriched his scholarly appreciation of the art. He was a respected authority on it long after his career swamped his creative energies.

Balaji first joined *Marg* under Mulk Raj Anand. He moved subsequently to the *Times of India* and in 1954 to the *The Illustrated Weekly of India* as a sub-editor under C.R. Mandy. He published several short stories at this time, and articles under the feature-head 'They Call it a Day'. Balaji then made an unexpected lateral move in 1961 when he joined a reputed advertising company as copywriter. Seven years later he became creative group head of its Madras unit, and ten years later one of its directors. As a 'creative', Balaji's interests were wide. He was a superb photographer and artist. One of his commercial films for a match company was described as a 'tour de force' and won both the CAG and the Advertising Club of Bombay's awards as the best commercial film in 1977.

Abhimanyu, written over several months, is his first full-length novel.

Abhimanyu

K. P. Balaji

Disha Books

DISHA BOOKS
an imprint of
ORIENT LONGMAN LIMITED
Registered Office
3-6-272 Himayatnagar, Hyderabad 500 029
Other Offices
Kamani Marg, Ballard Estate, Bombay 400 038
17 Chittaranjan Avenue, Calcutta 700 072
160 Anna Salai, Madras 600 002
1/24 Asaf Ali Road, New Delhi, 110 002
80/1 Mahatma Gandhi Road, Bangalore 560 001
3-6-272 Himayatnagar, Hyderabad 500 029
Birla Mandir Road, Patna 800 004
S.C. Goswami Road, Panbazar, Guwahati 781 001
'Patiala House', 16-A Ashok Marg, Lucknow 226 001

Published in Sangam Books 1978
Published in Disha Books 1992

© Orient Longman Limited, 1978
ISBN 0 86311 266 8

Printed in India at
Swapna Printing Works Private Limited
52, Raja Rammohan Roy Sarani
Calcutta 700 009

Published by
Orient Longman Limited
17 Chittaranjan Avenue
Calcutta 700 072

Prologue

ABHIMANYU was the son of Arjuna, the third of the Pandava brothers in the epic *Mahabharata*. According to the story, he was a noble prince, the nephew of Krishna, and the most likely heir to the Pandava throne.

It is said that when he was still in his mother's womb, Krishna visited his sister and with divine prescience, forecast the course of events which would lead to the battle of Kurukshetra. He spoke of the fratricidal war between the Pandavas and the Kauravas, and how the latter would make their battle array: the 'padmavyuha' in the shape of a many-petalled lotus. He explained the tactics of breaking into this circle of mighty warriors—but then, inexplicably, finding his sister asleep and noticing that the child in the womb was 'listening', fell silent.

Abhimanyu was sent into battle by Yudhishthira, the eldest of the Pandavas. Relying on his foetal memory, the prince fought his way in, wreaking havoc in the Kaurava ranks. And then he was trapped and killed.

The story goes on to relate that, fearing Arjuna's terrible vengeance, each one of the great warriors on the Kaurava side shot an arrow into the body of the young prince, so that not one but all of them would have to share the guilt for his death.

Abhimanyu

1

Govindan Nair freewheeled his bicycle over the last twenty-odd yards to the Taj Cycle Hire and Repair Mart, listening with a certain impersonal pride to the wheezy hum that the sprocket wheel made against the gentle restraint of the chain. He marvelled at the machine's smoothness, as he bent forward now like an eager jockey, lending it his weight and will, urging his mount to draw upon a final, hidden source of power that Nair, if no one else, believed it possessed.

He even nearly made it all the way to the shop this day, almost realizing a private if somewhat boyish ambition to establish beyond doubt the incredibly good mechanical condition of the ageing bicycle he rode. But at the last moment a pedestrian panicked in his path; Nair clutched the brakes wildly, swerved this side and that in an effort to retain his balance, and then, giving up suddenly, swung his fat leg over the bar and landed solidly and inelegantly on the dusty road.

He felt angry and thwarted. His calf muscles ached and a spot right below his left breast hurt horribly where the curving end of the handle-bar had jabbed him. His hands shook with the nervousness of near-disaster as he turned round and glared at the man who had crossed his path.

The man himself was rubbing his side vigorously and looking at Nair belligerently. 'Can't you see where you are going?' he snapped. 'This is a municipal road, mister. Why don't you go and join a circus?'

Nair was ready with a sharp retort, but then he changed his mind. Ill-mannered ruffians! The roads were full of them these days. Could even be a Communist, for all one knew. No point in getting into an argument with that lot! Next thing you knew, it would become a tussle between the haves and the have-nots and a crowd would gather.

Nair held the other man's gaze for a moment, and then turned away in disgust. He straightened the bicycle and pushed it gloomily over the rest of the distance to the cluttered portals of the cycle shop.

'She almost made it,' he said aloud, distractedly, feeling desolate and a bit foolish now, as he stood under the signboard which proclaimed in a fading script that satisfaction to one and all was the avowed motto of the establishment, of which Syed Mohammed Ali was the sole proprietor. 'All the way from that turning,' Nair continued doggedly, half-addressing Ali, a dark form shiny with sweat and oil, like some primitive idol nearly lost in the dusky interior of the shop. 'On her own, mind you ... without even the gentlest push on the pedals—but that idiot . . .'

Ali emerged, his hands dripping with kerosene, his bare chest flecked with smears of grease, and cast his glance up and down the road. He pursed his lips and squinted at the light outside—the final golden benevolence of a dying day—and then turned to Nair with a friendly nod. 'How quickly it gets dark these days!' he remarked rather irrelevantly.

Nair felt irritated and quickly handed over the bicycle to Ali. 'People don't look where they are going,' he said. 'Just carelessness. It has nothing to do with the darkness . . .'

'Who?' Ali asked, puzzled.

'Oh, nothing . . . Well, some fellow on the road.' Nair

patted the bicycle impatiently.

'Ah, yes, the cycle,' Ali said as he wheeled it round to a side and put it on its stand. He looked at it speculatively for a moment. 'It is a good one,' he said, nodding his head slowly, assessing its worth without sentiment, as though it was Nair and not he himself who owned it. 'Nothing much to look at, but the best in the shop.' He turned round, studied Nair's face, still puzzled by the expression of dismay on it. 'It is high time you bought it for yourself,' he continued placatingly. 'How often have I told you that! There are many more years of good service in it.'

Nair grunted noncommittally and rubbed the sore spot on his chest.

To be quite frank, he thought, he did not need any recommendation. It was just that he wasn't a millionaire. He was only a clerk in a Government office. Well, not a clerk but a supervisor, but that too was not anything to shout about. Not where money was concerned, anyway. True, in all fairness to Ali, the price he quoted was not high and he had offered to take the money in instalments. But what was the use? A good bicycle, even an old one, cost nearly a couple of hundred rupees these days. And surely, a householder like himself had more urgent things to think of than these luxuries!

For the past ten years or so, Nair reflected, he had hired it from the shop every working day at a flat rate of ten rupees a month, taking it in the morning on his way to office and returning it in the evening, surrendering with it any delusion of ownership that he might have entertained during the few hours of possession. How much did it all come to? One hundred and twenty rupees a year. One thousand and two hundred rupees in ten years! He was flabbergasted at the enormity of the sum and quickly checked once again in his mind whether his calculation was correct. For a fleeting second, he wished he had walked every day to office and saved all that money. Or taken a bus, even though cycling had become a habit with Nair long before the town had begun to boast of even a rudimentary bus system. How disturbing it was to think that for want of a little will power he had squandered away a small fortune! And to what purpose? A little convenience, yes, and, let him admit it, the dubious dignity of arriving in front of his juniors in office on a bicycle!

Nair sighed. Such thinking was of no use. It got you nowhere. What was gone was gone. Hadn't he often felt cheated and left out, not by Ali or anybody else, but by life itself? He had been like a man on a bridge, watching the river flow on, without the power, or the will, to stop it. He had seen bigger things than bicycles get away from his grasp. What was the point of complaining now?

'You could pay in instalments,' Ali persisted.

'What?... Oh, yes. Well, I must do something about it, Ali. But not now...'

Ali was a good fellow and he meant well, Nair thought. He felt a little ashamed of his irritation with Ali a while ago. Indeed the cycle was as good as his own. After the first few months, Ali had never let anyone else use it, not even on a holiday, and by and large, not even in cases of emergency. The only thing that had discouraged Nair from taking it home was the fear of theft. There was no point in inviting trouble. He preferred rather to walk up and down the short distance between the shop and his home every day.

Ali went inside the shop and Nair followed him. 'These are hard days, Ali,' he said. 'You know that very well. Difficult to make ends meet... Prices going up all the time. And a son in college...' Nair paused, suddenly self-conscious at the mention of a son in college, unable to suppress a faint glow of pride.

'How is he doing?' Ali asked politely, turning to a dismantled machine on the floor and squatting by its side. He decided then that the light was too dim and said over his shoulder: 'Could you put on that switch there... right behind you ?'

Nair groped on the wall absent-mindedly, found the switch and suddenly the shop took on a new dimension in the glow of a bare electric bulb hanging down from the ceiling at the end of a short length of flex. He examined his fingers to see whether they had picked up any grease or dirt from the switch, looked around for a piece of clean rag, and finding none, rubbed them gingerly on the wall.

The place was congested with bicycles, except for the circle under the light where Ali worked. Shoved away in a corner was a tangled heap of twisted frames and mudguards lying in rusty neglect, while the floor was littered with tools and odd nuts and bolts and dismembered pieces in varying stages of repair. From the ceiling, near a wall, a frame hung on old chains, its surface glowing with fresh paint. The bicycles in good shape—four or five of them which Ali apparently gave out on hire—were lined up at the entrance. Nair glanced around and located a stool, and after making sure that it was free from grease and dust, sat on it.

In the light, Nair looked stocky and well-preserved, with a cherubic face adorned by an old-fashioned toothbrush moustache. He was dressed in a style which was fast becoming obsolete in the town—a coat over a shirt and dhoti—a legacy from British days when a coat was a symbol of dignity for any Government servant above the clerical level. His long strands of thinning hair, plastered down and carefully manoeuvred into place in the morning, now showed a natural tendency to curl in defiance of his attempts to hide a widening bald patch on the crown. He was proud of his teeth, so white and well-formed as to be mistaken for dentures in a man in his early fifties. Nair's coat was of cheap cotton, frayed at the collar and cuffs, but it was clean and starched and his dhoti was spotlessly white.

'How is he doing, your son?' Ali prompted. He knew that Nair liked to talk about his son. Parental pride was something that he could understand. He himself was a father—though only of three girls, a lesser privilege but a source of pride for him all the same.

'Oh, he is doing all right,' Nair said, looking round on a chance that there might be others eager to hear what a father had to say about a son in college. He met no inquisitive glance, and with a vague sense of disappointment, he turned back to Ali. 'He is a bright boy, that one, though it is I myself who say it. Won a prize last time, in English too, at that.' He paused and scratched the back of his neck thoughtfully. 'But, nowadays, I am not so sure, with all this trouble in the air . . .'

'The young ones enjoy trouble,' Ali chuckled. 'That's why they go round looking for it. But your son . . . he is a quiet one . . .'

'Children need excitement, you see,' Nair went on, a little defensively, not quite liking the turn the conversation was taking. 'Though it was all different when we were young. Oh, we fought with each other, or were chased away for stealing mangoes, or ran away from class and raised hell in the temple tank.' He smiled, searching his memory for other instances of harmless juvenile delinquency. 'You know, there was a boy in my class—seventh standard it was, I think—so long ago, too, thirty years or forty, yes, nearer forty . . . well, smart fellow. Good at his studies and all that, working pretty high up in a Bombay firm these days . . . Well, this fellow, he hated the Sanskrit pundit, a Brahmin, black as ink and with a tuft on his head, a sadist if ever I saw one! Would be in a vile temper the day the local barber shaved him, which was once a week, and would beat us black and blue for no reason. Or maybe he quarrelled with his wife, the boys said. She was a real shrew, the wife, served him right though . . .'

'What happened to him?' Ali asked, feeling a little impatient, putting aside a spanner with which he was working.

'Well, this boy—I don't remember his name—but he came up stealthily behind the pundit one day with a pair of scissors and... snick! ... the tuft lay on the floor.' Nair's stocky frame suddenly shook with mirth, and for a moment he seemed in danger of toppling over from the stool. 'It was there, the tuft, like a dead rat on the floor... and the pundit ran all the way to the Headmaster, with his dhoti flying in the air!'

Ali laughed with gusto. He himself had never been to school and his attitude to teachers alternated between awe and resentment, and a fall in dignity for one of the tribe struck him as particularly amusing.

'What did they do to the boy?' he asked, when both of them had calmed down a little.

'The boy? Oh, well, the Headmaster nearly skinned him the next day in front of the whole school...' Nair paused, sobered. 'And no one, not even the boy, uttered a sound. You know, his bottom was so sore for days that he couldn't sit on the bench.'

Ali nodded sagely. Those were the days when Headmasters were tyrants. Even he knew that. The boys feared their teachers, even if there were a few exceptions like this one in the story. What would have happened today?...

'Times have changed,' he reflected. 'These days no Headmaster would dare do it. They—the boys, I mean—would take out a procession and shout slogans. And who could question them? They no longer respect their elders.'

Nair suddenly felt uncomfortable and looked away, vaguely regretting the story now and the moral that it had unexpectedly exposed, like a worm in a fruit. Ali was right. It was a different breed of boys that you found in schools and colleges these days. You never knew what they would be up to next. They talked a different language and they seemed to fear no one, not even their parents. Whose fault was it? People like Ali, Nair knew, who had no children in college, would perhaps blame the parents. Even the other day someone had said in the paper that discipline, like charity, should begin at home. Must have been some politician, ready as always to put the blame on other people. Nair felt resentful and apprehensive. Did he also have to share, though obscurely, the guilt of all fathers whose sons in school and college were potential, if not actual rebels against the established order? Would he too one day have to eat the bitter fruit?

There would always be trouble to keep the prophets of chaos busy, Nair thought hopelessly. What was it now—the language issue, the rice ration or what was the name of that godforsaken border village? Parkinsonpet? Yes, that was it. The unseen worm burrowed all the time, relentlessly, pursuing its own selfish ends.

Nair got up. 'It is getting late, Ali. I should be on my way.'

He stood there uncertainly for a while, watching Ali's back now bent over some new task, unconcerned, Nair thought, with the problems of the world. He felt disillusioned. What kind of a world was this which seemed to harbour within itself the very instruments of destruction? He suddenly thought of his son—where was the boy now, and doing what? He had been behaving rather peculiarly of late. He felt a sudden eagerness to be back home, in the company of his wife, amid the safe humdrum goings-on which he had, during these years, learnt to accept as domesticity.

Dusk was falling, a powdery blackness settling with silent haste over the narrow, straggling streets, as Nair began to walk home. Here and there lights had tentatively begun to twinkle from wayside shops and electric posts. Nair walked briskly, his short fat legs working like a pair of scissors, the corners of his dhoti making little whipcracks in the breeze. There was a little of the dusk in his mind as he walked, thinking of his son, of the cost of living, of the hard day's work in the office, and of other days to come—bringing what unknown perils ?

The crowds and bustle on the road only added to his sense of doom. Buses, cars, lorries, hand-carts, and those insufferable autorickshaws nosing along like puppies at their heels ! What pointless hurry and scurry ! Screeching brakes and angry shouts . . . These people looked as though they were racing away from some impending catastrophe ! Fools ! Fools ! Every one of them !

This was the town he loved—he still loved—a town which looked as if its best years were already behind it, tucked away in history books, once a home of heroes but now a garish parade ground for black-marketeers and gold-smugglers. Why blame the younger generation ? What models did they have to emulate ? The new aristocracy of petty crooks and corrupt politicians ?

Nair looked with distaste at the glass fronts of the shops on either side, reflecting the squalor of the streets. Neon lights were everywhere, their vulgar effulgence transforming people into pale ghosts. Ahead of him, a little withdrawn from the press of the street, rose a mosque as though on crude crutches, its half-finished minarets partly hidden by scaffoldings, a garish imitation of Moghul splendour, built not so much in glory of Islam but as a challenge to the oppression of other faiths.

Politics. That was it. Everything was politics. It was a miasma that enveloped all, tainted everything it touched. There was evidence of it everywhere, on walls with slogans written in tar and whitewash, vying for attention under cinema posters displaying a surfeit of feminine charms. Nair felt helpless and vulnerable as he walked, surrounded, he felt, by invisible forces of evil.

Politics. Processions and speeches and stone-throwing. The streets were the scene of new battles—fought for whose gain ? A news-vendor was even now trotting along, shouting incoherent words of excitement. Nair knew him by sight, an old man in tattered khaki shorts and horn-rimmed glasses, getting his share of a living out of the public's insatiable gluttony for sensation. There were juicy bits about the kidnapping of a college girl and an opposition leader's challenge to the Government on the Parkinsonpet issue. Nair resisted the temptation to buy a paper. He did not want any part of it. Not today, in any case.

Nair had never, even in his youth, looked upon politics with much indulgence. Far from it. He had fought shy of it ever since it had been his good fortune, when he was still in his teens, to get a respectable job as a clerk in a Government office. Supplies and Disposals. The place had almost been like the last outpost of British colonialism. The big boss was a tough Englishman retired from the army, whose game leg had permanently disqualified him from military service. He was contemptuous of the natives, but good to those who swore allegiance to the Raj. Britain was at war and talk of sabotage was in the air. Nair had seen Gandhi once, and that too from a great distance, and the red-faced Englishman every day in office. His choice of loyalties had not been difficult.

Forty silver rupees a month when a bag of Nellore rice cost just five rupees ! Pension at the end of twenty-five years and a new status and dignity in the community ever since the day the appointment letter was signed. What more could one ask for ?

What had politics done for him ? Or this thing they called Independence ? The department had changed its name and boss several times. New rules had waived the twenty-five year service clause and extended his retirement age to fifty-five. But in material terms, what did it all amount to ? In thirty-two years of back-breaking work, Nair had laboriously climbed the ladder of promotion, from clerk to head clerk and section supervisor. Just three short-spaced rungs, held on to tenaciously, quoting rule and precedent, fighting nepotism and the pulling of strings, bargaining, pacifying, antagonizing . . . and at the end of it, eight hundred and forty-two rupees after deductions. And a bag of Nellore rice—where was it today ? At any price ?

Nair had feared politics then as he feared it now, even if for different reasons. With a secret sense of guilt, he had condemned Gandhi and the rest of them, echoing the words of those to whom he had pledged allegiance, firm in his belief that freedom was only a politician's catchword and that Congress could have as well declared war on the gods. Forty silver rupees at the end of the month was reality you could touch and feel. True, as the months went by, he had been wracked by doubts and a growing sense of treachery to his own people. And yet freedom had meant for him only one thing : freedom from want and insecurity. That was the truth as he saw it—the truth of a middle-class existence. There was no place for heroism in it. And he had never tried to be a hero. Nor had ever been one. Not even, he reflected sadly, to his own kith and kin.

And now politics, it appeared, was invading his own home, sitting with him at dinner, haunting his hours of rest, isolating him from all that he had fought for in life.

Politics was brought to his home by his son.

Nair slowed his steps as he turned left into a narrow lane, and groped over the blocks of stone laid side by side across it to prevent erosion when the monsoon converted the pathway into an angry stream. Every night, at this point in his journey home, Nair felt thankful to the municipality for having replaced the old oil-fed street lamp by the brighter and more dependable electric light. He did not grudge credit where it was due. At the last municipal elections, he had cast his vote without prejudice and sentiment in favour of a Harijan candidate who had promised to convert the lane into a proper road. It would be done one day, he was sure of that, benefitting a lot of people in the area. He himself had volunteered, as indeed had all his neighbours on either side, to give away free a strip of his land for this purpose. He walked now with the anticipated glow of a generous and sensible thing accomplished, and presently arrived at a creaking wicket gate which let him into the small compound in which his house stood.

It was an unpretentious house, single-storied and tile-roofed, with a pillared verandah in front. The walls were whitewashed and plastered except at the rear near the kitchen, where outsiders would hardly see it. Flowering shrubs and crotons decorated the front, while to a side, set in a built-up platform, grew a *tulsi* plant, a concession to his wife's religious sentiments. Every morning, sitting on the verandah reading the newspaper, Nair would look over the edge of the pages with a smile of condescension at his wife, freshly bathed and smelling of sandal paste and flowers, standing palms together and head bowed, her lips moving softly in prayer. He himself was above it all, but still the sight gave him a sense of security.

'It is no palace,' Nair used to tell his friends, trying not to appear proud and obvious. 'But it is good to have a place of your own to come to in the evening.'

The house had cost him eight thousand rupees in those days and much of the money had come from the cash and property that his wife had received as her share when her joint family holdings were partitioned. Nair had felt elated and indignant by turn all through the weeks and months it had taken to complete the partition formalities : elated that his dream of building a house of his own was a few thousand rupees nearer fulfilment, and indignant because her people had treated him with scant respect and had pettily and— well, if you wanted his honest opinion—fraudulently tricked her out of a good portion of her share. He had fumed and fretted, reluctant and a little afraid to enter openly into the fray, accused her of indifference and even disloyalty to him, and then given up the struggle and surrendered with as much grace as he could muster in the circumstances.

'Their needs are greater than ours,' his wife had pleaded philosophically and somewhat illogically, defending her clan to his utter irritation and exasperation.

'It is not their money!' Nair had thrown up his hands. 'I don't want their money, anyway. It is yours. It is the principle of it that matters. And *they* are the ones who are so proud of their family . . . of their traditions . . .'

'One gets only what one is destined to get,' his wife had quoted a proverb.

'Yes, yes, that is all very well for you to say! And next thing you'll throw the *Gita* at me. And meanwhile they'll cheat you out of your birthright!' Nair had wiped his face wearily. 'In any case, why should I talk? Who am I to talk?'

The real trouble, both of them knew well enough, was that Nair had married considerably above his station. Kalyani Amma's family at that time was not precisely prospering, but it was old and widely respected. Extravagant and idle males had brought it to the edge of ruin, and the rebellious young, throwing family loyalties to the winds, had pressed for partition. It was the intervention of well-wishers and friends (Nair privately called them stupid busybodies) that had saved them all from litigation. What a blow it would have been to family prestige! Accusations and counter-accusations against one's own kith and kin in a public court!

In comparison, the community had looked upon Nair as an upstart; a nonentity who was lucky enough to have landed for himself a secure Government job. The British were notoriously indifferent to such things. Nair had no family to speak of and no landed property to call his own. Which self-respecting father would have given away his daughter to a man whose antecedents were unknown?

But Kalyani Amma's father had thought otherwise. She was the fourth of his nine children, not endowed, he feared, with either much beauty or wit, and a secure income of forty rupees a month in those days was nothing to be scoffed at. Family considerations were discreetly set aside. The astrologer who was summoned pronounced it a good match. The neighbours—the best of them—attended the wedding and a little condescendingly (so Nair thought) blessed the couple with long life and plenty of children, expressing the opinion that it was a satisfactory alliance.

All things considered, Nair was inclined to agree with them. Kalyani Amma was a wife who, he thought, would be credit to a far more worthy husband. True, once the wedding ceremony was over, her family treated him first with condescension and later with ill-concealed indifference and even hostility. Nair was perplexed and offended at their constant attempts to 'put him in his place,' though not all of them considered it demeaning to touch him for a loan now and then or to pull a string here and there to get them out of trouble with offcialdom. He could never come to terms with the subtle manoeuvres of the aristocracy. Out of his helplessness, he put a large share of the blame on his wife. It was her fault that he was not treated properly in her house. If they showed him no respect, it was because they had no respect or regard for her. He began to react to their pinpricks, paying back hostility with hostility. As time went by, he saw very little of them. Only his wife visited them, against his wish almost, on special occasions and ceremonial days.

And then one day he was the owner of his own house, and he cut himself off completely from her clan. There was at least one place on earth where he was totally and indisputably master.

As he climbed the steps to the verandah, his wife came out of the inner room and waited for him. He took off his coat and held it out to her to be carried inside. He removed his chappals and looked round for the pot of water that she normally kept on the edge of the verandah for him to wash his feet. She had always been a stickler for neatness. She did not like him to carry the dust of the bazar into the house.

His favourite easy chair was there and he sank into it with a sigh of relief. In a while his wife would bring him his cup of tea and perhaps sit with him and talk to him about the day's events. This was a ritual he loved, when he could talk feelingly of his minor victories in the office or give her an account, fretfully and without restraint, of the inefficiency, negligence or stupidity of his superiors. Sometimes he talked about Ali and of his own ambition to own a bicycle. His wife was a patient listener, seldom interrupting him but egging him on with unobtrusive comments, allowing him to let off steam and cool his mind even as the sporadic but gentle evening breeze cooled his work-weary body.

Today, with the tumbler of steaming tea placed by his side, she did not wait for him to speak but went inside the house. He recognized this as a bad sign and felt disturbed. He heard her moving about the house—familiar sounds that a woman at work made, the clink of pots, a cupboard opening, the swish of starched clothes . . . For a moment he thought of calling her, but changed his mind. If there was trouble, it was better to let her take her own time to talk about it. Otherwise, he knew from experience, she would only baulk, side-step his queries or give evasive answers. With a sinking heart Nair realized, as he waited in the semi-darkness outside, that there was only one kind of trouble which made her act like that. Her son. Their son. What had the boy been up to now?

He noticed that the window of the eastern room was dark, which meant that his son had not yet returned from college. It was eight o'clock. Nair felt a sudden surge of anxiety, and then anger, as he thought of other late nights, which were getting more frequent and more disturbing these days. Must be politics and friends and all that foolish talk about strikes and agitations ! Nair felt the blood pounding in his head. It was time he had a talk with his son.

High time indeed.

But why blame the boy, he thought helplessly. It was his wife's fault. She had always spoilt him, defended him at the wrong moments and without reason, philosophized when sharp words were called for. Who but he himself realized how much of a financial strain it was to send a boy to college these days! Only he knew—no one else did, not even his wife—how much trouble he had undergone to get his son a scholarship. The petitions, the degrading appeals he had to make to some men of influence in the town, the self-demeaning tales of personal woe and hardship that he had to unburden in front of the admittedly sympathetic principal, Father Joshe of the Missionary College! It was the fear that his son might never be able to have a decent education—something that he himself had sorely lacked in life—that had kept Nair going till the end of it.

'Your son has a good record, I realize,' Father Joshe had said, looking appreciatively at his high school report while Nair himself struggled to suppress a glow of pride on his own face. 'But there are many deserving cases like that, you know. More deserving in some respects—I mean financially.' The principal's eyes twinkled as he looked at his visitor. 'Don't you people always accuse us of being partial to Christian students?'

'Oh...I...well,' Nair looked up in confusion, then saw the expression on Father Joshe's face and relaxed. 'The fact is that I cannot afford to send him to college. It is the truth.' He looked sadly at a paper-weight on the desk in front of him. 'I—I want the boy to have something that I myself have missed in life. My father himself was poor and he was old-fashioned...'

Father Joshe nodded and put aside the report and the application. 'I shall do my best. I can't promise anything, the Board has to decide it. But I shall keep in mind what you have told me.'

Nair knew that, submitting to local pressures, the

Government had decided to take over the Missionary College, one of the oldest and most prestigious educational institutions in the State. It was largely patronized by the affluent, because the college admittedly charged exorbitant fees. It had provoked a student agitation in recent times, but Father Joshe had been adamant: 'An institution of this nature can be run best when it is more or less financially self-sufficient,' he had maintained. 'We can't—we don't want to—depend on doles, no matter where they come from. That way this place will be more accessible to students with merit. And let's face it, we are more than generous with scholarships.' He had refused to step down.

Controversy had raged for a time in the newspapers and on public platforms, for and against official meddling in matters that the bureaucracy was considered least qualified to conduct. But one thing was unanimous: the missionary was definitely in disfavour, his methods were efficient but suspect, and his motives were too outlandish to merit discussion. True, a story had gained currency for a while that the whole trouble had started with Father Joshe's refusal to admit a Minister's son (who, the good Father thought, should properly be handed over to a corrective institution), but this was dismissed as mischievous propaganda. At best, it was cited as an illustration of how the devious missionary mind worked and to what depths it could descend when its private interests were threatened.

'Religious colonialism must go,' Congress leader Raghava Menon had solemnly told his electorate. 'I am not underrating the good work done by many missionaries, but . . .'

'In a couple of years from now,' a Marxist leader had thundered, 'I promise you, there will not be a single frocked priest on these hallowed premises . . .'

He was not quite right, of course. A Board of Management, of which prominent local citizens were members, was set up, but after a short and chaotic session, it had judiciously decided to request Father Joshe to continue as principal till such time that a suitable replacement could be found. The number of other frocked priests had dwindled steadily, but it was apparent that Father Joshe himself would play the thing ungraciously to the bitter end. He was often obstinate and perverse at the Board meetings. He was impervious to persuasion of any kind, he couldn't be 'influenced' and he still talked vaguely of merit and the future of the young generation.

As Nair walked towards the college gate, a little overwhelmed by the size and what he later described to his wife as the austere dignity of the buildings around him, he had felt less and less reassured and more given to a helpless despair. He even regretted the time he had wasted, waiting in the anterooms of some of the members of the College Board. He should have told Father Joshe about that too, at the interview. What would he think when he found out that Nair had been pulling strings behind his back ? Would that spoil his son's case ?

Two weeks later he had received a letter from the College. They could, on consideration, offer Kesavan a half-fee concession (special fees excluded) and called the boy for an interview. But Nair knew he had won. This was only a formality. Half fees then it had to be. He could not grudge his son that.

Where was the boy today—now, at this moment ? He should be at his studies, preparing for his examinations... Nair suddenly checked himself. Probably that was where the boy was, with his friends, in some home or the hostel. Combined study, they called it. Yes, that must be it. His son had sense. He was a good fellow, well-mannered and hard-working. He was very popular in college, too, Nair had every reason to believe. He did not exactly approve of some of Kesavan's companions, particularly the ones who preached revolt and fought with the professors. But a boy of his age ran into all kinds of companions in college. Not all of them from the best stock, the way education was going proletarian these days. He must learn to use his judgement. That was part of the process of growing up. Nair liked to think that he believed in giving the younger generation a certain degree of freedom. That helped them to stand on their own feet, as Nair himself had learnt early, perhaps a bit earlier than necessary, in his own life.

He felt a new confidence flow into his mind which had been a while ago dark with forebodings. He regretted that he had previously been less than fair to his wife, and therefore in a way to himself. The problem, if there was indeed one, had little to do with parental indulgence. It was true that Kesavan was an only son, but it was equally true that Nair would never be the one to shirk his responsibilities. He did not have the least doubt about it. Why, one of these days he would definitely have a good talk with his son—as he had so often promised his wife. The trouble was that he had been looking for the right moment, but these days he hardly ever saw his son. Come to think of it, not even on Sundays and holidays! How was the boy spending his spare time?

Discipline, like charity, should begin at home. Who said that? Must be someone who had no children of his own, Nair decided. The time had not yet come for panic. Indeed, there was no need for fuss, no need yet for an angry scene with his wife or son. He sighed. He felt a new sense of relief as though, in some inexplicable but all the same logical way, sitting in that easy chair, letting a soporific breeze lull him into a pleasant state of ennui, he had still done his duty by his family.

Only much later, after he had dinner and was getting ready for bed; and his wife had still not spoken about whatever it was that was troubling her, did Nair again have that vague premonition of disaster.

2

The house had no electricity. It was indeed one of the few residences in the neighbourhood which had not profited when a member of the town municipal council, eager to retain his seat, had promised to move heaven and earth to bring modern amenities to his electorate.

The task, however, had turned out to be as onerous as it sounded, and soon after his election the man apparently had lost interest in the project. The heaven in this case was, of course, the august Electricity Board to which notoriously, only a few chosen mortals had access. The purely terrestrial details were to be handled by a local office, where again, typical of most Government departments, everyone seemed to have the authority to say 'no' or 'may be,' but few, if any, had the power or the sense of commitment to say 'yes'. The area under question was a new suburb of the town, inhabited by the lower and lower-middle classes; patently a low-tax community not important enough to merit mention even in the annual State electrification project statistics.

Petition after petition was sent without result. Supplicants representing the community wandered virtually from pillar to post (in Nair's own terms) and wasted a lot of time and energy in the electrical engineer's office, angry and abject in turn. Forms were filled in, again and again, on the same cheap stencilled stationery with undecipherable —and often contradictory—instructions. Clerks lolling in chairs or engaged in long-drawn-out conversations with colleagues waved the petitioners on from table to table and eventually out through the door, promising that the next day might turn out to be more propitious for such purely nuisance-value errands. The question of bribery was desperately but briefly discussed, but unfortunately even among the petitioners no agreement could be reached on the right amount. It had, of course, to be a collective effort, and arguments broke out on who should contribute how much.

Matters were thus at a stalemate when the less civic-minded of the local population decided that direct action was called for. Old oil-burning street lamps were broken. A lamp-lighter was manhandled, some innocent passers-by were held up at knife point and robbed, and the lane leading to Nair's house from the main road suddenly became a police problem. Letters to the editor of an influential local daily appeared, one indignantly written by Nair himself. The engineer, if only he could be caught attending his office, was threatened by post that he would be gheraoed. The situation was becoming very unsavoury indeed and the municipal council member at last decided to act. The actual electrification was completed in another year and a half.

Kalyani Amma, sitting on the verandah in the faint glow cast by the street lamp outside the gate, knew only too well how sore a point it was with her husband that lack of funds denied him the benefits of a project to which he himself had contributed so much, at least in spirit. After six years, they still had to depend on the dim and messy kerosene lamps which gave pleasure only to moths throughout the year and to unmanageable hordes of flying ants after the first rain of the monsoon. Nair would go after them, a newspaper rolled up and held aloft in one hand, striking at them with a tenacious inaccuracy, missing the lamp itself by what appeared to be a miracle. They evaded him—even as did the prestige attached to a house with electricity. Nair fretted, made calculations and sometimes, in idle and optimistic moments, even planned where the light points should be, arguing with his wife with undue vehemence till she saw the futility of it and gave up. He talked off and on about loans and economization. But his hopes, like the house itself, remained dim. In the early days Kalyani Amma would try to console him by saying that at least they did not have to worry about the dangers of electric shock or the inconvenience of power failures, which were in fact frequent in their town. But nothing could brighten her husband. He continued to look upon it as a personal failure.

Kalyani Amma shifted uncomfortably in her husband's easy chair and sat up as she heard footsteps on the road, but they went past the gate, leaving her once again to her loneliness and misgivings. A while ago she had left her husband sleeping in the bedroom and had come here to wait for her son. Was he really asleep, or was he only pretending? Should she have told him what had happened today? But she had sensed, the moment he was back home, that her husband was in an irritable mood—perhaps some trouble in the office—and she had decided not to worry him with her own anxieties. Nothing would be gained by haste. She wanted time to sort out things in her own mind.

What was keeping her son so long? She would have been frantic with fear about his personal safety if these late hours had not become so frequent in recent times. Her husband had dismissed them as 'combined study', but she had, as his wife, sensed his irritation and helplessness. She also knew that he held her partly to blame—that she was over-indulgent and defensive where Kesavan was concerned. She sighed. She wished she were a man and knew the ways of the world and the pitfalls young men had to face... But what was the use! She was only a woman, and a simple one at that. She could only plead with her husband to have a talk with the boy. She had often done that, and yet when he had snapped at her and asked her 'What about?', she had no answer. She did not really know. Only her mother's instinct told her that something was terribly wrong.

Firmness. Persuasion. That was all a man's job. Of course, things were vastly different in her own time. She recalled that in all her life she had spoken perhaps just a dozen sentences to her father. In fact, she hardly ever saw much of him. He came and went, virtually a visitor. His presence was known only from the murmurings that came from her mother's bedroom late in the night. He was not an unkind man, she was convinced of that; it was just that the taboos and traditions of the joint-family system set up unbreakable barriers. But one thing was certain; she had loved her father, in her own way, and feared him—though today she would have liked to interpret that fear as respect.

How much fear, or respect, did Kesavan feel for his father? Kalyani Amma devoutly wished she knew. There was really no way of knowing. The two of them were hardly seen together, much less spoke to each other these days. When his father was around, Kesavan seemed to have only a vocabulary of monosyllables. She had tried to draw them into a conversation, even an argument to be quite honest, goading or provoking them, only to be shouted at by one or the other. Was she becoming the only common link, and that too such an inadequate one, between father and son? No, no, that was not true, she told herself hastily. This was but a passing phase. It was part of growing up, that uncertain stage between adolescence and manhood which brings a mental isolation and a distrust of adults. Kesavan loved her, she had not the least doubt of it ... and yet how often would he speak cuttingly to her, wound her sometimes at the slightest provocation? How often had he complained bitterly about her nagging?

But she was his mother, and she had found it easy to forgive him, at least in retrospect, even though she had snapped back at him in momentary anger sometimes. And there were also the times she remembered so well, when he would turn playful and tease her out of her wits, or sit with her and talk to her about a hundred and one things, half of which of course, she did not understand: of mathematics and books, of science and the stars, of distant countries and customs, why, even of stupid football matches. (He had given up in despair once trying to explain to her why it was important for twenty-two otherwise normal people to chase a ball all over a field!). When he was in a conciliatory mood, he would speak with respect about religion and the *Gita*, and she loved to watch his face when he was so earnest and serious. Religion was a subject close to her heart and she would turn teacher, telling him stories of the heroes of legend. He was a boy, her son, and in spite of his worldly airs, there was an innocence about him which seldom failed to bring tears to her eyes. Where was that young boy of yesterday, and who was this stranger in their midst?

She shifted in the chair and wiped her eyes and softly blew her nose. All sentiment and nonsense from a foolish woman! She was his mother and she could not afford to fail him. The problem was as simple as that. She just could not afford to be weak. Why was it that everything was so different between father and son? At first she had been hurt and perplexed by her husband's attitude—his evasiveness, his eagerness to avoid a scene and what she had angrily considered then as his abject surrender of responsibility. He was not a weak man, of that she was sure, though his courage was of a kind that only those who were close to him could appreciate. He had a resilience which no amount of buffeting in life could quite destroy. This too she had seen. He could also work up a lot of heat, though strangely, she had often thought, only on issues that did not seem to concern them directly at all! At such times she had been told that not much sense or wisdom was expected of her as a woman. She did not know the world. But then, she had protested, she knew her world well enough. It was the father's duty to discipline the son, however unpleasant the task might turn out to be. A mother could go only this far, and no further. Was that a failure on her part?

Govindan Nair had refused to budge. Perhaps he was just soft, Kalyani Amma decided. For one reason or another, he had avoided a confrontation with his son, pretended that there was no real problem and accused her of being a fussy woman. Was he really right? Again, she wished she knew. All she could see was the growing restraint, if not antagonism, between the two of them, and she had helplessly turned from one to the other and back again in a vain attempt to bring them together. She had used reasoning, cajolery and admonitions, she had stormed and sulked by turns, she had even wept on occasions; but she was not sure whether it had done any good at any stage. Oddly, at the end of it all, she had withdrawn, feeling more an interloper than a mediator. Hostility seemed to divide and at the same time, strangely unite them, unconsciously perhaps, but certainly against her. In a man's world she was the outsider—her woman's intuition had told her that—and she had stepped back in confusion. Was that some cowardice on her part?

A man had his pride, she knew that. Whatever he might say, however much he might talk about freedom, he did not like to be treated as an equal by his child. What was a woman to do then; what was her responsibility? The two of them meant all the world to her, why weren't they all she now had in the world? Her own people had turned their backs on her, and she had been cut to the quick by their pettiness and greed and the insulting manner in which they had treated her husband. She had been hurt, though with a perverse loyalty strange even to herself, she had defended them, the people her husband had contemptuously referred to as 'clan'. She felt a sudden sympathy for him; she knew his weakness and his strength, and she knew of his loyalty to her, and also of his dependence on her, never acknowledged but always there, to sustain him in times of stress. That was a wife's duty as she understood it; that was the fulfilment of her marriage vows.

She remembered him now as a suitor, the first time he had come to her house. There were two friends with him and the menfolk had talked at length in the outer room, only her mother making an occasional comment as she stood listening just inside the door. Kalyani (she had not yet earned the appendage 'Amma' then, a sign of respect for the married woman) had felt no excitement, not even much curiosity, only a dull fear that she was going to bungle whatever it was that was expected of her. Those people could very well have been arbitrating an outsider's fate. She had seen other girls in the house go through the same ritual, and often unsuccessfully.

She was by no means a favoured daughter of the household. She was one among many grown-up girls in a large family, which was old and respected but at that time well past its glory, already hostile to the outside world with its growing sense of decline. Its affairs were in chaos, its prospects were bleak. Girls were a liability till such time when they could be found husbands. And the most favoured grooms were among the newly rich whom the men of the house looked upon with open contempt, but concealed envy, trading security for prestige with a supreme air of condescension.

Kalyani had made a mercifully brief appearance in the outer room, decked in whatever little finery she possessed and firmly pushed into the room by her mother, but she was too confused to identify among the three visitors the man rash enough to want to share his life with her. She stood with her face bent, studying a crack on the cement floor, while people around her fumbled for suitable words to be spoken in her favour. They sounded more apologetic about her shortcomings, she felt, than enthusiastic about her attributes. She came away with a feeling that everyone, including perhaps the prospective groom, was relieved to have her out of the room.

When she first heard that the proposal had been finalized, she was clearly given to understand that she should consider herself fortunate. She had neither asked, nor was she told, who he was and what she was to expect out of the alliance. She had to put together her own picture of it from bits and pieces of conversation she overheard between her own mother and her aunts or other well-wishers, from hints, or when they were in a more communicative mood, comments from her married sisters, or from the more lively but less informed gossip of the servants. To have exhibited any open curiosity would have been taken as immodesty in a girl of her age and upbringing. As was expected of her, she listened to all without comment, prayed occasionally in private, and otherwise went about her own business in the house.

The only perceptible change in her usual pattern of life was the sudden interest she seemed to be getting from the older women of the house. They all seemed to become acutely conscious of her shortcomings and extraordinarily eager to correct them.

'Why don't you comb and do your hair properly, Kalyani? God knows he hasn't endowed you with any great looks. Do you have to make it worse?' an aunt would say, in a tone that suggested that this sloppiness was a personal affront to herself and an attempt to thwart her plans for a better life for the girl.

'Not even a *pottu* on her forehead,' her mother would exclaim. 'One would think there is going to be a funeral in the house—not a wedding. Go and put it on, this instant!'

'For heaven's sake,'—this from a married sister, a

mother of three at twenty-one and prematurely old in looks and demeanour, 'show some cosideration for the man who is kind enough to take you away! Why don't you wear a better blouse than that faded one? Do you want him to think that we are a family of destitutes?'

It went on and on. Her mother, she knew, was jumpy and easily upset, worried to distraction about the coming event, hoping that the marriage would come through in spite of her worst fears. And the others—they were easy to forgive, too, at least to be ignored without rancour, for she knew that that was their way of talking and they had her good at heart. Regard and gentleness were also there—but from unexpected quarters. The men of the house, status-conscious and awkward before the younger women of the family, knew that she would soon attain a special stature—that of a married woman. To the public at large, she would hereafter be 'Kalyani Amma', married to a man of substance and standing in the community. Even her father was kind to her, in one of his rare moments of affection. He spent money, which he could ill afford at that time, in buying her a gold chain with a small but beautiful stone-studded pendant. (She still had it, having refused to sell or pawn that piece of jewellery, even when Nair was in dire financial difficulties.) After her marriage she would leave the house and go with her husband to the town—a clear portent of the imminent break-up of the joint family and the coming years of discord. The departure would have, in the minds of the people, the solemnity, if not the sadness, of a death.

Cousins of her own age treated her with envy, suddenly alienated by the prospect of her good fortune. The old servants bowed to her with mock dignity and forecast in a bantering tone: 'Now the little girl has grown up and is going away, leaving us poor people behind! She will go to the town and forget us; and one day when we visit her she'll be angry with us and ask her servants to turn us out! God grant us that we do not live long enough to see that black day!'

Govindan Nair was no Prince Charming. No one in the house expected him to be one. He came with a small group of friends and one or two men of no great consequence who were apparently distantly related to him. The people of the house mentally winced; they were appalled that this was the only 'family' he could round up. But they had earlier been warned by the match-maker and were eventually ready to ignore it even in the face of supercilious questions from the less polite guests. Nair wore a new silk shirt and a starched cotton dhoti, and the womenfolk considered him quite presentable. Everyone assembled had a fairly close idea of his social position and monthly income. The first was nothing much to speak of, the second was satisfactory according to current reckonings. All in all, it was a good match. Good enough to rouse a sense of satisfaction among the male guests and a lot of envy among the female.

So while the pipes and drums played an auspicious and popular tune from a little beyond the periphery of a closely-packed circle of guests, the bride put a garland of flowers round the neck of the groom, and he, in turn, with trembling hands seen only by those standing closest to him, tied the sacred *tali* round her neck, took her hand in his and circled the ceremonial lamps thrice and came back to the starting point, now suddenly looking as though he did not know what to do or where to go next. It was the dispersal of the guests, hurrying to find a place at the feast and eager to go home as early as possible, that told him finally that the ceremony was over.

Kalyani Amma imagined she heard a movement from within and got up, wondering whether her husband was awake. If he caught her sitting alone in the darkness outside so late in the night, he would be sure to kick up a row as the neighbourhood was not very safe after dark, and worse still he would begin to wonder what was keeping her awake.

She got up and went inside, bolting the front door behind her. She groped her way through the darkness to the bedroom, careful not to bump against any furniture or otherwise make any noise. For a moment she stood undecided, then she raised the wick of a lamp that was burning on a side table and looked at the man sleeping on the cot.

He lay on his back, hands crossed over the chest as though protectively, breathing, mouth agape. She looked at the receding forehead, the greying hairs at the temples, the lines round the eyes and mouth. His lips dropped a little, giving him a petulant look. She felt a sudden tenderness for this man, sleeping unaware of her scrutiny, weary from work, shaken by life, childish in some ways even in the afternoon of his life. He had always been trustful and loyal to her even in the face of difficulties which so often seemed to shatter his hopes and aspirations. She waved away a mosquito that had settled on his chin. He grimaced at the same moment and groaned, then turned on his side and was lost again in sleep.

Her eyesight had not been very good of late and she picked up the lamp gently and held it close to a small alarm clock on a shelf on the wall. The time was 11.40 p.m. She felt increasingly anxious and angry with her son. Well, it was going to be today, she thought, no matter how late it was. She had had enough of this nonsense, his utter callousness. Kesavan had gone too far, much too far. She could not put up this pretence any more.

What she was going to say to him when he came back, she had no idea. It was up to him to offer explanations. But an explanation she would have even if she had to drag it out of him.

She jerked up her head, startled. The wicket gate made a familiar scraping sound against the ground as someone—it had to be her son—closed it and secured it with the latch. She carried the lamp with her as she came out of the bedroom, walking slowly, careful again not to make any noise or trip against something, rounded the central table in the middle room and stopped at the door which opened onto the verandah, just as footsteps outside reached it and paused. Obviously her son stood there hesitating.

Kalyani Amma put the lamp on the central table and turned the wick still higher, filling the room with light. She walked over to the bedroom door and closed it softly. When she turned, she noticed that the cup from which her husband had drunk milk before retiring was still on the table; she was dismayed that tonight she had forgotten to take it back to the kitchen and wash it, as she always did, before putting it away. The feet outside the door scraped on the floor impatiently. Kalyani Amma walked over to the door and unbolted it.

Kesavan entered, gave her a quick look, then went towards the table. He stood near the lamp, as though seeking reassurance from its brightness against the darkness outside through which a while ago he must have come walking, alone. He idly picked up the cup, found it empty and put it back. He must have mentally braced himself then, for he turned round and looked at his mother, a little sheepishly, hesitantly . . . and then challengingly.

How thin he looked, Kalyani Amma thought—and haggard! He had never been one for eating much, unlike his father—and yes, more like her. He had her same bony features, sharp, straight nose and high cheekbones which made his black eyes intense and luminous in the light of the lamp. He had a high forehead, with a line in the middle between the brows, now shaded by the side light to look almost like a caste-mark. His Adam's apple was prominent in his thin neck, and it moved as he swallowed uncomfortably under her scrutiny. In a few more years, she thought with a sudden stir of pride, he would grow into a tall man—

again unlike his father, who was short. Kesavan had taken more after the men of her own family.

'Have you eaten?' she asked, turning her gaze away from him.

He hesitated, and then said abruptly. 'No . . . Well, I did have something, but that was earlier in the evening.'

'Are you hungry?'

'If . . . if there is something to eat . . .'

She walked past him into the kitchen and lighted a new lamp. His food was there, rice and curry, kept in vessels with tightly closed lids to keep them warm. She took down a jar of pickles from a shelf and also a large, old biscuit tin from which she took out fried pappads. She picked up a jar of buttermilk and poured some of it into a glass tumbler. He would not eat rice without it, she knew, and he always liked to drink a mouthful or two of it at the end of his meal.

There was no dining table. She had never acknowledged the need for one in spite of the protests from her husband and son. The kitchen was already cluttered, she had argued, and she would get a dining table when she had a proper dining room. In the original plan of the house there was provision for it, but by the time the actual construction had got well under way the capital was running out fast and some compromises had to be made. It was to be taken up later, when better times came, and she was still waiting.

She spread a small mat on the floor and was putting the plates down in front of it when Kesavan entered. He had removed his shirt—the night was warm—and had changed his trousers for a dhoti. He had apparently just washed his face and feet. Water was dripping from the back of his head and neck, in rivulets down his back, and she went to him and wiped it with the loose end of her upper cloth. Kesavan sat cross-legged on the mat, gathering up his dhoti over his knees as he did so.

She began to serve him food; first rice, then curry, then pickles and pappads.

'The vegetable vendor didn't come today', she said apologetically, explaining the meagreness of the fare.

He merely grunted and started eating in his usual hasty manner, not really caring what he ate, much to her chagrin always. She sighed, looking at his thin torso now bent over the food. The collar bones and ribs were clearly defined. At the back the spine could be seen like a low, uneven ridge.

She squatted by his side, on the bare floor, turned round and reached out for a glass of water for him. 'It is nearly 12 o'clock', she said.

'Is it?' he asked, as though surprised, not looking up. 'I mean, is it as late as that?'

'Yes', she said slowly. 'It's as late as that.' Her tone had turned vaguely ominous, but she waited in vain for him to respond. Only his pace of eating increased a trifle.

'Don't gulp down your food,' she said, and then after a pause, 'Where were you till now?'

'I was in the college—in the hostel.'

She noticed the unprovoked sharpness in his voice, but ignored it. 'Studying?'

'Well, yes . . . not exactly.' He shifted in his seat uncomfortably, apparently resentful of being cornered into telling a lie. 'We were talking over things.'

'What things? About your studies—examinations?'

'No.' He picked up the glass of water and drank.

'Then what other things?'

'What does it matter?' he exploded, looking up at her sharply, his eyes angry and defensive. 'You wouldn't understand these things anyway!' He picked up the buttermilk and drained it in one gulp. He got up, went out through a back door and presently she heard water splashing as he washed his hands and rinsed his mouth.

She began to collect the empty plates and tidy up. She picked up the mat, rolled it up neatly and put it away. She piled up the plates and walked with them towards the back door to wash them outside; then she changed her mind and put them on a side on the floor. They could wait till tomorrow.

As she was bending down she heard Kesavan come in and walk past her into the central room, and thence to his own room. She closed the back door and pushed the bolts in. She went over to the place where Kesavan had been sitting on the floor, sprinkled some water and wiped the ground clean with a duster. She took her own time doing these things; there was no great need for her to hurry. He would not go to bed till he was sure that she herself had gone to her room and closed the door.

Some nights, when all was quiet, she could get the faint smell of cigarette smoke before she fell asleep.

He had lit a lamp and was sitting in a chair, reading the evening paper when she entered his room. He did not look up. She went to his cot, straightened out the crumpled sheets, patted the pillow into shape and put it back in its place. The night was turning out to be stuffy and she could see mosquitoes, diabolical little black dots on the whitewashed wall.

'I want to talk to you,' she said as she sat down on the cot.

There was a soft rustle of the newspaper and his voice came from behind it. 'Now?'

'Yes, now.'

'It's late, isn't it? I'm feeling very sleepy.'

'I just want to ask you a few things. Now is as good a time as any other, I suppose. In any case, we don't see you at all during daytime these days.'

He lowered the newspaper and looked at her : 'I'll be here all of tomorrow morning—I think.' He obviously did not want to make it sound like a promise.

Tomorrow was the second Saturday of the month and her husband would be home. So it had to be now, she decided. 'There was a man to see you here today. In the morning. After you had gone to—college.'

'Oh? Who was it?'

'I don't know. He gave his name as Gopalan. Who is he?'

'He is—an acquaintance. He might have wanted to know about some things that are going on in the college.'

'Then he should have gone to the college, shouldn't he? Well, come to think of it, he didn't look as though he has ever seen the inside of a college—or a school, for that matter.'

'Oh, he isn't riff-raff', Kesavan laughed shortly. 'You needn't worry about that! He is a highly respected man.'

'Respected by whom?'

'By everyone. I mean, by most people. He is a—a local leader.'

'He was very shabbily dressed. And I didn't much like his ways. In fact he came up on the verandah and sat down in your father's chair without invitation. I didn't like that at all.'

'Mother, you can't judge a man by his appearance. He is not exactly rolling in wealth but he is quite a clever man. A very interesting one. He is widely respected, I told you that.'

'He has no manners. I am a woman and I was alone in the house. He had no business to sit in Father's chair.'

'Oh, he wouldn't have—he couldn't have known that it was Father's chair,' Kesavan said placatingly. 'To him it must have looked like any old chair. He must have come walking a long distance and perhaps just wanted to ease his legs.' He looked at her slyly. 'And as for you being a woman alone in the house, I am sure he had no evil intentions. . .'

'Don't talk to me like that! I'm your mother, don't forget that!'

He suddenly got up from his chair, came over and sat by her on the cot and put his arm around her waist shyly—and then hastily withdrew it. Kesavan was not normally given to such familiarities. She herself was surprised—pleasantly surprised.

'Times are changing, Mother,' he said as he went back to his own seat. 'These times are not like those in feudal days. You can't expect people to stand at the gate, hands crossed, coughing politely. Gopalan is not of our caste, but what does it matter?'

'Yes', she said conceding the point for the moment. She did not really know why, but she had taken an instant dislike to the man. It was not his shabbiness, but a certain indefinable air about him. He looked as though he couldn't be trusted. What people Kesavan was hobnobbing with these days!

'Well, that is not really what I wanted to talk to you about,' she continued. 'He told me you were not going to college these days. I asked him why he had come in the morning to see you—and that was the answer he gave.' The man had realized his mistake immediately, she recalled now. He had mumbled something—that he thought Kesavan might not have gone to college because of some study leave, or something like that. But he could not fool her. She knew that examinations were still too far off for any study leave to begin. 'Well?'

'I'm going to college. You know that.'

'No. I don't. I'm asking you. Are you attending classes?'

It had been a shock to her. The amazing part of it was that it had never, ever occurred to her or her husband to question Kesavan about his comings and goings. They had just assumed it . . . taken things on trust. The college was quite some distance away—part of the journey was by bus. She had no way at all of knowing. Nor her husband. It was as though an edifice has suddenly cracked—no, crashed down, opening out a whole lot of possibilities for mischief. And that Gopalan's saturnine face had sent a cold shiver up her spine. . . Kesavan! She just could not believe it!

'Why don't you answer?' she persisted. 'I asked, are you

attending classes?'

'No... Not for the past few days, if you want me to be precise.'

'I want you to be precise. Now tell me... and tell me the truth. Why were you not attending classes?'

'Just like that.'

'Just like *what*?'

'Well, if you want to know the truth: I have been suspended from college for a few days with some other chaps.'

'Suspended? What is that?' But she knew instinctively, without his telling her, what it meant. Oh, God, the shame of it!

'We've been asked to keep away from college for a few days, that's all. It's nothing to worry about.'

'Oh, I see.' His calmness only made her bitter.

'I don't think you do, Mother,' Kesavan said softly. 'You know there is some trouble going on about a place called Parkinsonpet. There was some disturbance about it in the class. Honestly, I had no part in it.'

'Then why were you sent out? Did you tell your teacher?'

He smiled at her naivete. 'The others were my friends. We were looked upon as a gang. So I too had to go.'

'But why didn't you say you were innocent?'

'Look, Mother. I told you they were my friends. I couldn't let them down...'

'Strange loyalties you have!' she shook her head in frustration. 'But what about your loyalty to me—or to your father? Couldn't you at least tell him?'

'I thought there was no need to—trouble him.'

'Trouble him!' Her patience suddenly gave way. 'Do you know how important it is to him that you are going to college? Do you know what trouble your father takes? Do you know anything at all! You wouldn't. Why should you? You want fees. You want books. You want clothes. Have you even wondered where these things are coming from...

where he finds the money to buy these? Oh, you are beyond belief! Do you realize what trouble he had taken to get you admitted in college? What indignities he had suffered to secure a scholarship for you?'

Kesavan got up and paced the room. 'I know all that, Mother. And I am grateful.'

'You ought to be grateful. Have no doubt about that. . . And I don't like the tone in which you say it.'

'How do you expect me to say that? Weep with gratitude?' He had stopped in his stride.

'If you talk like that,' she said, looking steadily at him, her voice icy cold, 'I will slap you. Don't think you are too old for that!'

She saw him flush, and she paused, composing herself. 'What have you got against your father?'

'Nothing.'

'Then why do you talk like that?'

'Like what? What did I say now? ' He still sounded vaguely rebellious. 'I said I know what trouble he takes.' He walked over to his chair and slumped into it wearily.

'Your father is a good man, Kesavan. I am his wife and I know it.' Her lips quivered and she fought back the tears that she suddenly felt smarting in her eyes. 'I have spent the best years of my life with him. Twenty-three years. . . He had always been good to me—to us!' She paused and wiped her eyes. 'He had always loved children. . . and not necessarily his own either. I could give him only one. . .'

Kesavan said nothing. He was sitting with his head bent, staring at the floor.

'He was the happiest man when you were born. The fuss he made. . .and the nights he would sit up, watching over you, worried about a sneeze, pacing the floor with you in his arms when you cried, complaining, always complaining, that I was not gentle enough with you. I would laugh at him in those days. Our doctor used to say that it was your father who needed medicines when his child was ill. He used to be

Abhimanyu

so distraught with anxiety.'

She remembered all that now and many things more. How her husband used to spend hours playing with the growing boy, carrying him on his shoulders, spending money that he could ill afford on toys and clothes, basking in the child's affection, even jealous of his mother at times... How he would make plans for his son, wanting to make him a district collector one moment, a doctor or an engineer the next, worrying about his studies and health... Perhaps, she thought in recent times, it was a mistake, a tragedy that children grew up. They drifted away. They forgot everything too soon. They change with a shattering suddenness. Overnight, almost, they become aliens.

'You are all that he has, you remember that,' she repeated. 'He never had much luck in life. Even marrying me, for instance. I have never said it to anyone—I am now telling you that. Ours is an old family—I mean *my* family. They are not rich and powerful any more, but their old attitudes are still there. Your father had always been conscious of it—they had made him conscious of that... And I can never forgive them for that.' She paused and looked at him for a moment: 'Success and wealth are not everything in life. Doesn't the *Gita* say that the only right we have is the right to do our work? We have no claims on the fruits of our labour. We must realize our duty and do it. To the best of our ability. I want you to remember that.' She looked at him challengingly.

'Sometimes,' Kesavan said softly, 'one doesn't know clearly what one's duty is.'

'That is only because one is not honest enough. Or has no real faith,' Kalyani Amma said. 'God always shows us the way if we are humble enough, sincere enough...' She saw Kesavan shift in his chair. 'All right, all right. Not God then. You yourself. You are a student. Your duty is to study. Is that too difficult to understand? Other things can wait.'

She was silent for a while. Then she asked him gently:

'What will happen now, my son? What will you do?'

He sighed. 'Nothing, Mother. You have nothing to worry about. This will blow over...'

'And then...?'

'Well, then...' he smiled at her. 'I'll remember my duty.'

'Is that a promise?'

'Yes... you can take it as that. As much as I or anyone can foresee the future.'

She went over to the lamp and looked back enquiringly at him. 'Are you going to sleep now?'

'Yes, yes. My God, you've kept me up late!'

She turned down the wick of the lamp. 'Blow it out if you don't need it,' she said. 'You know how difficult it is to get kerosene these days.'

When she was at the door, he suddenly said, 'And one more thing, Mother. I wish you wouldn't speak about this to Father just yet. Things are bad enough as they are. I really don't think we should make him worry...'

She said nothing. She looked at him and closed the door softly behind her as she left.

3

Comrade Gopalan, Secretary of the town branch of the newly-formed Militant Socialist Party, sat alone at a table in a restaurant, reading the morning edition of the *People's Voice*. It was too early in the day for many customers, so Gopalan did not care for interruptions. The proprietor was an admirer of his and he would see to it that no unwelcome visitors disturbed Gopalan.

The paper in Gopalan's hand was yellow—not with age, but because it was the cheapest newsprint available in the country. Its types were smudgy and hardly readable, yet the clientele it catered to had always found it worth their while to decipher the news reports. Snappy headlines, uninhibited but cunning enough to be almost always on the safe side of libel, provoked, scandalized and sometimes, when the situation warranted it, shocked readers into a word-by-word perusal of what was printed below.

Truth was all right, Gopalan thought, as a subject for pulpit talk, but there were varying interpretations of it. The *People's Voice* had its own, and it kept at least one libel lawyer busy most of the time. The yellow sheets were a kind of badge of dedication, like khadi cloth was for some Congressmen. Gopalan smiled wryly. After all, it was further proof that the pursuit of truth was not altogether a profitable business in this world. It was indeed a miracle that the newspaper still continued to get its newsprint quota. Well, perhaps not a miracle. The publishers had to thank Gopalan largely for it. Like many small town newspapers, the Editor himself owned a majority of the shares. Advertising was a rare windfall and it had been a touch and go affair most of the time. Gopalan had studied the set-up and found it profitable to cultivate the Editor. It needed only an hour's frank discussion for the two of them to conclude that they were men of the same ilk. They had the same views on journalism—purposeful, straight-faced journalism. Indeed they had the same views on many matters of importance : on power and violence, on politics as the tool of the modern man. They had an extremely precise idea how a newspaper, struggling for funds but edited with imagination and verve, could fit into the scheme of things.

The strategy Gopalan had outlined was masterful. The first thing was to get the newspaper officially banned. Not with any kind of trouble that could really stand up in court, but with borderline cases. All that it needed was to corner a high official with a bad conscience and then blackmail him gently. Not even much money was involved. Gopalan had carefully scrutinized a list of possibles and eliminated all but two for varying reasons : an M. L. A. and a high police official. The newspaper had a good story and unless something drastic was done about it, it was sooner or later going to print it. Gopalan himself organized the negotiations through a third party. Payment was not even vaguely hinted at. The mediator had warned that it could only make things worse. He was—God forbid!—certainly not on the side of the newspaper. They were, well, he did not mind saying it in private, a bunch of crooks. He understood the predicament of the officials. Times were difficult for everyone and they were, he fully conceded, working for the larger benefit of the people and country. Minor misdemeanours should indeed be overlooked by a grateful populace. But, oh, these newspapers! They were scandal sheets really.

They were out to prejudice the public mind ...

It had all been much simpler than Gopalan had hoped. The two men had swallowed the bait. With more speed than sense, they had moved the right circles to get the newspaper banned. No one had really cared then—some obscure rag somewhere. The newspaper office was raided, its files sealed and its Editor was arrested and let out on bail. The provocation was a carefully worded charge of corruption against a harmless district collector, drafted with the help of a shrewd lawyer. And the same legal brain steered the case out of court in less than three months with nothing more than a warning from the judge. The Court observed while dismissing the suit, that the newspaper must choose its words with circumspection as people are liable to read between the lines. Official ineptitude, even if proved, should not be confused with dishonesty. The Government did not find it worthwhile to press for an appeal.

The outcome for the newspaper was more than satisfactory. The *People's Voice* shot into prominence and circulation moved up to an economically feasible level. Allocation of newsprint quota became a 'freedom of the press' issue and even other more sober newspapers, if not with conviction at least with considerable self-interest, pleaded vehemently against the throttling of the press, without mentioning names, of course. The *People's Voice* was firmly on saddle. Now it needed more than a small libel case to dislodge it.

The Editor was grateful, though Gopalan rarely ever asked for any favours in return. He did not have to. As an up and coming politician he wanted a hold over a newspaper, but he was not a business baron to own one. Mutual interest, he had always known, could also be a currency with great purchasing power.

Today, sitting in the restaurant, Gopalan's face was expressionless as he slowly, methodically read the paper. He was a man in his late thirties, dark and lanky, sharp-nosed and hollow-eyed, with a two-days' growth of beard on his cleft chin. He had a shock of black curly hair and his high brow was deeply lined. His tall frame was loosely clad in a white kurta and dhoti of coarsely spun fabric, both of which could have been improved in looks with a little soap and water. With a bony, long-fingered hand he scratched his chin now and then as he read, making a soft, scraping sound.

Nowhere in the paper had he seen his name; he had checked that, as he always did, when he had first scanned the paper. It was now over two weeks—perhaps even a month—since the paper had printed anything he had said. It was not wilful omission, Gopalan was sure of that. When he chose to speak, the newspaper could always count on a lively copy. The interval now was certainly too long for comfort. He was an astute politician. He knew the tricks of the trade. It was never good to be out of public eye for too long. Particularly not when elections were virtually round the corner.

Gopalan folded the paper carefully and put it aside on the table. The cup of tea had turned cold and he could see a thin film forming on the surface. He pushed it away with distaste and called out sharply to a passing boy to bring him another cup. He liked his tea, just as he liked politics, steaming hot.

The proprietor hovered near him solicitiously, personally took the cup and looked enquiringly at it.

'Oh, there is nothing wrong with your tea,' Gopalan said, smiling. 'It became cold. My fault. I didn't see the boy place it on the table. I was reading the paper.'

The boy had joined them by this time, and he stood aside, apprehensively, fearing the manager's wrath. Gopalan smiled at him reassuringly. 'It is all right,' he said to the manager. 'It is really not his fault, poor fellow.'

Poor, wretched underdog! Gopalan thought, looking at the boy's receding back. Skinny, stunted, certainly below twelve. An age at which boys like him would be playing, or going to school... what a way to begin your life, in that soot-filled, stinking kitchen at the back. Gopalan looked round to see that the manager had returned to his desk. He looked distinctly disappointed at having missed an opportunity to snarl at the boy or clout him and thereby re-establish his own credentials and good faith with this man whom he admired so much. He had examined the new cup closely, almost eager to spot a blemish, but finding none had placed it gingerly on the table in front of Gopalan like an unnecessary peace offering.

How much did the boy earn, Gopalan wondered. May be nothing. Or perhaps a meal and a place to sleep at night. In a sudden mood of generosity, he thought he should speak to the manager about it, then he changed his mind. It might be looked upon as uncalled-for interference. The restaurant business, at least in some cases, he was sure, was unlike managing an estate or running a factory. It has its problems. This one, in particular, did not exactly present a picture of prosperity.

It was indeed a small and shabby show. The glass panels at the front were thickly smudged with soot and dirt. The furniture—half a dozen tables of all shapes and sizes with equally dilapidated chairs to match—looked like cast-outs from a junk shop. The whitewashed walls had turned a brownish-yellow with age and displayed large, jagged patches where the plaster had peeled off. The manager's desk was virtually a period piece, a cross between a table and an almirah, rising chest-high and panelled all round, with decorations of garishly-flowered glazed tiles. The clink of coins came from it now and then as the manager idly but lovingly dipped his fingers into the till, while he kept a watchful eye over the establishment or turned his gaze occasionally to the road outside. Above the desk were glossy prints of Gandhi and Lenin in glass frames; judicious co-existence, Gopalan reflected wryly. A man likes to play it safe these days. If you were in business, it was bad policy to be dubbed either this or that or any other. You had to cater to all kinds of people, even if you made no secret of where your innermost sympathies lay. Perhaps it needed some kind of courage. The overall impression the place gave was of sordidness, and Gopalan had always found it easy to forgive sordidness.

As he sipped the boiling brew in the cup, Gopalan's thoughts once again returned to his own immediate problems. Yes, he liked to liven things up a bit. His colleagues always blamed him for straining at the leash. They counselled patience, a wait-and-watch game. Patience! Gopalan's face curled into the semblance of a smile. Patience had never been his outstanding virtue. He had always dismissed it as a weapon of the weak. He considered himself eminently a man of action, of decisive action.

It was on this point—political action with its hidden fist of violence—that Gopalan and a group of like-thinking men had finally broken away from the socialist theoreticians and revisionists to form the Militant Socialist Party. The fist was, for the most part, still hidden, but it had been assiduously trained to hit with devastating efficiency when the need arose. Personally, Gopalan was fed up with the namby-pambies. They were not going to achieve anything in a hundred years! Since when had public debate become the weapon of the revolution? Gopalan chuckled contemptuously. Just look at the old guard, he had hissed at his companions. You scratch them and find the petit bourgeoisie underneath. They had the superficial zeal of the convert but none of the sterner stuff that made leaders of men. Neither they nor their idle talk of revolution was genuine.

His listeners, most of whom knew Gopalan's own background well, believed him implicitly. No one had to tell them that it was men such as him who inspired devotion unto death...

As in the case of many people, Gopalan could recall his childhood only as a chain of isolated events, without any clear chronological order. He was the fourth in a family of seven children. His father was a tailor—a good one, he remembered, successful and always conscious of it. He was a proud man who took pleasure in his work, who bowed down to no one.

The children were allowed to visit the shop, at least when work was slack, and they would take delight in gathering bits and pieces of coloured cloth, listening to the busy drone of the sewing machine and marvelling at the dexterity and apparent abandon with which their father cut what looked like very expensive material. He stitched clothes for both men and women; the latter particularly praised his skill; but he would make children's dresses only as a special favour. There was not enough percentage in it. 'Nanu-tailor', the people in the street used to call him and they always treated him with respect. He never drank, unlike people of his class, and seldom smoked. He only liked to chew paan, with that dark, specially prepared aromatic tobacco, and he was forever humming and grunting inside the shop, afraid of opening his mouth and spotting the cloth with red spittle. If speech was essential, he walked to the front of the shop, looked first this side and then that, and then holding his lips pressed between the first two fingers of his left hand, spat expertly, always hitting the middle of the road, much to the delighted awe of the children. Then he would turn round and speak, and because of these lengthy preliminaries, anything he said had the solemnity of a pronouncement.

Gopalan, unlike his brothers and sisters, loved his father with a single-mindedness which was later to characterize almost all his emotions and attachments in life. His day was made when his father singled him out for a good word; he felt insecure and lost when he didn't merit even a smile.

After school he liked to run errands for his father. He always felt privileged at such times, especially if he was rewarded for his troubles. A few paise to buy sweets or a top or a kite. On his birthday or on the first school-going day of the year, he would be the proud possessor of a new shirt, elegantly striped and with that heady smell of freshness. It was a luxury that boys of his class could ill afford. Gopalan had been baffled by the complaints they used to make about their fathers; of men who drank a certain stinking liquor and beat their wives and children, started fights in the streets at night and were hauled away by rough-handed policemen. The shame of it! No wonder his mother was the object of much envy in the street.

Then the blow fell.

One day, when his father did not come home in the night, Gopalan was at first perplexed, then frightened—then distraught with agony when he learnt that he would never again come back to their house. The shop was closed for a while and then it was taken over by a new man who continued the tailoring business. He was a fat man with a large moustache who did not care to have children standing on the road and looking forlornly into his shop. He first shooed them away, and then threatened them with his huge black scissors.

Where had his father gone? The grown-ups had shown a reluctance to discuss the subject. Was he dead? Perhaps that was it, Gopalan had thought. He was dead and the boy wept for him, broken-hearted and inconsolable. It was almost a week after his father had disappeared that he had the first inkling of the truth. He had hardly seen his mother in those days—and whenever he did see her, she looked grief-stricken or angry—or sometimes even as though she was out of her mind. She snapped at the children and once even beat up one of them so severely that a neighbour had to intervene and draw the child away. Gopalan had never dared to ask even for food when he was hungry—much less

Abhimanyu

about his father.

But the night he came to the conclusion that his father was dead, Gopalan could not sleep and he lay on the mat, afraid of the darkness, trying hard to suppress the sobs that wracked his small frame. After a while, he heard someone at the door and saw his mother looking into the room.

'Is that you, Gopalan, mumbling?' she asked. He hardly recognized her voice. It was hoarse, as though she had a heavy cold. He could see her form silhouetted against the door, and her hair was dishevelled and wild. He bit his lips and stayed silent.

She came into the room quietly and began to look among the sleeping children. She came near and sat down by his side. She touched his face gently and then her trembling hand travelled over his body, soothingly. He felt his courage return. This was the mother he knew, who was kind and gentle even though she was harsh with them when they did something to make her angry. He had done nothing now. He had tried not to make any noise. Only he had felt sad and abandoned when he thought of his father and he had cried—even as he was crying now, louder and louder, till his mother put her hand softly over his mouth and spoke consolingly. 'What is it? What is it, my son?'

He spoke, and his words came out with great difficulty, as though a hand—a fat, hairy hand like that of the man with the moustache—was choking him. 'Is our father dead?'

His mother did not say anything for a while but she went on patting him gently. 'No. He is not dead. He has left us—I don't know where he is gone. He doesn't care for us any more, that is all.' She too began to weep.

He could have laughed with relief... that his father had only gone away somewhere—and was not dead. He loved them, of that he had no doubt. He was sure to come back. He would come back the next day—or the next week. Gopalan wanted to reassure his mother, but he only held on to her in the dark and said nothing.

In the bright light of the day, his fears appeared still more unfounded. His father had nowhere else to go—his mother was probably sick. She was tight-lipped again and irritable, and thinking of the night before he was embarrassed and gave her a wide berth. The older children were also uncommunicative. Perhaps they did not know anything and when he persisted they cuffed him and asked him to leave them alone. He did not mind that. He felt light-hearted—almost gay—and he went and bought some peppermints with the few paise that a neighbour had, with unexpected kindness, given him. For an odd reason, he was conscious that he was attracting a lot of attention even from strangers.

He went and sat in a quiet corner, in the shade between two houses, to eat his sweets in peace, and think things out. He kept an eye on the street to see whether his father would be passing by, by chance, on his way home. What a relief it would be to run up to him and greet him! The new man in the shop was a mystery. He looked as though he had come to stay, as though the shop was his!

His father had nowhere else to go! . . . What was it that someone said about another woman? He could not understand it. All the women he knew were still there—in the neighbourhood. His father was not with any of them, he himself had checked that. Why was it then that his classmates had laughed when he had told them that his father would return one day? Did they know something that he did not know? He had also overheard some neighbours encouraging his mother to find some work to support the children. 'You cannot neglect them,' they had said, 'even if the man could. You cannot let them starve.'

At the end of the month, his father had not yet returned and Gopalan knew, in the way children know some things without recourse to adult logic, that his father would never come back.

He never again asked about his father. When some friends tried to give his mother hope that the man would one day return to her when he got 'tired of it', he dismissed it as foolishness but kept silent. When, as the days and weeks and months went by, he saw his mother struggle to keep the family together, suffer indignities...when he saw the gradual undermining of her health as a result of overwork and worry—he did not ask any questions either. He bore the vicissitudes with a despairing patience, with a grim indifference, just like any other member of the family. When he was one day stopped from going to school, or when his youngest brother died in the agony and loneliness of the night because they could not afford to call in a doctor on time or pull wires to get him admitted in the overcrowded Government hospital, he still asked no questions. Sometimes he sat and thought over these incidents and he came to the conclusion that some were born to suffer just as some others were born to enjoy, for no fault or merit of their own. His mother blamed it all on Fate and when she was in a despairing mood, told her children that there was no God and that it was all a lie and that no one could believe in a God who was merciless to the poor. She would then clap her hand over her mouth and beat her chest and declare that she was a mad woman to talk in that way and that God was merciful, who would understand her agony and forgive her.

Gopalan did not believe her, though at such times his heart went out to her in sympathy. There was no God, he was convinced of that. There was nothing in the temples except those mute stone images and fat priests who were interested only in making money out of other people's foolishness. He always found enough truth and reason around the dilapidated chawls in which he lived now, in the wreckage of other lives such as his, to support his argument. He was the brightest boy of the family and he kept his thoughts to himself. He recalled with shame the times he had gone to a temple, with his father and mother, and had watched with wide-eyed curiosity the demonstration of piety displayed by the people around him. For some curious reason, the folk he knew and lived with had no access to the inner precincts, and he had often wondered what really went on in there. Perhaps God preferred the rich because they were clean and soft-spoken and well-mannered. It was their God then, and he wanted no part of it.

Typical of many people of his class, Gopalan's mind took the short-cut from the innocence of childhood into the maturity of the adult. Only his body seemed to go through the slow biological processes of adolescence. He had of course long ago given up school, but he took delight in learning to read and write, to fumble with the intricacies of arithmetic, or delve into the mysteries of everyday science. He studied for himself with the help of other school-going children of his own age, or with borrowed books and he read them avidly in the smoky light of a chimney-less kerosene lamp at home. Of what material use this learning would be, he had no idea; but he knew this was one of the differences between the rich and the poor. He never had a chance to test his knowledge or measure its depth. Information, scant as it came, was piled helter-skelter in his undisciplined mind. Gopalan's ideas of the world and his concept of human affairs shifted with every tide and current like an island of sand at a river-mouth. The life he saw around him made little sense in the light of his new learning. The people were crude, passive and had the resignation of the condemned. They were a rough lot, even his own kith and kin; they lived and fought like dogs. Pot-bellied children, loud-mouthed women and drunken men! They wallowed in filth. He felt disgusted, but knowing the emptiness and tragedies of their lives, he was also moved to pity—and at times by an impotent rage. They were not bad people, even if some of them seemed to get into trouble with the law; but then as he had seen, the law too was corrupt. Violence and squalor was a way of life that had been somehow imposed on them. There was something wrong, somewhere. He could not place his finger on it.

Then Gopalan discovered Marx and Lenin, through the kindness of a world-weary schoolmaster of a neighbourhood elementary school. It was a revelation. Here were the answers to all his questions, in cold print, in unsentimental prose. He felt he was reborn to a far fairer and nobler inheritance than he had ever dreamed possible. The shifting sands had at last found their permanent place, with the latitude and longitude fixed firmly on his mental map.

He sympathized with the underdog, because he himself had started life as one. But he was also a self-made man and believed that what the have-nots needed most was a sense of purpose and the courage to fight for their rights. He learnt more; and with new knowledge came new convictions and a new faith, and determination to put his ideas into effect. Thereafter Gopalan's mind grew according to a recognizable pattern, well-conditioned and disciplined, along what appeared to him as logical channels, gaining a certain poise and assurance which early enough began to make him stand out from his companions. Life had given him shrewdness if not mellowness, convictions if not confidence. These and a newly-discovered ability to express himself in forceful words put him on the road to leadership.

Much later in life, looking back upon his early years, Gopalan was convinced that the vicissitudes by themselves had no big hand in shaping the career he had chosen, in spite of the inevitable sentimentalization that any successful man could expect from adulatory chroniclers. He would have arrived here anyway, by a different if devious route. He would have championed the underdog, and, with clenched fists and resounding voice, spoken eloquently for the revolution. He was never afraid of violence—in a battle, he said, you counted the spoils and not the dead. Everything had a price—he had discovered that early enough in life. And the better the thing, the higher the price. Only cowards were afraid to pay it. He had no use for cowards. The world had no use for them either; not in the world that he visualized, where men were equal and free from want and fear. A little blood-letting would do no one any harm. He and others who thought like him would pull down old temples, displace the old gods and build anew, with steel and concrete, where equality and fraternity were the litany, and work was worship.

In the early years of World War II, Gopalan went to jail as an avowed enemy of the British Empire, a bedraggled nonentity condemned as a third-class prisoner, sharing his cell with felons. He did not resent this discrimination; he felt contempt for the privileged political detenus. It hardened him while, he suspected, it only strengthened the appetites of the others. He thought of greater sacrifices in times to come, while their minds dwelt upon the ease and personal gains that freedom would bring. He led a hunger-strike against the atrocious prison conditions, and was tied to a post and whipped for his troubles. A native warden whom he had called a boot-licker of the imperialists gave him a kidney injury which was to trouble him from time to time for the rest of his life. He read books and distributed leaflets smuggled in with the help of corrupt prison officials. He held discourses. He knew the agonies and fears of solitary confinement, but he held on to his sanity by recalling, and sometimes repeating aloud, the inspiring words of the leaders he admired. 'Workers of the world unite,' he shouted and shouted, till the very walls of the cell trembled, and a warder came and began to rattle the door.

He had been to jail, on other occasions too, even after his country awoke one morning to freedom, and chaos. Democracy, they called it, an asylum ruled by its inmates, men driven by power and greed, scheming, casting their votes and conniving at keeping the underdog an underdog, breaking the will of their victims with taxes and tear gas and corrupt tribunals. Enough of this farce called democracy, Gopalan had often cried to his followers. You have to cut this canker out—even if you have to spill some blood.

But it was one thing to shout from platforms, and quite another to fight in the streets of what he called a police-ruled state. Slogans were impotent against lathis—faith, however fervent, did not stop bullets. The revolution had to bide its time, wait for better weapons and better opportunities. With ruthless cunning, he had to strike terror in the hearts of his opponents. He had to bully the popular conscience out of its habitual lassitude, its pernicious state of atrophy. He had to shock and wound it into alertness. He broke away from the conventional communists and laid the foundation for a party dedicated to what he called purposeful action. Step by step he made his plans, winning a small victory here or losing a battle there, waiting for his chance to reveal his deadly hand. He knew he was up against desperate vested interests, with homilies on their lips and murder in their heart. They were the leaders of sheep and their most potent weapon was still the ballot box. Gopalan grimaced. The ballot box, indeed! Tampered with, he was sure, stuffed with worthless bits of paper, faked in the offices of his rival parties, representing in sum total nothing but a massive hoax played on a helpless people.

So be it. He would fight them with their own weapons. At least for the present. He was a master of strategy. He would create confusion in the enemy ranks. He could, he was sure, still beat them at their own game. While he made preparation for the final assault, he could amuse himself by finding out with just how much grace the capitalist-imperialist clique would bow itself out of power.

Gopalan looked at his wrist watch. The time was well past nine. He felt impatient, and a little insulted. He did not like to be kept waiting. Where were those boys? He had himself gone to one of their houses the day before, and had virtually been pushed out of the compound by that woman, who must be his mother. He had nothing against her—a bourgeois type, with her nose high up in the air—but a woman all the same, like his own mother. He had not thought it wise to tell her about Kesavan's predicament. Perhaps she already knew that her son as well as a few other students were under suspension from the college. No, he remembered now. Gopalan was conscious of dropping a brick when he had asked whether the boy was at home and that was when the woman became defensive, and then faintly antagonistic. He was a good boy, that Kesavan, intelligent—oh, very quick-witted and sincere. . . though, Gopalan had to admit it, a little too thoughtful and indecisive for his own good. But all boys these days were like that. They were slow to mature and bear a man's responsibilities. They were either dumb or turned out to be obnoxious smarties. Too much pampered at home, he was sure. That was the trouble with the middle class which unfortunately still dominated the educational institutions. They faced no challenges, they fattened on cod-liver oil and their responses were sluggish. They had to be guided, provoked, roused. . . only then did they get the courage to act.

He would deal with the Principal, in his own way, in his own good time. Damned Christian God-lover! The students were afraid of him—not afraid, perhaps, then what was it? Respect? Regard? Gopalan had guffawed in their face.

'Why are you afraid of him?' he had taunted them. 'Of punishment? What can he do to you—or anyone for that matter? Not a thing, if you unite. Students united is a force to be reckoned with—not by the college authorities alone, but by the Government itself. Remember that. You must think like men. Act like men. A great responsibility rests on you.'

What responsibility? To make older people see reason,

he had appealed to their pride. 'The future is yours, and you cannot let the country go to the dogs. You cannot let greedy, selfish men play havoc with your lives! This is the basic issue you are fighting for, don't forget that, no matter what the immediate provocation is. You cannot let them ride rough-shod over your conscience, can you? Only cowards and little children run away from bullies. You are neither. You are men. Men on the threshold of life. Don't let anyone treat you like children. You must stand up and fight.'

They had fought—on previous occasions, though not with the vigour that he would have expected and encouraged. On the issue of fees. On the question of language. Why, even when examination papers were tough or when a professor was too harsh with a student. Small battles, but decisive ones. Once or twice, it was true, they had retreated. But who was responsible for that? Not Gopalan or his party. Everyone exploited the students. Old monkeys using the young ones to pull their chestnuts out of the fire! On such occasions, Gopalan himself had not spared the boys.

'Never get into a battle unless you are sure of winning it,' he had warned them. It was not a precept that he himself could always afford to practise, but he himself was playing for much bigger stakes. In this case he had only been watching the fun from the sidelines. As a well-wisher of the student community, interested only in seeing justice done.

'Who are your leaders? What are they after? You have been tricked and you don't even know that! They use you when they wanted to fight for the so-called freedom of the country. Now that they themselves are in power, they don't want you to embarrass them—or to thwart them. Give them the peace to enjoy the spoils of your war!'

The student crowd had roared with anger and shouted slogans. Gopalan had waited, as though he were a man of great patience, disheartened, dispirited at the sight of what was manifestly a mental debacle on the part of the national leaders. What had been the occasion? Ah, yes. It was just before the protest against enhanced fees was launched. It was a state-wide affair with, it was reported, the tacit blessing of the ruling party. The target was the private colleges. The movement was disorganized and weakened by faction fights. But the students had had their share of fun, cutting classes, throwing stones and a total disruption of examinations. As far as Gopalan could judge then, the strike had achieved little more.

He had given it to them, then. Straight from the shoulder, so to speak. He had not spared anyone, not even himself or his own party. They were also, after all, on the wrong side of the generation gap. Why should he let go of an opportunity to prove that he knew where the blame lay; and he was fair enough to acknowledge it.

'Our minds are not as quick as yours,' he had said with feigned dismay. 'We are getting old, perhaps. Or complacent. We should have seen it coming and acted in the best interests of our young friends. But forgive us. We are your elders and you should take our decisions without question. We have our own axe to grind—inside the Assembly and outside it. But, pardon us again, some of us are in league with the college authorities,' he went on with heavy sarcasm. 'We lower the standards of the free Government colleges—and give the green signal to some favoured private institutions to put up the fees and bleed the students and their parents white. Education is costly. We are not citizens of a genuine socialist state. Colleges need funds and more funds. Why, some of us need a part of those funds to fight our election battles! So you must bear with us and pay without question!'

'Never ! Never !' the cry had risen from young throats. Gopalan had seen it as the first tremors of a juggernaut quivering into life, pulled along by a new force of unity bonded by a common purpose.

What that purpose was, he himself was not clear. Or was

not prepared to set out in words now. There would be time later for polemics. Yet only few of the students had the patience for vague and involved theorizations. They wanted action. They wanted a target.

'We shall fight for our rights,' they had roared again.

Gopalan, wisely, had counselled patience then. He had let them strain at the leash, but he had no intention at that time of letting go. His party set great store by organization. Nothing worthwhile was achieved in a hurry, without careful preparation. He would only test the force, but not use it. A time would come for that later. No, he had not spared anyone, then or thereafter. The strike had come about, and after a few days had ended tamely in a compromise. The colleges had relented, the Government had relented and the arbitration committee had dragged on the issue till all the sap of rebellion was squeezed out of it. The students lost interest and their parents were impatient and nervous. The revised rates were still high, but they were prepared to buy peace.

Gopalan had openly expressed sympathy but secretly smiled with satisfaction. It had been, when all was said and done, a lesson for everyone. Particularly the students. It had been a part of their training, a try-out on the testing ground. A few beatings would toughen them up. And who really paid for this training? Not the students. Not even the parents. The cost of living was spiralling anyway and what difference did a few more rupees make? Gopalan laughed at the thought. The Government paid. The party in power paid. His own rival, that idiot Raghava Menon, who sat so smugly in the Assembly, had paid. Or he would pay. Now. At this moment. When the next general elections were so near!

Gopalan looked up from his reverie to see four young men cross the street and walk towards the restaurant. At last they were here ! One of these days he should teach them, without giving offence of course, the virtue of punctuality. That was part of the self-discipline they needed if they were to be of any use to anybody. Kesavan was not with them, but he did not give that a second thought.

The four boys walked with firm steps, heads held high, faces grimly set. Little would the people of this town imagine, Gopalan thought, looking at them, that the first wind of unrest had already begun to blow and that it would soon strike this lethargic, indifferent community with the force of a gale.

4

Raghava Menon finished his breakfast as he always did, with three teaspoonfuls of honey, carefully measured out of a glass jar with a black plastic screw-cap. He looked at the label appreciatively—'pure Coorg honey', it said in white letters against a golden brown background. Menon smacked his lips with satisfaction. He liked honey. It was one of the few gastronomical indulgences that he could permit himself at his age—fifty-eight he was, though his friends always said that he did not look a day older than forty-five.

The honey helped his digestion, or so the family doctor had assured him. It also seemed to impart a little of its golden glow to his complexion. Menon was strikingly fair and he must have been a handsome man in his youth. His hair was thin but still jet black and his features were small and regular, though now a little lost amid fleshy cheeks and a clean, immaculately shaven double chin. His teeth were healthy and very white, and he still took pride in displaying them in a wide smile whenever the occasion presented itself. In repose, his small, well-shaped mouth was petulant, a little Nero-like, his detractors said. Menon was only amused, perhaps even a trifle flattered. After all, was not Nero a flourishing emperor of Rome?

Menon heaved his bulk out of the chair and walked over to a wash-basin fixed in a corner of the dining room for his exclusive use. He wore a dhoti of fine-spun cotton and his body was bare except for a towel that he wore over his left shoulder. The hair on his chest and back were startlingly black against a white skin. Only very close scrutiny would have revealed that even they were dyed. As he stood with his hands held under the running water from the tap, his paunch pressed against the edge of the porcelain washbasin. 'Baldness, hair on the back and a paunch,' these, according to an old vernacular proverb, were the visible signs of prosperity in men. He had so far one of them, he would say smilingly to his wife, sometimes, in the privacy of their bedroom. The other two, he was still too youthful to acquire.

He took a handful of water, sipped it and gargled noisily with his chin held high, like a bird drinking. He heard his wife behind him, collecting the plates from the table, and he knew that she herself would wash them now and put them away. It had always been her pleasure, she called it a privilege to serve him food, to clean up after he had finished, though there were enough servants in the house to do that. She would maintain that it was a wife's duty to serve her husband. She had neither the time nor the inclination to learn new-fangled ways from the younger generation as represented by her own daughters. They needed ayahs for everything. They read English books, though she herself had yet to see a woman who had profited by them. They slept most of the time, leaving everything to servants. How their husbands could put up with it, she had no idea at all.

Menon was touched by his wife's sense of duty, but he would ask banteringly, 'Then why do you want so many servants in the house? I am not a zamindar, you know that!'

'How many of them are there?' she would protest immediately. 'Just the cook and the girl—who else? You can't really count the sweeper woman among the servants ...Though God knows, the way servants behave these days, it is better not to have any. Not one! and you say you are not a zamindar,' she would smile at her husband.

Menon laughed, thinking of it, as he walked past, gently patting her cheek as he did so. She bent back embarrassed, looking round to see if anyone had noticed this demonstration of conjugal felicity.

'Shame on you!' she said coyly'. . .and after all these years! With four children, and one of them a big officer, remember that! Acting as though we were just a newly-married couple!'

Menon guffawed and stood looking at her speculatively. A fine woman! Past forty and still not a wrinkle on the face, not a strand of grey hair on her head! Big-bosomed and wide-hipped—a contrast to the thin-as-a-pole, anaemic women of the younger generation. Why, take his own daughters. The elder one. Fussing about cream and sugar all the time. Eating raw vegatables and covering up the haggard look with make-up. . . oh, he knew she used it when she was away from home with her husband in the city. He did not personally like it and his own wife, if she knew about it, would be scandalized, but that was progress, he had been told. Thank God his wife did not need any make-up. . . He looked up to see her watching him.

'What is it?' he asked.

'Some people don't know what is happening in their own house, to their own children,' she said smiling broadly. 'What is it?' he asked intrigued, and a little alarmed. 'Some news from Calcutta?' That was where his eldest daughter was with her husband, who was an executive in an oil company.

'Yes,' she said, looking at him almost shyly now. 'There is a letter from her this morning. She is—well, she feels a little giddy in the morning, it seems, and she has no appetite. . .'

Menon's face cracked into a wide grin like an over-ripe melon. God, why these women had to be so devious and coy while talking of pregnancies, he would never know! He felt a sudden excitement, a pleasant warmth spread within him at the prospect that he might soon be a grandfather. 'Have they seen a doctor?'

' I don't know,' she replied. 'The silly girl doesn't say that. Do you think it means something?'

'Of course, of course. Do you remember the first time you. . .'

'All right, all right. No need to go into details. . . We must ask her to come home at once!'

'What on earth for?' Menon asked.

'Oh, she is so far away. . .'

'Don't be silly!' He saw his wife's face fall, and he quickly changed his tone. 'Look, there is nothing to worry about—at least at this stage. . .'

'How do you know? The first four months, one has to be very careful.'

'I'm sure they will be careful. I shall speak to her tonight on the telephone. Calcutta is a big city, you know. There are good doctors and perhaps she can have her delivery here. . .'

'What do you mean, perhaps. She must have her delivery here. She is my daughter.'

'Of course, of course, I am not denying that.'

'She needs her mother.'

'Well, yes, I agree.' He was not at all sure that his daughter would agree. And his son-in-law was a man whom Menon looked upon with awe—and mild irritation at times. A quiet, pipe-smoking young man with slightly outlandish ideas. Very modern and all that and from a very good family, but somewhat westernized after a degree from abroad, and rather, Menon suspected, self-centered. He hoped his second son who was at present in the States would turn out to be different.

'You tell her that when you speak to her tonight,' his wife insisted.

'Yes, yes,' he promised absent-mindedly, not keen to let this develop into a controversy.

She walked away slowly towards the kitchen, after putting the jar of honey back in the refrigerator. In a short while he heard her voice raised as she said something sharply to someone—possibly the servant girl or the cook.

Menon came into the drawing room and sank with a sigh into a heavily upholstered easy chair. He took the towel from the shoulder and wiped his face and chest with it. He looked round for a stool, pulled it close and put his feet up.

The room was well-appointed, with quiet taste, thanks to the insistence of his youngest daughter Nandini, his favourite, though he seldom admitted it, and non-interference by his wife who considered the drawing room, accessible as it was to the outside world and her husband's many visitors, not quite her personal concern. Still daughter and mother had had arguments over it, as when his wife had wanted to put up old family group photographs on the wall...or at least a large picture of Lord Krishna painted by a local artist and framed in glistening gilt. Menon had for once unequivocally taken the side of the daughter against her mother.

'Let her do it the way she wants. She has good taste in these things.' He had not been sure of that at all, but when later friends had complimented him on the room, he thought that he was certainly a good judge of his daughter if not of interior decoration. He could trust that girl.

She was pretty, very pretty, he thought, and full of life, with an undertone of seriousness which won her many friends —and many admirers in college, if one were to believe gossip. He was not exactly surprised or displeased, to be quite honest, but one had to watch out there! There was too much freedom between boys and girls in college these days. Gone were the days when a word exchanged with a girl or a smile from a boy would have raised speculation, perhaps even a riot! One could not control them now. They considered themselves old enough to look after their own affairs. Not that he had any apprehensions about Nandini. She was a sensible girl, far more sensible than the older daughter who was a bit of a scatterbrain, Menon feared. Thank God, she was well settled. As soon as Nandini was out of college, he should look for a husband for her. From a good family. An IAS at least. The new crop of company executives were all right; they seemed to live in comfort and style. But the Government was still the safest bet, and the IAS had a lot of prestige, if not glamour. Though with the new system of selection—he himself had advocated openly the cause of Harijans in keeping with his party policy—a lot of riff-raff got into it these days. He wondered what Nandini's own views would be on the subject. For all his patriarchal air, he knew in his heart of heart that she would have her way in the end. She could also be tough, that one !

Dreamily, he looked forward to another leisurely day spent at home. The Assembly was closed for the winter break and he enjoyed these holidays in his home town, away from the bustle of the capital, savouring boredom, satisfied that this was a well-earned rest. Rest ? Menon pursed his lips and closed his eyes as though with a sudden sense of weariness. There would always be callers, petitions, recommendations, sometimes reporters, or functions over which he would have to preside. And birthdays when he was the honoured guest, or weddings at which he blessed the couple while the proud parents looked on. Occasionally flash-bulbs flared and he would worry, wondering whether they had caught him with a pleasant expression. The local cameramen had a habit of catching a person with the eyes closed or the mouth wide open. Really Menon did not mind all this fanfare and fuss. You had to pay a price for being a celebrity in a small town, and he was one for paying it graciously.

After the next elections, Menon pondered now, he

would probably find himself in the Ministry. Even last time, it had been a narrow miss. His party could not forget the fact that he had the solid, middle-class Nair community behind him in this town, his constituency. He had bowed out with grace that time to make way for an influential and, yes, Menon admitted it, a rather brilliant Harijan candidate. You had to play a give-and-take game in politics. That way you lasted longer and stayed healthier. It was never a wise policy to embarrass the party bosses. You had to take a wider, if less immediately satisfactory, view of such things. And Menon had always asserted that he was not carried away, beyond sense and logic, by ostentation and power.

He had earned his present position and the privileges that came with it. He never doubted it. Let his opponents say what they would. Back in the thirties, he had given up a promising lawyer's career to put his all in politics. He had not even attempted a compromise, like some others, to run both careers at the same time, doing justice neither to one's ideals nor to one's clients. It was all or nothing, one or the other for him. It was true that he was financially very sound even without his law practice, having inherited considerable ancestral property. But still, those were times of uncertainty and the future had often looked bleak. What promises of success were there then? What assurance of a life of ease later? None. None whatever. He, as so many others like him, had no thought of any future gains other than the unconditional freedom of his country. Patriotism was not a catchword then. It was a strange and new feeling that sent one's blood pounding through one's veins. When the volunteers sang 'Vande Mataram', it would bring tears of joy to his eyes and a sense of glory to his heart. What a song it was! A pity they did not make it the National Anthem. 'You are our knowledge ... You are our dharma ... You are our very life ...' Where was that India gone now?

No, it had not been easy. There were relatives and so-called well-wishers of the family who had run him down as though he were a criminal. They had forgotten all that today, but he had not; or else they would not be coming to him for favours now! There was his old mother, not knowing what it was all about but shamed beyond belief by the fact that he had gone to jail, refusing to take him back into the house... and his father, brooding, always unsure of his loyalties, his mind deep-rooted in the belief that the Empire was impregnable... But Raghava Menon had stood by his convictions, never flinching, never doubting the greatness of Gandhiji or the high destiny of the party to which he belonged. He had often wondered whether his mother, in her last moments, had forgiven him. He had never known. He was serving a term in the Vellore jail then. The authorities had been kind to him—perhaps his father had pulled some wires— and he was given special permission to go home and visit his ailing mother.

That was the last time he saw her alive. He had felt nothing then, only compassion for the old woman who lay in bed, shrivelled up, stricken by paralysis, her eyes fixed and vacantly staring at his face. He had looked long and deep into them, trying desperately to discern some glimmer of recognition, some sign of emotion...

'She recognizes you,' his father had said. 'We have been seeing her like this for a long time... we know the signs, however faint they are.' He bent down and then shouted his son's name several times into his wife's ears.

But did she hear? Menon doubted it. Even the doctor, when questioned, had merely shrugged.

'Is there any hope at all?' he had enquired, feeling a lump in his throat, knowing the hopelessness of it all even before the doctor replied.

She died three weeks after he returned to the jail at the end of his parole.

He had felt no bitterness, not even any great sense of loss. His mother had been a true matriarch of the old school: proud, unbending, generous, and obstinate. The

Abhimanyu

family meant everything, her brothers and uncles were gods. The Emperor, irrespective of the colour of his skin or the distance of his seat of power, was perhaps still 'king' to her; and to wage war against royalty was treason. She had probably never forgiven him, Raghava Menon thought. He did not feel any emotion about it. There were too many others like him, around him, who were called upon to make greater sacrifices. And oddly his mother's death seemed to have released his father from the bonds of loyalty that had tied him to her. He supported, and even encouraged his son, and was proud of him till the time of his death exactly seven years later in free India.

Easy life! Menon snorted. It was not easy then; nor, when you came down to practical terms, was it easy now. Let his enemies grudge him his success, his low but steady rise to eminence. They were all upstarts, like that fool Gopalan! Arrogant, impertinent...dogs that stand by on the roadside and bark at the caravan. They hated his guts. They wanted to see him destroyed. They were just envious, embittered men. Spokesmen of the rag-and-bone community who had wild dreams of one day ruling the land!

Raghava Menon felt at this moment supremely secure and impregnable. He had no fear of the rabble. He was too much of an aristocrat, by birth as well as by disposition, to succumb to their taunts. This was his home town— these were the people who knew him as one of their own kind. They would never let him down.

Menon picked up the morning paper from a side-table and looked at it. The Americans had started a new offensive in Vietnam. Somewhere in a northern state, a few more legislators had crossed the floor—cheating, Menon thought, of the worst kind, forgetting that they represented an electorate which had voted them into power on the merit of their original party affiliations...A Minister announced the prospect of a good harvest that year. (And high time, too, Menon said under his breath, his wife had been pestering him just yesterday to use him influence to get more rice for their home.) The students had been up to mischief in Andhra. . .

He suddenly put the paper aside. Students! Yes, they were up to mischief everywhere ! . . . Here . . . Now. . . In this very town! No serious trouble yet, thank God, but trouble all the same. And of all things, about that obscure border village, Parkinsonpet !

Stupid ! Utterly stupid ! All that fuss over nothing; a five-mile stretch of land and a group of huts that no one but a few half-starved wretches had so far cared to call their own ! Not worthy to be made an issue, and yet . . . and yet . . .

Menon felt an impotent anger at the students, and then at his own party bosses up there in Delhi. It was their fault really. It was they who unthinkingly played themselves into the hands of dangerous, unscrupulous opportunists like Gopalan. Who had to pay the price for their mistakes? Who else but the people here, people like himself?

Parkinsonpet! What a name! What a place! An old District Collector Parkinson used to set up camp there as a base for a shikar in the forest-covered hills to the north. Menon wondered whether the place had ever been entered in any revenue records at all. It was neither hill nor plain, too rocky for cultivation, inhabited by a few aboriginal tribals doing coolie work in the villages or cutting wood on the sly from reserve forests and selling them at distant markets. Even wild animals skirted the territory when they came down to drink at the river that flowed two miles below. What made people set up habitations in such places, Menon had wondered. Now, of course, they had found the place good for teak and a little rubber, and there was talk, wild talk in all probability, that there were valuable minerals in the place. Was it gold or mica dust that glowed in the sands of the river ? No one had really checked. And now it was too late for a proper survey. The rumour had been good enough for propaganda, and two states had staked a claim over the village.

It was utterly beyond reason and logic and Menon suspected that all the parties concerned were aware of it. Somehow, it had risen from obscurity amid bargaining, negotiations, claims and counter-claims, into a prestige issue. When had it actually happened. Menon did not know. No one knew. No one really cared. Everything was a prestige issue these days, though it was never clear whose prestige was involved. Individuals and organizations and eventually State governments made the issue their own. It was easy to raise a controversy in the Assembly; and the Ministers made it worse by unthinking, evasive or ill-informed answers. Then the Press took it up and gave it a new dignity on the front page. Oddly the lesser the authorities were inclined to discuss it, the better copy it made for newspapers! Next thing you knew an Opposition member went on a fast, and the stage was set for trouble.

It was the same story on the other side of the border too. There, Menon knew, a Minister had to face a no-confidence move and quit. The Centre could have, and should have, settled the issue long ago. Menon himself had recommended giving up the village. If there really was gold, it would only go into the national coffers; why break your head over it? Why be left with a bunch of tribals who would be clamouring for rehabilitation? But there would always be people who hesitated at crucial moments, who lived in constant dread of Opposition attacks. Before he knew it, the issue had gone beyond the bounds of reason.

Menon knew that the Opposition, which in this case really meant Gopalan, would make an election issue out of it. They were all ganging up to oust Menon from the Assembly. They would hit hard and hit below the belt if an opportunity arose. Why else did they have to work up the student community? What had the boys got to do with it? About fees, yes, about language, yes...but about a border village—that was sheer impertinence. They were growing too big for their shoes. They were just turning their resentment of discipline into a holy war against their elders ! That was the sum total of it. Football matches were becoming too dull for them.

It should all have been nipped in the bud. It was really the fault of the principals and teachers and professors you ran across these days. A gutless community ! Inefficient, indifferent... assuming a kind of holier-than-thou attitude when all you tried was to appeal to their reason. What was that man's name?...that Christian missionary ? Father Joshe, yes, that was it. The college had been the hotbed of trouble for some time. And yet, 'Don't blame us, Mr Menon,' the man had said. 'Student indiscipline is no longer a problem to be confined within the college walls.'

Pious nonsense! And whose fault was it, pray?

'They get politics with their mother's milk,' another smart alec had said sarcastically: 'Politicians, I don't mean you personally, Mr. Menon... Education is now becoming a by-product in our college. And, frankly, politicians should take a large share of the blame...'

Menon had remained silent—angry, provoked, but at a total loss for words to retaliate with. There was some truth in what the man said. And the whole truth, if one wanted it, was that everybody was to blame. Politicians. Parents. Teachers. Even the Government. They would never be stern when sternness was called for. When the students threw stones, the police looked away with embarrassment. They could get away with anything these days ! They always got the public's sympathy. Boys would be boys and all that nonsense ! The parents were really the guilty ones. When we were young, he thought, we would not dare go home with a complaint against a teacher, genuine or otherwise. There would be no skin left on us...

His wife entered and said : 'There's a man to see you.'

Menon looked round without interest. 'Who is it ?'

'I don't know. He gave his name as Govindan Nair.'

Abhimanyu

Govindan Nair? Menon could not place him. The name was familiar, but it was a common enough one. A new petition perhaps, or was a stuffy little library being opened somewhere? Menon sighed. There was never an escape from this kind of thing.

'All right,' he said to his wife, who stood by waiting. Then it suddenly occurred to him. It was probably someone known to her. Then he had it! 'Do you know him?' he asked again suspiciously.

'No. Never seen him in my life! He had come over to the back and was asking the servant questions. It seemed he did not want to disturb you and wanted to make sure that you were free...'

'All right, all right,' Menon said. 'I shall see him.'

When the visitor entered, Menon was sitting, absorbed in the newspaper. He lowered it a little and studied the other over the edge of the paper. Govindan Nair cleared his throat. He had an umbrella in his hand and he looked round for a place to put it down in...then, finding no encouragement from Menon, he changed his mind and remained standing, fidgeting with it.

'I do not think you remember me...' he began hesitantly.

Menon scrutinized the man, surely a stranger? He took in Nair's faded coat, his clean but coarse dhoti and bare feet. The man must have politely left his chappals outside.

'No, I don't seem to know you,' Menon said, somehow not making that remark rude but only a plain statement of fact.

'I am a supervisor in the Supplies and Disposals office.'

So that was it. A recommendation for promotion? No, that could not be. The man looked too old to be worrying about promotions. Perhaps an extension of service, or a cancellation of a transfer...?

'Actually,' the man was saying, 'it is not about myself

that I have come, intruding on your valuable time.'

'Then what is it ?'

'It is—it is about my son. You wouldn't remember, but last year you were most kind to help us get a scholarship for him.'

'I see.' He did not see at all, but he went on all the same. 'You want a job for him. I can tell you...'

'No, no, no...He's still in college. Thank God I don't have to worry about a job for him— yet,' Nair said ingratiatingly.

'Then what is it ?' Menon's tone became a trifle impatient. 'Why don't you say what you want ?'

'He has been suspended from college.'

Good Lord, Menon thought. What a lot of preliminaries to tell him that ! He looked at his visitor with a new interest.

'Why has he been suspended ?'

He saw the other man hesitate. This must be the hardest part of his story. Nair cleared his throat again and looked round helplessly. Then his eyes met Menon's. 'He is impetuous...a bit foolish. Gets easily carried away at times, but he is, he was a good student. Very good at English and mathematics...' He began to fumble under Menon's steady gaze. 'He...like so many others...talk of politics...and that strike last year... No, no, it was early this year...'

'I see,' Menon now mercifully cut the other short. 'Politics, is that it ?'

Nair was looking out of the window. In the compound, some workmen were spreading paddy, boiled and still steaming wet, on bamboo mats to dry in the sun. A big-hipped woman, standing on the mat and bent nearly double, was swinging her hands from side to side, in a wide arc, combing the paddy with her fingers.

Menon followed the other man's gaze and said. 'That is paddy from my village. I...I get special permission to bring it here. The ration rice doesn't agree with us.' His voice turned a trifle challenging. 'You agree with that, don't you ?'

Nair gave a start. 'Of course. The rice you get in ration

Abhimanyu

shops these days stinks...and it is full of stones. I was not thinking of that,' he ended on a faint note of apology.

It was just as well that you were not thinking of that, Menon thought. Procurement of paddy was in force and there was a ban on inter-district movement of any food grains. He had no permit, special or otherwise (imagine a thing like that getting to the notice of the wrong people !) He brought it from the village all the same, and the officials never really bothered. Well, Menon said to himself, one must have some privileges...

'Yes, about your son,' he continued reflectively. 'A good way to pay me back, isn't it ?...if, as you say, I recommended him for a scholarship. Did he get it ?'

'He did, and I am deeply indebted to you. But now, I am afraid the college might... You know—'

'Yes, I know. The college might cancel it. What else do you expect ?'

Menon suddenly sat up, pulling his feet away from the stool on which they rested. For a moment, he even felt sorry for the man in front of him. The interview had started off badly. But who was responsible for that ? Facts had to be faced. Here was one of them; at least the father of one of then, squirming under his gaze, asking for what Menon considered just punishment.

'The boys are becoming too much of a problem, let me tell you that, Mr Nair. Whose fault is it ?...yours ! Let us face it. It is the parent's fault ! You don't know how to bring up your children. You give them too much freedom. You let them sit on your head. What is the use of running to us when things get out of hand ?' Nair blinked helplessly, feeling miserable. 'He is a good boy. I am his father and I say it without hesitation. People get into the wrong company sometimes.'

'Wrong company ? My children never got into wrong company, Mr Nair. I saw to that.' Menon snorted. 'Is he a student leader or something ?'

'Oh no! Nothing like that! He is just...Well, the boys like him, I think. He is very quiet and studious...and last year he won a prize for—for something...'

'Not a prize for stirring up trouble?' Menon said with heavy sarcasm. Nair looked at him, his face broken up into a painful smile. Then quickly he turned his eyes down. 'He is my only son. His future means a lot to us, to my wife and myself. All that he needs now is proper guidance.'

'And you expect me to give him that guidance?'

'No, no. It is my fault. I admit that. You have many other problems, Mr Menon. I know, I know,' he anticipated the other man's protests. 'I mean, perhaps I have neglected him a bit...'

Menon laughed. Then he asked: 'Has his scholarship been cancelled?'

'Not officially, as far as I know. But the principal has warned him. My...my wife told me so. We are very anxious. I am a poor man, Mr Menon. I cannot afford to send him to college. The scholarship is a great help, and I must thank you for that. If you could put in a word, I am sure...'

'Which college is it?'

'The Missionary College. Father Joshe.'

'Oh, that man!' Menon did not say anything more for a long time. He looked out of the window. The workmen had gone now and with a mild feeling of irritation, he noticed that a few crows were already gathering on the branches of nearby trees. He wanted to call someone or even step outside, but he felt it would be rather undignified to be seen by this man shooing away crows.

'I shall think over it,' he turned to Nair. 'Father Joshe is an adamant man. If he has made up his mind.' Nair stood looking forlorn and downcast. Hesitantly he put his palms together, in a gesture of supplicaton. His eyes glistened and for a moment Menon wondered whether the man was going to cry. 'I will never forget your help. I shall always be grateful...'

'Yes, yes,' Menon said impatiently. The crows outside were getting bolder. Two of them had actually hopped down from the branch and were on the edge of the mat almost, bending their heads this side and that, on the alert for intruders. Nair had retreated outside the door. He held the umbrella in his left hand and was putting on his chappals, his right hand pressed against the wall for support. He hesitated, made another supplicatory gesture and then turned round and began to walk towards the gate.

Menon noted with distaste that there was a sweat-mark where the man had rested his palm on the wall. Damned nuisance! To imagine that Menon would take it up with that Father Joshe! Served the boy right if he was dabbling in politics...

He remembered the crows and stepped down hastily from the verandah on to the compound. They were pecking at his paddy now—black, destructive devils! He began to shout and wave his hands frantically, watching them fly away in a flurry.

5

Father Joshe walked with measured steps down the verandah of the Missionary College, his heavy leather shoes making a resounding bump on the cement floor at perfectly regular intervals. Sunlight, coming in at a slant between the row of heavy, squarish pillars on his left, lay in shiny rectangular patches along his path. As he walked, the shadows of the pillars swept over his flowing white gown like dark hands blocking his path. Father Joshe wished obstacles in life were as ephemeral and easy to pass as these !

The heavy shoes were a mistake, his juniors used to remind him from time to time. They warned the students of his approach well in advance, and gave them time to compose themselves and wish him good morning in an altogether irreproachable manner, with the correct inflexions in their voice. Father Joshe smiled. He fully agreed with his colleagues; they were right, of course; but he continued to wear the same type of heavy-heeled shoes. He was always for giving the boys a fair chance.

He was not much of a disciplinarian, Father Joshe often reflected ruefully. At least not in the same old sense... Hmmm... That was a concession, he thought, he was making to himself. And yet discipline, like anything else, must also be subject to a change of definition from time to time. What old sense ? He was an old man, there was no denying that, but he was still living in the present ! You could not separate mischief from the boys. Why, after twenty-five years of service in this institution, he had come to the conclusion that you could not really have one without the other. Indeed, if he were pressed to admit it, he would have said that he liked a little mischief in his boys, as long as it did not cross the bounds of propriety, of course. Was that leniency, or perhaps indulgence ? He was not sure. May be it was not a very wise attitude for the head of a highly respected educational institution. Of late he had begun to have serious doubts about his wisdom in such matters.

The verandah turned left at a right angle, the regularity of the footsteps was broken but for a moment, and Father Joshe was again walking with the same measured steps down a stretch just like the one before except that the sun no longer lay across his path. He stopped at the fifth door on his right—a half-door, in fact with the bottom section of frosted glass of a pattern that had long ago ceased to be the fashion with building contractors. To a side of the door, a small panel of polished wood carried the legend 'Principal' in raised brass letters with an in-and-out indicator below.

Father Joshe paused for a moment before going in and looked across the college quadrangle. It was too early in the morning for students, and in any case it was a Saturday and only a few special classes would be held. He did not quite approve of this practice of special classes. The professors must try to finish their portions during the allotted periods. But with all these breaks in classes because of strikes and hartals and so on, no one really had any choice. This was also bad for discipline. It created a disorientation in the student mind. It permitted sloppiness on the part of professors. Both were bad. Very bad.

He had remembered that it was a Saturday as he passed the Staff Room a few doors earlier. He did not expect anybody to be in and he had walked on, without bothering to enter and wish his subordinates good morning. He did not much care for protocol. He always found it an encumbrance. If anyone chastised him for it occasionally, it was only Joseph, his personal peon, who, Father Joshe now noticed, had not yet arrived and was not at his usual post outside the door. He realized with a mild resentment that today he would have to open the door of the office himself. Just behind the half-door was the teak-panelled main door, which Father Joshe opened with a key he took out of the folds of his gown. The spring-loaded swinging panels were getting in his way and he pushed one aside irritably only to be smacked in the back as he turned. He muttered something under his breath, and then crossed himself hastily. There was a way of doing these things. Now, with great deliberation, he pushed open the left half of the swinging door, and held on to it while he fumbled with his other hand behind it to find the catch which always held it open when he was in the office. He saw Joseph's stool on one side, pulled it along and placed it outside, against the closed half of the door. He walked in, dusting his hands, round the plywood screen which hid the door from where he sat, and walked across the room to his desk.

He briefly glanced at the wooden crucifix on the wall over his chair and crossed himself. He gathered his voluminous gown around him and sat down, looking reflectively at the table. There was dust on it, and for a moment he appeared undecided. Then he picked up a magazine from the table and peremptorily dusted the top with it. He put it aside, not altogether pleased with his effort. Joseph should have been here earlier than this, he thought. But then he remembered : it was not often that he himself came so early to his office and the peon had not been told the day before. He pursed his lips and looked moodily at the windows. He himself would have to get up and open them.

Inside the room Father Joshe looked towering, taller than he had seemed among the pillars on the verandah. He had a high nose which stood out like a ridge, dividing his

Abhimanyu

rugged face into two sections, as it were. His eyes were bright and shining, and, but for the expression in them people would perhaps never be able to make out whether he was smiling or scowling, for his mouth was virtually lost amid a heavy beard that came down nearly to his chest. He had a high forehead, deeply wrinkled, so high in fact as to have lost its identity under a general description of a bald head, with a fringe of hair, which was, like the beard, heavily streaked with white. His hands which stuck out of the gown were bony, long-fingered and sensitive.

The windows let in a little bit of the sunlight and a refreshing whiff of the cool morning breeze. Now that he was about it, Father Joshe went over to the single-day-a-sheet calendar that hung on the wall facing his desk and tore off the top sheet. With a jolt, he remembered that he had only three more days to give an answer to the ultimatum given by the students' union.

What answer was there to be given anyway, he thought, as he went back to his chair. He was not quite clear in his mind what this was all about. They were not talking this time about fees or the language issue, or anything else that Father Joshe had anything to do with. A place called Parkinsonpet was vaguely mentioned, and the students wanted the college to be closed for a fortnight as a sign of protest. Protest against what ? Not having enough holidays in the year ! This was ridiculous ! And with examinations not too far away, it would be ruinous for the students ! Didn't they realize that ? 'We want to show our solidarity with the free-thinking people of this state,' they had said. What on earth was that ? Father Joshe wished his boys would demonstrate solidarity over the issue of studies !

There was, of course, the immediate question of the four students who had been suspended. He had done it after due consideration, and, in actual fact, under pressure from some of the professors. The boys had—at least one or two of them had—according to the report he had got, shouted slogans while a class was on and had spoken rudely, and, yes, insultingly to the professor who had tried to restore order. In the pandemonium that seemed to have been let loose, a large number of the students had walked out and, worse still, made abusive and vulgar remarks at the girl students who had stayed behind. Father Joshe had been particularly incensed by this last act of what he called juvenile crudeness.

His first reaction, however, was to get a little worried about the professor —assistant professor, in fact. The man had never got on with the students, never been quite able to control the class. What else could you expect when a teacher seemed to fumble over the problems that he himself had set for his students ? It was not because the man was inefficient, Father Joshe was convinced of that. He had a brilliant academic record. He had some experience in a suburban college, but what his performance had been there, Father Joshe did not have any idea. It was difficult to judge from a certificate. He had seen that sometimes a good degree, oddly, created a mental block in young professors. It made them take a supercilious attitude towards the boys, and not being much older than their wards, the latter resented it. Probably in this case, Father Joshe thought, the problem might be purely one of nerves...of wilting under the steady, and often provocative, stare of a few dozen pairs of eyes. Father Joshe himself knew, from his early years of teaching, that it could be quite unnerving. But a teacher had to get over it. He had to win the respect of the students, if not their devotion. He must at all times carry the class with him. Threats, and even punishment, were of use only up to a certain point. Beyond that, the problem boomeranged and became one of competence. Father Joshe had his own views on the matter, based on personal experience : the ideal teacher was born...up to a certain level one could be trained...the rest just did not click. They were not meant for the profession. Degrees did not have much to do with it. But the way things were turning out, colleges had, more and more, to make do with misfits.

He had called the young man aside and advised him. He had counselled patience. He had himself walked down the verandah several times when the assistant professor was conducting the class. He had tried to outstare the students who had chosen to turn round and watch him pass. He had even called a few of them to his office and threatened them with punishment. But things only seemed to get worse. And, to top it all, he had progressively become aware of feeling among some of the professors that he was soft-hearted; that he was too indulgent towards the students.

Father Joshe sighed. Where was the middle path that the wise men of old had extolled?

He was sure of one thing, and he was prepared to assert it in any form: the present-day younger generation was in no way different—neither worse, nor perhaps better—than the previous ones. If anything, they were a little more intelligent, a little more mature than their fathers were when they were young. He did not have the least doubt about it. They were exposed to a wider spectrum of knowledge and experience, and their reactions naturally were less predictable. It was a pity that the so-very-wise older generation did not take this simple fact into consideration when condemning the young or making plans for them. No, he was not condoning arrogance or impertinence, nor was he acquiescing to a spirit of sheer rebellion. The boys deserved consideration . . . yes, even respect, why not? They were young but they also had in good measure what is known as human dignity. There would always be the bad ones in any generation and it was everyone's duty to spot them and weed them out. That outright condemnation of the young, as though they were all a bunch of juvenile delinquents, always angered him . . . no matter if it roused the enmity of a few.

The problem that now faced him, of course, was a special one. He could have dealt somehow with a straight case of indiscipline. He himself was being fast educated on the psychology of strikes and student demonstrations. Last time, was it about fees, or about the language? He had been amused, though he had tried his best to look shocked and angry, when some boy in the crowd had called him an 'old fogey' and an 'imperialist agent'. He was a bit of an old fogey, there was no denying that, Father Joshe had thought, but what was—who was—an imperialist agent?

He heard a noise at the door and presently Joseph came in, bearing a tray with a cup of coffee. 'Good morning, Father,' he said, looking sheepishly at the dust trails on the table. 'I didn't know you'd be in so early.'

'Good morning, Joseph. . . and God bless you for the coffee. I really need a cup.'

'You could have told me yesterday. . . '

'What?... Oh, that's all right. I forgot. I have to see a man. . . and it seems he can come only at 8.30, though I told him it was a bit too early for me. You know him? His name is Gopalan.'

'That Communist?'

'Is he a Communist?'

'Well, I really don't know, Father,' Joseph said a little shamefacedly. 'Some party or the other. They're all the same. All trouble-makers.' Joseph began to dust the table and Father Joshe got up and stood aside.

'We seem to be having too many trouble-makers in our midst these days, don't we Joseph?. . . . I have vaguely heard about him, but I haven't met him.'

Joseph flicked the duster contemptuously. 'Probably this is the first time that man is seeing the inside of an educational institution! Riff-raff, that's what they are. . . Does he want to join the college?' Joseph smiled. Though he looked upon Father Joshe with awe, some levity was permitted when they were alone.

'I hope not!...' Father Joshe laughed. 'We have enough trouble-makers as it is. Actually, I don't know what he wants. He didn't say. He was rather gruff on the telephone. It must be about the suspension, don't you think?'

'They're all busybodies, these politicians. They are up to no good, I can tell you that, Father. You should have refused to see him...'

'Oh, I couldn't do that, Joseph. I shouldn't. We must be patient with our—er, opponents.'

But as Joseph finished dusting and walked away, Father Joshe was inclined to agree with his earlier statement: politicians, by and large, were up to no good. He himself had come up against them; yes, even though he belonged to the religious order. Intrigues and back-biting and slander. Partisan attitudes even in the course of one's service to God. Sabotage of worthwhile projects and common horse-trading of loyalties! Violence of the mind was as sinful as violence of any other kind, Father Joshe thought. There were times when one had indeed to be godly to feel merciful towards one's fellow-beings...

The students had apparently shouted slogans concerning Parkinsonpet. But Father Joshe was not sure whether it was just because the border village was in the news, or because they merely wanted to annoy the assistant professor and the slogans came in handy. How were these boys concerned with Parkinsonpet and what was the point in raising slogans in the classroom? Then a thought occurred to Father Joshe: where did the assistant professor come from? His name suggested that he did not belong to this state. For that matter, in local politics he could be considered an 'alien' even if he was born and brought up here and his ancestors had one or two generations ago migrated from their home state and settled in this place. When the linguistic reorganization of states was in full swing, such people had turned out to be the ' niggers in the woodpile.' Flushing them out, or at least a campaign to do that, had been an election weapon that had saved some parochial leaders from political obscurity !

But when he had the so-called student leaders in his room the day following the incident, Father Joshe had decided against asking them about this. There was no point in putting a new idea into their heads–and no virtue in giving a semblance of dignity to what he considered plain delinquency. Father Joshe remained non-committal—even neutral—during the interview.

'I take a very serious view of any breach of discipline and decorum inside the college premises,' he had said, looking at the young offenders who stood self-conciously at a little distance away from his desk. He had resisted the temptation to ask them to sit down, in spite of the fact that he knew the interview would be a long one.

There were four of them, named by the assistant professor as the ring-leaders of the riot. Father Joshe wondered why Kesavan was among them. He had never pictured the boy as a trouble-maker. The other, he had more or less expected. There was Chandran, the Union Secretary; Basheer, who was the best football centre-forward the college had seen for a long time ('Forward in the field, backward in the class!' Father Joshe had needled the affable Muslim youngster occasionally!), and Mathew. Mathew, Father Joshe had opportunity to know personally, was a 'bad 'un'. His father owned a vast estate and was considered to be rolling in wealth. The boy himself had done some rolling in the same class for three years and he remained in the college only because his doting parent had very strong influence over some of the Board directors. Well, there was no getting away from it. You could not avoid types like that turning up now and then in any college.

Chandran naturally took upon himself the role of being

Abhimanyu

spokesman for the group.'We didn't shout in the class, Father.'

'Then who did ?' In actual point of fact, Father Joshe thought, this might be quite true. These 'leaders' would be too careful to be caught with unassailable evidence like that!

'Some of the boys in the class did—we don't know who they are. But the professor asked us to leave the class.'

'What for?'

'He didn't specify, Father.'

'He is under no obligation to specify,' Father Joshe said and changed the subject. 'And you left the class?'

'No, Father.'

'Oh, I see, you refused to obey. May I know why ?'

'He didn't tell us why we should leave the class, as I told you, Father. We thought—well we strongly felt that it was obligatory on anyone's part to indicate the charge before he metes out punishment. Just because he didn't like us...'

(My friend, you're quite slippery, Father Joshe thought. No wonder they have made you the Union secretary!)

'This college,' the principal continued aloud, cutting the other short, 'is not run on the basis of personal likes and dislikes. I would like you ro remember that. If he asked you to leave the class, you must leave the class.'

'But I did leave the class, Father.'

'Immediately?'

'Well, no Father. I requested him... '

'So you stood there and argued. That was very wrong, Chandran.'

The boy did not reply to that, but merely looked away. 'And what about you ... and you ... and Mathew?' It was Mathew who answered, in what Father Joshe noted was a slightly defiant tone. 'We walked away in protest, Father.'

'In protest against what ?'

'He rubbed out what we had written on the blackboard, Father.'

Chandran turned round sharply, looking warningly at Mathew, but it was too late.

'So he rubbed out what was written on the blackboard, I see. That was his first offence, eh? Do you realize that the blackboard is kept there for the use of professors? Expressly for their use?'

Chandran tried to open his mouth, but Father Joshe silenced him with a wave of his hand.

Mathew was confused, realizing that he had somehow ventured out too much, but went on: 'I do realize, Father. But this one was on a side and no one uses that side, except the Maths professor.'

'What had you written on it?'

'I hadn't written anything on it, Father.'

'All right. What was written on that board?'

Mathew looked at Chandran, who in turn cleared his throat and said: 'Somebody had written: We will fight for Parkinsonpet.'

'That was all?'

'Well, not all, Father. There was—something else.'

'What was it?'

'Well, it said ... I would rather not say it, Father.'

'Why, Chandran? If you had written something—all right, some unknown person had written something on the board for the whole world to see, why make me an exception?'

Chandran braced himself: 'It said, we'll do something to all "Kithakones".'

'Kithakones? Who are they?'

'It is a . . . a term used for those belonging to the state across the border, Father.'

'A derogatory term, I take it?'

'Yes, Father.'

'I see. Do what to them?'

The boy still hesitated.

'I want you to be specific, Chandran, do what?'

Chandran looked at Father Joshe helplessly for a moment. Then he said rather sharply: 'It said, we'll castrate them, Father.'

Father Joshe looked out throught the window. Under the shade of a tree, he could see a group of students looking intently this side. He glared at them till the group dissolved and one by one walked away. He turned back to Chandran.

'Do you think you are competent to carry out this—er—delicate operation, Chandran?'

'I didn't write it, Father.'

'But you protested when he rubbed it off, didn't you?'

'No, Father. He came into the class, looked at it—and the girl students giggled. I think that was what provoked — all right, Father, I'm sorry . . . and then he asked the class who wrote it on the board. No one answered. Then he asked me specifically who did it. I said I don't know. . .Then he ordered me to leave the class.'

Father Joshe decided that it was now better to close the interview. 'This is all wrong, Chandran... and Kesavan. I didn't expect to see you in this. I am suspending all four of you for one week. After that you'll apologize to the professor and get his permission to sit in the class again.'

He nodded at them in dismissal, and turned to some papers on the desk. For a moment he was aware that they were shuffling about and waiting undecided. Then he heard them leave.

Just as they were at the door, he called out: 'Kesavan!'

There was a pause, then a whispered conversation behind the screen which hid the door, and then Kesavan came in. Father Joshe busied himself with the paper till he was sure the others had left.

'I am disappointed,' he said, looking at Kesavan. 'And I am angry.' He really felt sad. Kesavan was one of the brighter boys. He had been slack of late and Father Joshe had been worried. It was with the good students that the reputation of a college rested.

'Are you aware that the college authorities had been kind enough to grant you a scholarship?'

'I had not exactly thought of it, Father.'

'Well, you can think about it now. Next time you are here for this kind of thing, we will have to reconsider even the half-scholarship. I am not threatening you. I have too much regard for your good sense to issue threats. But we give that kind of encouragement only to deserving students. Deserving in every way. Is that clear to you?'

'Yes, Father.'

'Good. You may go now.'

When the boy had left, Father Joshe pushed aside the paper and leaned back in his chair. It was a pity, he thought. All this nonsense... Take that piece the boy had done on Hamlet, for instance. Father Joshe had thought that it deserved a better outlet than the college magazine. A very mature, even sensitive bit of work, that.

Two days later the Student Union had come forward with that preposterous ultimatum. They wanted the college to be closed for a fortnight as an expression of their protest against the recent Government decision to appoint a one-man commission to go into the Parkinsonpet issue. 'The appointment of the commission is a provocative gesture, a stalling move to thwart the legitimate claims of the people of the state,' the ultimatum had said.

There was a sub-condition: the suspended students should be taken back unconditionally and the assistant professor should be reprimanded. If the answer was not 'yes' to all these demands, and not conveyed to the Union within the stipulated time, the students would go on a strike which would later be extended, with the co-operation of like-minded citizens' organizations outside, to a hartal and other legitimate demonstrations of protest...

Preposterous it certainly was! Father Joshe had not yet put it up to the college board because, in the first instance, he was not in a position to know how serious the threat was.

Would it get out of hand, and if so, how quickly? What course of action could he recommend to the board? A stepping down?... He was quite sure his own pride was not involved. Student agitations were becoming too serious a problem to be judged or settled on a basis of personal vanity. They could flare up into anything. They had to be contained at the earliest possible moment. But how?

This was one of the main reasons why he had agreed to see Gopalan on the other man's terms. Father Joshe wanted to be clear what dark forces were behind this.

He studied the man Joseph had ushered in a minute ago. Gopalan was only ten minutes late (Deliberate? Father Joshe wondered.) and on entering, he had looked round the room and pulled up a chair for himself with a supercilious air, not waiting for an invitation. He had merely grunted something in reply to his host's greeting. He sat, bent a little forward, his elbows resting on the arms of the chair, his legs crossed and displaying dust-covered chappals. Joseph had backed out cautiously, a disapproving look on his face, perhaps not quite sure whether he could trust this man alone with his master.

Father Joshe did not appear to notice Gopalan's shabby appearance, nor did the visitor seem in the least self-conscious about it. They treated each other with politeness, perhaps a little unctuously polite in the case of Gopalan.

'I would like to come straight to the point, Father, rather than waste your time or mine with any preliminaries.'

Father Joshe picked up a file in front of him and placed it slowly on a side. He was amused to note that he was feeling a little odd, though he would not have liked to call it nervousness, under the steady stare of his visitor.

'I would very much appreciate that, Mr Gopalan. In this case, I think it would be the best way to begin.'

'This is strictly not my business. I mean, what I am going to say. You might consider me an intruder.' Gopalan looked round, a faint smile of sarcasm on his face. 'I am not familiar with the workings of a great educational institution. In fact,' he glanced challengingly at the other, 'I do not have the advantage of a formal education at all.'

(But you have other considerable advantages in this deal, Father Joshe thought.) Aloud he said :

'A formal education, unfortunately, does not guarantee making us either better men or wiser men, Mr Gopalan.' He smiled. 'I do admire self-made men. Who doesn't ? Many of our own preceptors had themselves been ... '

'What I meant was, you shouldn't think I have not given serious thought to the matter I want to discuss. I am a politician, Father ; what we say can sometimes make or break us.'

'Quite ! Incidentally, that applies to all of us. You have your responsibilities just as we have our own.'

'It is good that you mentioned responsibility, Father. One's responsibility primarily is to be fair and just. It is all the more so, isn't it, in the case of the head of an institution like this ? Perhaps then you would not take it amiss if I say that there was no justfication for imposing a punishment on the students out of all proportion to the... error they had committed.'

Father Joshe felt a stir of anger and hastily suppressed it : 'What are you referring to, Mr Gopalan ?'

'To the suspension, Father, you know that very well.'

(Yes, I know that very well, Father Joshe thought. But what business was it of yours to question it ?) He sighed. He must not lose his temper—at least not so early in the day !

'Indiscipline is fatal in an institution of this kind, Mr Gopalan. It has to be checked. I am sure a man in your position will appreciate that.'

'I am only expressing doubt about your definition of indiscipline, Father. Isn't tolerance one of the virtues your religion preaches ?' Gopalan was smiling broadly now.

'It is. And as a matter of fact, it is a virtue that even your religion preaches, if I may say so... ?'

'I have no religion, Father. I do not believe in all that crap any more.'

'Well, so much the worse for you then. Religion, apart from metaphysical considerations, is a solace in times of trouble, Mr Gopalan.'

'Father, I do not want this to be a preaching session, forgive me...You were talking about tolerance.'

The principal's face coloured. 'So I was. Yes. Tolerance. But tolerance must not be mistaken for weakness, must it? Then it becomes dangerous.'

'You mean,' Gopalan's tone suddenly became hard, 'you have to resort to a show of strength?'

'I mean nothing of the sort, really, I want my students to turn their most serious thoughts to their studies. A moment ago we were talking about responsibilities. This is their responsibility. And we should all try to see that they discharge it.'

'The time has come, Father, when a matter that concerns the nation or even their own state is also their responsibility.'

'Then that time has come too early, Mr Gopalan, for them,' Father Joshe said sharply,' and I'll see, to the best of my ability, that they don't ...'

'Whether the time has come early or late is a matter of opinion, Father, and you are a foreigner, if you'll pardon me for saying so.'

'I will pardon you, but it makes no difference. I am a teacher. The boys are my responsibility. I look upon it as a sacred responsibility. It has nothing whatever to do with my nationality. Honest, sincere teachers look at it that way no matter where they are in whatever country. Don't you think I am competent to decide what is good for *my* boys?

'Your boys?'

Father Joshe was suddenly angry. He knew it was a false step, and the other man was baiting him to take it. He noticed with dismay that his hands had begun to tremble.

He took them off the table and placed them in his lap.

'Yes, my boys, Mr Gopalan. I feel responsible for them.' He had always loved children. Wasn't it a merciful God who had given him so many? This man, sitting before him with that sardonic smile on his face, would not understand a sentiment like that. He would not think twice before using the students as pawns in his game.

'Hasn't the Union served an ultimatum on the college, Father?' Gopalan was still smiling in his irritating manner.

Father Joshe ignored the question. 'Don't make the boys fight your battles, Mr Gopalan. Don't ruin their future for a small political gain you might make today. It is unforgivable. It is criminal. Surely they have a better purpose in life than that! To be the pawns in some dirty game. They are the people who will run your country tomorrow.' Father Joshe regretted that he had to resort to cliches made meaningless by people like this man himself, now sitting so smugly before him. 'Give them a chance to grow up into good, useful citizens. There is no excuse for jeopardizing their future. It is criminal—yes, let me repeat it, criminal — to distract them from their legitimate work.'

'I do not think this outburst is justified, Father. I do not think the students will agree with you. You can't have greater concern for their future than they themselves!' Gopalan appeared stung for the first time. 'On the other hand, if you are accusing me....'

'I am not accusing anyone,' Father Joshe said wearily. 'This is not the time or place for accusation. I am, yes, I am appealing to your good sense. May I call it your conscience?'

'My conscience is clear, I can assure you that, Father. We are living in a house of fire. You want to decide who has the responsibility to pour the water!'

'I am only saying that we should not feed the fire, if there is a fire, as you put it.'

'You will doubt it, Father, because you do not have to

look beyond the college walls. Some of us however, cannot take a narrow view like that !'

'Concern for the future of the younger generation is not taking a narrow view, Mr Gopalan.'

'You think only you have concern for them, Father ?' Gopalan was angry now, and Father Joshe found his own anger evaporating. 'You missionaries—I am sorry to say that —live with that colossal conceit. You propagate your religion to us with that conceit. You are bringing your civilized way to us with that conceit. We do not live any longer in the good old days of the Empire, Father. The white man's burden has eventually proved much too much for him !'

'There might be some truth in what you say, but that is besides the point. We are asking whether the boys should be called upon to make sacrifices beyond their...'

'Beyond their what ?'

'Capacity ? ... Perhaps their immediate interests ?'

'You are looking at it from a very restricted point of view. They will be called upon to make greater sacrifices—and I bet they will not stop because your noble feelings are hurt. You get that clear.'

Father Joshe felt very calm. He looked out of the window, at the trees, at the sun casting bright patterns on the ground, at the group of boys who were walking along the paths, chatting and laughing. Some of them were strolling on the lawn and Father Joshe was mildly annoyed. One of these days, he thought, the fine for trampling the flower-beds and lawns would have to be actually imposed, and not merely mentioned as a warning.

'What have you decided ?' Gopalan asked suddenly.

'About what ?'

'About the strike—the ultimatum ?'

'Well, the Union will be informed of the Board's decision in due course, I suppose.'

'There are other parties in this town, unfortunately, who

are interested in repressing the students. Father, I think it would be a mistake.'

'Repression is always a mistake, I agree.'

'I did not mean it that way. They—these people—do not care to have any student trouble now. Not on the Parkinsonpet issue, anyway. They would pressurize you to be firm, thinking that they can nip this in the bud that way. You are going to have trouble, Father, let me warn you.'

'I am afraid precisely of that,' Father Joshe said reflectively.

'You need not be afraid, Father,' Gopalan laughed. 'You can keep out of it, can't you ? In any case, your term is coming to an end soon. We all know that. What is there in this for you to fear ?'

Father Joshe lifted his head and looked at Gopalan. 'I have been in this country for over twenty-five years now, Mr. Gopalan. Will it be presumptuous if I say that I have come to love it in my own way ? Why, I grew up into a man on this very soil ! There have always been problems. Lack of funds. Lack of co-operation. Frustration. Politics. Oh yes, there's politics even in the field in which I operate, Mr Gopalan. After all, it was politics of a kind that put Jesus on the cross, remember ?... I have very often felt disheartened. Frightened. But not for the reasons you think... One thought has sustained me. Every year new boys come here, the old ones leave. Some of us here take the satisfaction that we send them away a little better equipped to face the world. If you want me to put it that way, I would say, better equipped to face the problems of your country. Is that incompatible with your own concept of patriotism, Mr Gopalan ?'

'That is a new thought, Father,' Gopalan laughed mirthlessly. 'The patriotic missionary...!'

Father Joshe reddened slightly. 'Well, don't resist new thoughts then, that is all I can say. You can take it that we do our duty, as we see it, to the best of our ability.'

'You mean we have no sense of duty, as you put it ?'

'I did not mean that. But is it your duty to incite the boys to create chaos, turn violent ?'

'We don't incite them. At least not my party. We only instill in them an awareness of what is right and wrong, and show them that they have to fight for that right, if need be, that is all. There will be a few casualties but that will be the case in any battle.'

'That is the point. Why turn the college campus into a battlefield and the students into soldiers ? The casualty, if you are honest enough to admit it, will have to be in their future. Is it worth it ? Why make them fight your battles ?'

Gopalan stood up. 'I don't think this discussion is taking us anywhere, Father. You are being carried away by sentiment. But I am warning you, the boys will fight and there is nothing you or anyone can do about it. You make things only worse by resisting.'

'Perhaps, And yet, as I see it, it will be my duty to resist.'

Gopalan laughed. 'What can you do, Father ?'

Father Joshe felt a tremor again. He had a foreboding that he was already on the losing side. He thought of his boys ... of riots ... of violence. There was indeed very little he could do to prevent it. For the first time, he felt hatred for the man who stood facing him. Uncharitably, he searched his mind for something cutting to say, something that would wipe away the smirk from the other man's face. Then he controlled himself. The man was right. It was their country. Patriotism from an alien was an affront. He was too weak to stem the flood. He felt a sense of futility, a helplessness and despair that was overwhelming.

'Yes, you are right, Mr Gopalan. There is very little hope for people who think like me, isn't there. But... ', he now said it very calmly, 'I will hope... And I will pray.'

Long after the other man had left, Father Joshe seemed to hear Gopalan's laughter echoing in his room. Rising in a crescendo, engulfing him in a flood of mocking sound....

6

The hostel canteen was not usually crowded on the afternoons of week days. Though 3 p.m. was long after lunch, it was still too early for tea. There were some rare exceptions to the latter rule, as there were exceptions to any rule, and Chandran was one of them.

He sat at a table alone, brooding, a cup of tea before him and a cigarette between his fingers. In his early years here Chandran used to a get a vicarious thrill from the fact that he was one of the few students who defied the warden's ban against smoking in the hostel premises. Of course, a lot of surreptitious smoking went on behind closed doors in the rooms, but that was altogether different, and perhaps even tacitly permitted unless the warden caught one red-handed. Doing it in the canteen was an open invitation to trouble, and serious trouble which could lead to expulsion.

What made Chandran unique was that, unlike his friend Mathew and some others who occasionally dared to break the ban, he was totally nonchalant about it. With him it was as though he was not defying a rule but purely exercising a privilege that came naturally to him. It was reflected in the manner in which he smoked, the ease and casualness with which he drew the smoke deeply into his lungs and let it out slowly through the flaring nostrils of his long, thin nose; or the utter cool indifference with which he blew smoke-rings up towards the ceiling. He did it all with the finesse of the habitue, not with the obvious bravado of the mere thrill-seeker. He would sometimes say, with the studied boredom of one who always found oneself a step ahead of one's peers, that he had started smoking when he was twelve; that he was a chain smoker who had to ignore such rules out of necessity, and not out of any adolescent desire to be different, or defiant.

All through the first year, Chandran had made no fuss. He was new here, and a rank 'junior' was unlikely to find support from the old boys, least of all when the effort was to establish a new precedent. If such a thing was called for at all, and there was still no majority opinion on this, the seniors would not have relished the leadership of a newcomer. Their own prestige would have been at stake then. With a total understanding of human nature Chandran acquiesced. Nothing would be gained by premature action.

He struck when the time was right. Which was during the latter half of his second year in the hostel. And the manner in which he organized and directed the attack, as well as the diplomacy with which he handled the post-victory phase demonstrated that Chandran was a natural leader. This was only a minor side issue, but it paved the way for his career in the college union and explained his rapid rise to power.

The person cast against him in this drama was Krishnan Nair, the canteen manager who ran the business independently on a contract basis. He was there even now, standing behind a counter of wood and glass, smiling a little uncertainly, his eyes narrowed and roving idly over the hostel quadrangle which lay in bright sunlight in glaring contrast to the late afternoon haze of the deserted dining hall. He knew that the warden would not come this side at this time of the day, but there could be some stray tutor who might be rash enough to have an exaggerated idea of his own authority and an ill-advised desire to prove it. Not that Krishnan Nair could foresee any great trouble for himself.

Perhaps nothing more than a moment of embarrassment, even if he did not choose to withdraw from the scene at the approach of danger. If he felt apprehensive about anyone, it could only be about the hapless tutor. The boys had a 'thing' about tutors, invariably youngsters promoted to a position of authority after the final year and undergoing apprenticeship under professors.

Krishnan Nair personally did not feel in the least vulnerable. After nearly twenty years, he considered himself a permanent fixture at the hostel. And he was proud of it. He had seen boys come and go, even as he had seen wardens come and go. Some of his old customers were now out in the wide world and held high positions in the Government and commercial firms. A former student who was an ambassador in a distant country still sent him New Year cards. In a reminiscent mood Krishnan Nair would bring them out and show them to the recent crop of boys. It was again through similar contracts that he had obtained jobs for two of his sons and a nephew ... No, he was not on the 'Staff' but his position in the institution was unassailable. Even Father Joshe, on those rare occasions when he visited the hostel, always stopped by to exchange a word with him, or enquire about him from one of the serving boys if Krishnan Nair was not at his post. Both of them at different levels, felt the same way about the college—an integral part of the institution and proud of its great traditions.

Krishnan Nair did not particularly care for Chandran, though one would not have noticed it in his manner or speech. Outwardly he treated all the boys equally. He listened with patience to their complaints about food, reprimanded a serving boy if he showed signs of inefficiency or impertinence, kept the place in reasonably good order and was secretly proud of the condition of the furniture and crockery. He had obtained special permission to put the counter, behind which he stood now; the glass front displayed an assortment of things inside : toiletry, stationery, envelopes and postage stamps, shirt buttons, shoe laces and tins of boot-polish, steel keychains and razor blades and various other items which the boys needed from time to time and considered too much trouble to buy at the bazaar. He maintained, with a self-satisfied smile, that his prices were more than reasonable as he got his goods from the wholesalers. He sold cigarettes, too, but these were stored away from sight in a bottom drawer to which only Krishnan Nair had the key.

He would have liked cash dealings, particularly with some of the boys, but the greater part of his business was made on a credit basis. He ran no great risk in this, because the college collected a security deposit from each student at the time of enrolment, meant to cover breakage of furniture, laboratory equipment, loss of library books and so on; but after Krishnan Nair had had a few distressing experiences with some deliberate defaulters among the boys, the college authorities had kindly raised the deposit and checked whether each outgoing student had cleared his canteen dues before returning the amount.

Chandran was one of the boys, Krishnan Nair would have predicted with a by-now infallible judgment, who was destined to forfeit a large part of the deposit. Not that he was dishonest or wilfully negligent. It was also apparent that he was from a well-to-do, land-owning family from whom sizeable money orders arrived with punctuality at the beginning of the month. Krishnan Nair suspected that the boy liked to break things—rules as well as property whether it belonged to him or not. Chandran never grudged payment. It was as though he just could not be bothered with such trivial matters. He was a free spender, generous when he was in a good mood, and it earned for him the awe and devotion of the poorer students as well as the habitual scrounger. It was rarely that he was seen without hangers-on. Chandran never demeaned himself by stealing, or perhaps he was too careful about his reputation. The glass flask in his room in which he kept drinking water or the beakers he used when serving his friends, all belonged to the college laboratory but were not 'flicked' by him. They were all presents from fawning admirers. He used them, though he felt a secret contempt for those delinquents. It was utterly adolescent, the way some boys stole chemicals and other useless things purely on a dare. Krishnan Nair also was also wary of kleptomaniacs. But there was no way of reaching his goods without his knowledge, except by breaking the glass front of the counter. They had done it only once—and it was mania of a different kind. It was a riot.

At this time, though Chandran had been in the hostel for more than a year, Krishnan Nair did not know him very well. The boy did not look any different from others and he was courteous and well-mannered, and a good customer. There was a little aloofness about him; Krishnan Nair had, wrongly as he discovered later, taken it to be the natural shyness of the newcomer. It was nothing of the kind. It was more the instinctive feeling of alienation of the leader from the common fold. His followers did not notice it, but many of his detractors considered it arrogance, though not one of them, after the first few months, would have bothered to raise the issue with him.

One day, without any preliminaries, Chandran had lit a cigarette in the dining hall after finishing lunch. It created a stir, surprise and amusement among the students present, and annoyance in Krishnan Nair. He went up to Chandran without much fanfare and told him to put out the cigarette. When Chandran ignored him, he quoted the hostel rule, at which he was asked to mind his own business. Krishnan Nair did not fancy getting into a scuffle. He could have, if it came to that, handled Chandran alone but not a crowd of boys. He announced loudly that he would not any longer sell cigarettes to Chandran.

'I shall settle this without any intervention from the

warden,' he said to those nearby. What was at stake was his own dignity and prestige. He would not put up with any nonsense from any of the boys. Right was on his side. He did not have the least doubt about his own victory.

Nothing spectacular happened in the next two days. But no student came to buy anything at the counter, and on the third day Krishnan Nair was a little worried and nervous. His dealings were now confined to a few of the really bad credit customers, and even they seemed to be in a great hurry to make their purchases and disappear at the earliest opportunity. The fourth day, it seemed, things returned almost to normal, but later there was trouble in the hostel. Four of the boys who had bought things from him found their rooms in a shambles and most of their possessions strewn in the corridor when they returned from their classes. Without bringing in Krishnan Nair or the origin of the controversy, the matter was taken up with the warden. Chandran, however, had a cast-iron alibi: he was with a professor clarifying doubts in his lessons when this incident had taken place.

Business slumped again.

It was not so much the loss of business as the indignity of it that worried Krishnan Nair. In the long run, he knew he would win; the boys would find it impossible to boycott him. He could ignore the sniggers and provocative remarks that he overheard during meal times. What really irked him was the elaborate courtesy, the tongue-in-cheek politeness that Chandran and his immediate friends showed him. They alone came to the counter and made lengthy enquiries about the price and quality of various things. They never bought anything; they handled the goods with great care, almost reverence, and returned everything to him intact. Then they would walk away, apparently unaware of the laughter and hootings that came from other students sitting at the tables and watching the proceedings.

At the end of ten days, Krishnan Nair announced a

drastic cut in prices. It was madness, he knew... but things were going too far for his comfort. The warden was aware of what was going on but he refused to interfere in the absence of any specific complaints or untoward incidents. When Krishnan Nair himself had met him, he did not bring up the subject, and he noted the amused smile on the warden's face, and as a matter of personal pride, hinted that if things were left to his own discretion, he would bring matters back to normal in no time.

He publicized the price cuts. He got pieces of white cardboard and displayed the new rates in bold letters written in black and at some places underlined in red. He was not displeased with the effect on the students. There was apparently a clear division of loyalties and open signs that the boycott would end. The stocks were finished in no time. If Chandran himself noticed the rush at the counter, he gave no indication whatever. The familiar, self-satisfied smile came back to Krishnan Nair's face; it lasted exactly two days.

Trouble—real trouble—started early one morning. Krishnan Nair, thinking the cold war was at an end, had removed the price reduction card and had gone back to the old rates. Mathew sidled up to the counter as soon as it opened and gingerly picked up three family-size tubes of toothpaste; a friend of his asked for six packets of razor blades. Then two more boys came and after a quick survey selected three jars of hair cream and four toothbrushes of very fine quality. Krishnan Nair was considerably surprised, but felt this might be one of his good days. The items were packed, and idly he noticed that there was a small crowd gathering at the counter. He was just entering these purchases in his account book when Mathew announced to a bystander that with prices so reasonable now, he was really stocking up for the rest of the year. He remarked that he came from a family of businessmen and he knew when to buy and sell. Krishnan Nair looked up, startled. He smiled a little uncertainly.

'Are you sure you want all that stuff—three large toothpaste tubes?' he asked.

'Of course,' Mathew replied, studying the small print on the packs. 'I have been reading up on dental hygiene. I am trying to cultivate a Macleans smile.'

'And me,' another ventured, 'I am going to shave and shave till I meet a girl who appreciates a satin-smooth chin.'

'Look, is this some kind of a joke?' Krishnan Nair made an unsuccessful grab at the packets. He was scowling now. 'I can tell you, there's no price reduction on these items. You have to pay the bazaar price!'

'You must be the one who's joking,' Mathew said, laughing. 'You had announced the new prices only . . . was it a week ago? Yes. We appreciated that. Why are you now talking about bazaar prices? They are cheats there. You yourself have told us that before!'

Krishnan Nair succeeded this time in snatching away a packet. No one was quite clear what happened in the next few minutes. There was shouting and arguing and pushing among the group of students gathered round. Somewhere in the background Krishnan Nair could see Chandran's head. He could also hear some foul words and equally foul and angry retorts. The crowd became bigger and more vociferous and angry. There was now a lot of pushing and pulling going on, and the pressure at the counter was almost overwhelming. It was breakfast time and there was quite a large number of boys in the hall. Suddenly, from nowhere, idlis began to fly and Krishnan Nair vaguely heard the sound of glass tumblers and plates breaking. A tea cup just missed his head and crashed against the wall behind. He panicked. He was a fat, short, hefty man and he elbowed his way into the melee. He heard the sound of chairs being thrown and the breaking of furniture. A few blows fell on his own back. His shirt was torn and it was with great difficulty that he clung on to his dhoti and prevented the students from stripping him in public. He screamed for help but his voice was drowned in the howl that rose all around him.

When he finally got back to the counter, tears of rage streaming down his eyes, he found the glass panes broken and the goods thrown all over the place. The serving boys hung around guiltily. Some of them had apparently come to his aid but had retreated in fear. The boys outnumbered them many times over. There was no point in getting hurt in a losing fight, and some of them, Krishnan Nair suspected, were secretly in league with the boys. He had his own problems with them, and they must have been waiting for just a chance like this. He was very much alone.

Chandran was among the few students who helped him and the serving boys gather the scattered goods. He was extremely solicitous. He called the students a bunch of scoundrels. In fact he said he quite agreed with Krishnan Nair that they were just plain bastards. Krishnan Nair flinched at the word, but he was too tired to care.

There was an official enquiry, of course, presided over by none other than Father Joshe himself, but the witnesses, at least such as those who volunteered to testify, were all rather reluctantly but firmly against him. The trouble, according to them, started because the goods sold at the counter were all of inferior, if not spurious, quality. The fantastic price reduction was quoted as an attempt to lure them into buying shop-soiled material. And when they had fallen for the bait, Krishnan Nair had again put up the price. This was bad enough, but when some boys had objected, he had, instead of calmly explaining things to the boys—if indeed any explanation was possible—unwisely chosen to abuse and insult them. There were three students who swore that he had used the word 'bastard'.

In the face of such overwhelming evidence, the warden, to whom Father Joshe had entrusted the enquiry after the first session, could do very little. In his report to the principal he even raised doubts about the advisability of continuing Krishnan Nair's stall. The boys' story was probably distorted, but he had no choice. It would perhaps be better in the interests of peace to avoid the root cause of trouble. The hostel should consider taking over the management of the stall, as it was also impractical to let the students go out of the hostel at all times on the pretext of buying things that they needed urgently from the bazaar. All in all, Krishnan Nair himself did not appear to be above reproach. He had fumbled when faced with the charge of abusing the students.

He knew he was beaten, and he was secretly pleased when none other than Chandran himself came to him for a compromise. The boy expressed regrets about the incident and agreed that the students would make a collection, unofficially of course, to repair the damage caused to the stall. They had no malice against Krishnan Nair. They had testified against him only to save themselves from punishment. They were now prepared for an honourable truce. Was Krishnan Nair prepared to accept it ?

After a few minutes' consideration, Krishnan Nair gave in. He was not asked to submit to any specific condition; in fact, he had to admit it, he was treated with respect and looked upon as the injured party. Chandran took the initiative in letting things get back to normal. He himself made purchases on the old terms and encouraged his friends and others to follow suit. Business once again boomed. The warden never raised the issue after a student deputation had seen him. And no one ever found out what the principal did with the report.

Chandran began to smoke cigarettes in the dining hall.

In singles and in pairs, the boys who Chandran had been waiting for patiently in the canteen joined him. He nodded at some of them, occasionally greeted a new arrival with a smile, but otherwise still sat immersed in his own thoughts, rarely if ever joining their conversation. Some of them apparently had cut classes, the others had the afternoon off. They were desultorily discussing professors and studies and the coming examinations.

Chandran finished his cup of tea and ordered a fresh round. He took a last pull on his cigarette and looked for a place to deposit the stub. He contemplated the cup speculatively, then decided against it. He did not want to drop the stub on the floor and extinguish it with his foot either. Both were against rules. He did not mind rules as long as he was the one who made them. He did not want to embarrass the canteen staff. He stubbed the cigarette carefully against the leg of the table, and then squeezed it between the first finger and thumb, scattering the tobacco and rolling the paper into a tight little pill. He dusted his hand against his trousers.

The last one to arrive was Kesavan, and Chandran's face lit up . . . imperceptibly he felt a little relieved. This was the cue for him to stand up briskly and adjourn to a corner table where their discussions would not be overheard. There were spies among the boys, probably even among the canteen staff. The group waited in silence as a serving-boy brought the tea and placed a cup in front of each one of them.

Kesavan sat on Chandran's left, quiet as usual, even a little moody. He had refused a cigarette earlier. 'Brutus', they called him, but a Brutus, Chandran knew, who would never betray Caesar. No one knew precisely what went on in Kesavan's mind, but it was, all the same, a mind which most of the students respected.

Chandran was particularly close to Kesavan . . . in fact, he considered Kesavan the only one fit to be called a real friend. They had not begun their association very promisingly. The first two years in college, they had been in different sections and as Kesavan was a day scholar, they had hardly had occasion to meet. In the third year they were still in different groups but they were together in the Shakespeare class. By this time Chandran was already a celebrity, and he resented the fact that Kesavan showed no particular inclination to speak to him or make friends with him as so many other boys did. Then they had occasion to cross swords at a debating society meet. The subject that Chandran had chosen was 'Ends justify the means' and he felt that he was particularly eloquent on that day. Kesavan was the last speaker on the other side, and it was clear that he had not volunteered to take part in the debate but had been pushed into it by the English lecturer. His side lost the debate, but Chandran felt that Kesavan had acquitted himself creditably. There were points he had raised which had oddly disturbed Chandran. He felt a strong desire to correct the other boy. Later they had private discussions on this subject, and then on other matters as well. Chandran felt for the first time that here was a boy who did not stand in awe of him. Here was someone in whose presence he did not have to strike a pose but could speak with candour and sincerity. Kesavan, in turn, recognized in the other a man of action, forthright and curiously idealistic, with amusing, original, and often startling ideas. In the weeks and months that followed, they became very good friends.

To their common friends, the boys appeared virtually opposites... in temperament as well as in looks. Kesavan was fair, fine-featured and of medium height. The boys teased him often about the girl students; that he could get their votes during college elections without even trying; that they watched him with open interest on the rare occasions when he spoke at the debating society meetings. He was by no means a brilliant speaker; he spoke slowly, introspectively, taking time to choose his words, relying more on logic than rhetoric, and quite often seemed to be on the losing side. He rubbed his nose with a finger and stroked his chin when confronted with a sound argument from the other side, and at the end of it all gave the impression that he had not said half the things that he wanted to say. It was rumoured that the girl students imitated him when they were safe within the four walls of the girls' room. As it happened, he was also the one, rarely, if ever, seen talking to the girls.

Chandran was strikingly tall for his age, lanky and dark. His eyes were narrow under arched, scanty eyebrows, which would have made him look rather sinister except that his long, hooked nose, thin lips and pointed chin combined to give the face a clownish look. His dropping moustache accentuated the effect. The perpetual smile on his lips gave the impression that he always had something in mind which privately amused him. His hair was cut short and it clung to his head as closely as a skull cap. He was reputed to have a devastating sense of humour, though, for some reason known only to himself, he did not choose to waste it on any debating society platform. There he was terribly intense and serious, and quick to take offence when bettered in an exchange. Perhaps he had no sense of humour at all, and it was one of those exaggerated judgments that students were likely to make regarding one whom they admired. Kesavan knew that, when in the mood, Chandran was capable of clowning and also, rather disturbingly, that beneath the surface calm there was an undercurrent of—what was it? Cruelty? Violence? There was a dark power that lay hidden. He did not know what it was.

But no one was ever in doubt about Chandran's oratorical skill. He spoke well and without hesitation. He was spontaneous and persuasive. His constant smile made him likeable, but it was deceptive, and he seemed to show the greatest deference to his opponents when his words were sharpest and intended to wound. His sarcasm was well known, and well feared too. It was like a scalpel sterilized,

Abhimanyu

delicate, razor-sharp and sure. He dissected his opponents' arguments with the same skill with which he cut open frogs in the zoology laboratory. He made them look helpless, exposed the fatuity of their reasoning, and having done with them, dismissed them with disdain. He was stung only by those rare ones who showed any signs of life under the probing scalpel. Then his lips set into a thin line, his eyes sparkled with fire, and his voice, never in need of a mike to boost its reach, shook the hall to its very foundations. This was the victory he relished most.

It always amused him that the girl students ran away from him. He was polite and at times gallant, but they never seemed at ease with him. They treated him, he often said to his friends with mock dismay, as though he were a vampire or a potential rapist. But he did not appear to mind it in the least. Perhaps it only increased his sense of power. He would stroke his chin and look up at the sky and shrug; the only thing he could do gracefully was to yield the field to the more romantically inclined among his colleagues.

But the boys admired him without reserve. He was a phenomenon. He could be at once serious and comic, thundering at the union meetings, clowning on the stage under the auspices of the dramatic society. On the Annual Day function, he would leave the audience in stitches of laughter and even Father Joshe was seen to laugh, throwing his head back, his huge frame shaking with helpless mirth. Chandran was by no means a model student, but it was widely believed that he was more intelligent than was indicated by the class reports. It was rumoured that he even wrote poetry, though no one, with the exception perhaps of Kesavan, had ever seen it. Chandran, of course, never admitted openly to such weaknesses.

He had lost his father early in life, and he had always looked upon himself as the man of the family — a feeling that was encouraged by his doting mother and sister. He was always consulted, though he was the youngest of the family and had shown scant interest in the management of their sizeable property. His mother, deeply religious and accepting the role of a widow with a certain grace, always seemed anxious to see him grow into a man and take charge of the family affairs. She did not resent his smoking, and piously ignored the rumour that he occasionally enjoyed a drink. He was imperious with the servants. The tenants lived in dread of him. What he needed, she thought, was a good bride which she would be looking for as soon as he was out of college. She had already enough horoscopes from good families to choose from. She looked indulgently upon his studies and considered them as little more than an expensive pastime which they could afford easily. He had no need for jobs. Marriage would mellow him, and he would eventually settle down as a man of leisure, a gentleman farmer, a power to be reckoned with in the affairs of the village.

Chandran sympathized with Kesavan and knew that his friend was in college by virtue of a scholarship. (Gopalan often used to say that the best thing a father could do was to die early and leave his property to his son !) Of course, Chandran's own case was different. He had seen little of his father, but from what had been heard, he too had doted on Chandran and had been most indulgent of his only male issue. Chandran had met Kesavan's father on several occasions and had, frankly, considered him a man of no consequence. Possibly even a bad influence on his son ! A glorified clerk, fumbling among old files, running errands for arrogant, stupid, newly-recruited Government officers ! He had neither the aristocratic bearing nor the calm competence of his son. Kesavan must have inherited these qualities from his mother's side. Chandran had looked with secret pity and wonder at his friend. What an embarrassment it was to have a father like that !

Kesavan was virtually the only student for whom Chandran had any respect. True, he often lost patience with him and stormed and thumped the table, but, almost against his will sometimes, he felt confused and let down when he did not have Kesavan's whole-hearted approval for something that he did or planned to do. His leadership was never challenged and, oddly, Kesavan gave in on crucial issues. But there was something inexplicable, something even generous about his surrender. He had a very independent spirit, which only those who moved very closely with him realized. His casual air and aloofness were deceptive. He made his own judgements. He did things irrespective of what others expected of him; as when he stayed away from the meeting with Gopalan. He had given no explanation, but Chandran knew that he did not come because he did not want to come. Kesavan was polite to Gopalan, but was wary of him. This Chandran had felt instinctively. What did his friend really think of the man and the party he represented ? There was no way of knowing. He could not get more than a succinct comment : 'He is all right. He has a case, I suppose.' A case ? A case against what ? Against social injustice ? A case against political corruption ? If Kesavan thought so, why could he not say so ?

It was the same thing when the students had gone on a strike a few months ago over the issue of college fees. Kesavan had joined them on principle, jeopardizing his own scholarship, but he had baulked at the first sign of violence and had pleaded for a peaceful demonstration. That was one of the few occasions when Chandran had seen his friend angry. He had threatened to turn a blackleg, well, not a blackleg really, but he had warned that he would openly dissociate himself from Chandran's group and canvass independently. The other students had taunted Kesavan, accused him behind his back of cowardice and living in dread of losing his measly scholarship. Chandran knew that these were not true, but he made no attempt to defend the other. He was angry with Kesavan, knowing in his own mind that he, as a leader, was giving up wilfully a tactical advantage to humour a friend. He had called off the strike and negotiated a compromise. It had taken him days to wipe out the disappointment and sense of failure he had shared with his followers.

This time, Chandran had decided, there would be no hesitation, no compromise. It was not merely because he had to retrieve a lost image. He had to remove the impression that the students had no sense of purpose or the courage to fight a battle to its logical end. He would show them, in Gopalan's words, that the student community in modern India was a force to be reckoned with and not merely a bunch of delinquents out for fun. They could teach the grown-ups a few things about how to run the country. How to get results. How to force an issue. The ends would justify the means.

'Any sort of apology is out of the question,' Chandran now spoke emphatically to the students gathered round the table. Some of them were members of the Union Council and the present group constituted a self-appointed Action Committee. 'Father Joshe is living in the nineteenth century. He can be terribly old-fashioned at times. The very idea!' He knew his companions were with him on this point, but he was not quite sure of Kesavan. He looked at his friend enquiringly.

Kesavan was studying the cigarette pack, turning it over and over in his hand. He merely nodded, not looking at Chandran.

'Will that mean that we will not be allowed to sit in the class?' a boy asked.

'Of course,' Chandran retorted. 'Apologize for what? For Parkinsonpet?'

'I say,' Mathew cut in. 'Where is this bloody place?'

'Oh, shut up,' Chandran said and the others laughed.

Abhimanyu

One boy picked up a matchbox, extracted a stick and lit it. Then in a sudden movement he brought the flame under Mathew's hand, which he hastily withdrew with a curse. 'That is what Parkinsonpet is like, my friend,' he told Mathew with a smile. 'A hot issue!'

'Oh, stop this!' Chandran exclaimed. 'And listen... We will not apologize. Never! I don't care what that baby-face thinks! We don't have to castrate him anyway! He has no balls!'

Everybody laughed. 'The point,' Kesavan said suddenly, 'is how Father Joshe reacts to the ultimatum. Has he said anything at all?'

Chandran shook his head. 'But I know what he thinks. He thinks Parkinsonpet is not our business. He is trying to reduce all this to a question of mere indiscipline. Impertinence towards a professor. Just a case for the cane as if he had been, as if all of us had been living in the old days! I can tell you one thing. This is strictly confidential. The Board is aware of how the students feel about Parkinsonpet. They don't want us to precipitate any deep trouble over this issue. At least one member had approached the principal, unofficially, of course...'

'Who is it?'

'Raghava Menon, who else? He has the Government behind him. He doesn't want any trouble just before the elections. Not over Parkinsonpet, anyway.'

'Who is he to pick and choose?'

Chandran ignored the query. 'If we stage any demonstration, you can expect the Government to come down on us with a heavy hand. The one-man commission is their idea—their idea of handing over Parkinsonpet to the other state on a platter, as Gopalan said. They think we are fools!'

'We'll show them who the real fools are!'

'Didn't Gopalan,' Kesavan cut in, 'see the principal?'

'Yes, he did.' It was Chandran who answered.

'What did he say? I mean the principal... I wonder how

Father Joshe took it, Gopalan being an outsider and all that ...'

'Look, my friend,' Chandran said sharply, 'there is no outsider or insider in this business. Not over Parkinsonpet, anyway. Let us not forget that. There is no need to confuse the issues . . .'

'All right,' Kesavan conceded, thoughtfully. 'I still wonder what Father Joshe said.'

'You want to know ?' Another member of the action committee interposed. 'It is a laugh ! It seems he will pray! He's a missionary all right !'

'It is not such a bad idea,' Kesavan smiled, and then turned serious. ' . . . for people who believe in prayers, you know . . .'

'Well, we'll teach him a lesson this time !'

'We'll teach him,' Chandran said irritably, 'and we'll teach others—when the time comes. This buffoon who is coming here—the one-man commission—'

'Is it true that he is a retired ICS man ?'

'God, what does it matter ? Maybe the fellow should have retired from life by this time ! We'll make him realize how strongly the people of this state, at least the student community feel about this issue. This has become our responsibility, and we must not shirk it.'

'That Raghava Menon is a crook, they're all crooks. They're the ones who should be castrated. Otherwise they'll sell the honour of our state.'

Chandran was immersed in his own thoughts for a while. Then he spoke, slowly : 'We'll refuse to apologize. That means surely we will not be allowed to enter the college. We'll make that a cue to organize a strike. The students are in the mood for it this time . . . Chances are it will not end there. Father Joshe will not voluntarily close the college. If the Board pressurizes him—that is, Raghava Menon pressurizes him—we'll just take the struggle out in the streets, that's all . . .'

'If that is the idea . . .' Kesavan began.

'I'm not saying that is the idea,' Chandran interrupted him. 'I'm merely examining an eventuality.'

'O.K. If that is an eventuality—why did we have to start the trouble inside the college?'

'That's a good question, Kesavan. But you must remember that we do not have a choice in this matter all along. Sometimes things happen without any premeditation.' It had been really Gopalan's idea, though Chandran did not mention it now. If the trouble started inside the college—in fact, it should—the rest, whatever that was, would receive a little more public sympathy. The college issue and the political question would all be so mixed up that in the melee no one would remember to ask that irritating question : What had the students to do with Parkinsonpet? Gopalan had been very convincing on this point.

There was silence again. Chandran lit a cigarette and looked at it speculatively. This had all to be thought out very carefully, planned to the last detail. Gopalan had extolled the virtue of organization. In the past few days, Chandran had been arguing within himself, sorting out his own lines of thought, planning and rearranging in his mind the means to an end already clear and beyond question.

'It is unlikely,' he said aloud, 'that Father Joshe will close the college, not this time.'

'Are your sure?'

'Of course I'm sure. Otherwise what was the point in our asking him to close the college as a sign of protest over the Parkinsonpet issue? Imagine what a spot that will put him in with Raghava Menon ready to chew his head off!' Chandran laughed. 'No, he won't close . . . You know what he said? He said he didn't know where Parkinsonpet was and he didn't care. He wants to give the professors a chance to finish their courses before examinations begin. I had this from one of the professors themselves. . . I don't want to name him.'

'What will Raghava Menon do?'

'What can he do! Gopalan thinks, and I agree with him, that he will try to prevent at any cost the students coming out on the streets. I told you, they want this to be strictly a discipline issue, confined within the college premises. Who really cares if a few pieces of furniture get broken!'

'Poor Father Joshe,' Kesavan said.

Chandran looked at him without expression. 'Why do you say that?'

Kesavan shrugged. 'The poor man is between the devil and the deep sea, isn't he? Of course, I'm not, not sympathizing with him, I just meant. . . '

'What sympathy—for whom? For Heaven's sake, what are you talking about?'

Kesavan smiled at his friend. 'Oh, don't mind what I said. Go on. He is the principal. He had it coming, anyway.'

'It's not a question of whether he had it coming. I have the highest regard for him. I can assure you of that. We are really engaged in something that doesn't concern him at all. This is not a college issue, let us keep that clearly in mind. And let us make it known outside the college. The Student Union will call for a strike—it will, and mark this, also canvass for a general hartal on the day that the one-man commission arrives. We'll have to work out the details carefully. Processions, leaflets. . . '

'Leaflets?'

'Yes. We'll get them printed in time. And posters. Gopalan will help us out on that. We'll draft the leaflet in a day or two.'

'What about the police?'

'What about them?' Chandran asked calmly. 'They would not enter the college premises. They have no authority, unless Father Joshe calls them. You think he would?'

'But outside?'

'Outside what? They can't prevent us from taking out a procession! They can't prevent us from distributing leaflets. We'll put up the posters at night. There'll be people to help us.'

'This will all depend on what the leaflets and posters say,' Kesavan observed.

Chandran shook his head. 'We have a case and we'll present it. That's all. There is supposed to be freedom of speech in the country!'

'Of course, there is,' Kesavan said, smiling. 'It is like what Henry Ford was supposed to have said: you can have any colour as long as it is not black. You can say anything as long as you do not embarrass the Government.'

'To hell with the Government!' Chandran exploded. 'What have they done for us? They can't give us rice. They can't give us sugar. They can't give us kerosene. They can only give us long lectures—and yes, taxes. You read the newspapers more often, the right ones. You finish college and go out and look for jobs . . . you'll know then what I mean. Anyhow, let us be firm on this: we'll not sit back and watch this Government hand over a part of our state to a neighbour. We have no use for such a Government. They can take their horse-trading elsewhere. We are not afraid of their laws—or their police, I can tell you that!'

Kesavan said nothing. Laws and police, he thought. Two things against which everyone wanted to measure their strength! It was a pity that the conscience of the Government, any Government, rested these days in the law court. Why was it that no one had yet discovered an easier way of reaching it without recourse to violence— whether initiated on your own side or provoked by the other?

7

The clock above the main college building proclaimed the time as just after 5 p.m. Kesavan had mumbled an excuse and left the 'canteen conference' before it formally ended; he wanted to see whether the library was open—which normally it should be—so that he could borrow some books. It was bad enough that he was missing classes; there was no reason why he should waste his time at home.

He had avoided the main gate and had entered the college premises through a side entrance used mainly by the students going to the playgrounds. He had not encountered anyone he personally knew, though a few stragglers had given him a look of recognition and interest as he passed.

There was hardly anyone in the college corridors either, and in any case some privacy was provided by the hedges lining the path along which he walked. Father Joshe liked a lot of greenery about, though as in the case of the shoes, some of his colleagues considered it a bad policy as it interrupted a clear view of the college from the staff rooms. The Principal had compromised by allowing the gardener to trim off the hedges at chest level.

Kesavan was in no real danger of meeting anyone he was anxious to avoid. The classes must have been over by four or four-thirty, as was evidenced by the hush that lay over the buildings like a pall. Coming right after that meeting, it appeared a little eerie to him. What trouble lay ahead for the college, for all of them? Were the students, he himself included, really concerned about Parkinsonpet? Or was their motivation a more deeprooted sense of frustration and futility . . . yes, and an undefined dread of the future? 'You go out and look for jobs' Chandran had taunted them. He could have given them statistics. But was it really all that bad ? Or did it apply only to mediocrities inside the college and outside ? With so many colleges coming up all around each year there were more and more young men looking for jobs. It was easy to get a degree these days—that is, if you chose not to be too dogmatic or idealistic about it. You could buy one, or manoeuvre one ... and in any case the students themselves were making examinations a big hoax ! What was the sense in staging a walk-out saying that the test papers were tough ? It had happened ... and it was happening everywhere. It was really ridiculous. On one such occasion in this very same college, Father Joshe had been furious. Kesavan had never seen him so angry ! 'You think,' the principal had thundered at them at a subsequent meeting, 'that a test paper is some kind of a whip that the professors hold over your head ? This is a malicious campaign against examinations by the below-average students in your midst ! Unfortunately mediocrities make up the majority ... Oh God, how can you all be so naive ! You think anyone out there in the world will buy your degrees when you obtain them through such means ? Don't set up that big howl about unemployment! A college degree is not a meal ticket, even if some people are trying desperately to reduce it to that level !'

Yes, a college degree was not a meal ticket, Kesavan had quoted Father Joshe often at student meetings. The statement was never very well received. He smiled at the thought. The very fact that he himself was considered a 'bright student' was an argument against him. He was not bright actually. He did not have that sharp, crystal-like brilliance that he admired in some of his associates. He was no fool, but then the majority was not made up of fools either. He was methodical. His application was—well—sound. He did not mind relying on these two qualities for success. They were the ones most likely to stand him in good stead in the long run.

Kesavan climbed the steps to the verandah of the science section and walked along the way leading to the main building which housed the offices and the library. The girls' section on his left was also practically deserted. Only a murmur, coming muffled as though from a great distance, indicated that there was some activity going on in the playgrounds. A match ? But they had not announced one, or did they, during the past few days that he had been absent from college ? Maybe not an important one, or he would not have seen Mathew at the action committee meeting. And not looking so calm either. Mathew would have been a nervous wreck by this time ! Nothing on earth could keep him from a football match. He was a true aficionado–loyal to the point of insanity where 'his boys' were concerned !

As he walked, Kesavan suddenly felt like an intruder. It was a very odd feeling, utterly strange to him in all these years. He stopped in his stride. He was an alien, or was he fast becoming one ?... in this world of Hamlet and the binomial theorem ? ... of test papers, nail-bitingly, and in the end creditably done ? ... of football and cricket matches doggedly fought and lustily cheered ? ... He felt a stranger, momentarily dissociated from it all ; he could not see why. Was it because of that rumbling that came from the playing fields ... or was it a disturbing air of finality he had sensed about the suspension this time ? . . . Kesavan smiled and began to walk. He was a little on edge today after that meeting perhaps. Maybe he was just 'home-sick' for the college.

And yet ...

It was not any anxiety about his scholarship or studies—Father Joshe would be fair. Tough but fair. Oh, there was a man he admired ! What a pity about his retirement ! Or, as the students said, was he really being squeezed out to make way for a puppet principal ? God, that was what the students should have been protesting about... ! Where would they again find a man like him? And if they did, would those politicians out there give such a man a chance? Puppet principal, it would be. Maybe he would give them meal tickets. . . It was all so confusing, and frustrating.

Oh, to hell with them all! Kesavan thought. Let them grind their own axes... that was not what was really troubling him. It was a vague, inexplicable, probably baseless stirring in his subconscious which told him that he was approaching a crucial point in his academic life. He could not pinpoint any single incident which provoked it ... Maybe, it was the set, unrelenting lines he had seen on Chandran's face, the hard glitter in his narrow eyes, a nervous clutching and unclutching of his hands as he spoke.What was going on in his mind? What was he planning to do? Did he know something that the rest didn't? Kesavan wished he could read his friend's mind. Chandran felt deeply and genuinely about Parkinsonpet, there was no doubt about that. There was also a new consciousness in him of his power over the students and a determination to regain the ground he had lost during the last occasion. The papers had called the last strike immature, disorganized and foolish, not because he had surrendered but because he had started it at all. Were the criticisms genuine? Or was it merely another instance of the brickbats, fair and unfair, that the world reserves for all failures? One or two influential columnists had actually supported the student movement. They had by implication condemned the missionary monopoly of education and the greed for money. They had lamented the loss of discipline and the incompetence of professors who failed to win the students' respect. (But how, Kesavan had felt, would students have respect for their teachers when the community itself has no respect for their teaching profession?)

An editorial had conceded that the students could well feel disheartened and frustrated. The world of adults was itself an unholy mess! And yet what had the students made of this public sympathy? Nothing. Only slogan shouting and some desultory and meaningless destruction of college property. It was a bigger farce than what they were used to on the Annual Day. (A direct hit at Chandran?) 'Let them forget politics and go back to their books,' the conservative *Motherland* had said. 'Let them work out their spleen on the football ground and leave politics to the grown-ups.'

Chandran had never been quite able to live it down. Kesavan, feeling partly responsible because of his stand on violence, had tried to soften it.

'Look,' he had argued, 'the *Motherland* is a "committed" paper. Everyone knows that. They are angry with you because they have lost a round with the missionaries. They toe the official line.'

'Yes,' Chandran agreed, 'but the Government has nothing against the missionaries. The Church is a different matter because it holds a lot of votes. What has poor Father Joshe got to do with it all . . .'

'Maybe you're right, Chandran. Father Joshe at best might only be a symbol. . . but this is really a very local issue. Only local interests are involved. The student community, as you yourself have said, is becoming a force to be reckoned with. Everybody wants to have a hold over the educational institutions.'

Chandran put his hand over his friend's shoulder conciliatorily. 'All right, have it your way. . .' He laughed. 'Everybody's itching to have a finger in the pie, are they?'

Abhimanyu

They had not discussed the subject again, but Kesavan knew that Chandran could not afford another fiasco. This time there would be no half-measures. No counselling. What price would Chandran have to pay for victory ?. . .

Kesavan hesitated before the library entrance. It was still open but he could see very few students inside. He walked briskly towards the counter.

The library assistant looked at him noncommittally from behind his enclosure, and smiled cautiously as he approached.

'I want to borrow some books,' Kesavan said, fishing in his pocket for his library membership card. 'Can I go in ?'

'I don't see why not,' said the assistant. There had been no instructions to him regarding the suspended students. 'Make it quick, though, we're almost ready to close for the day. . . Hey, come back,' he called out as Kesavan was walking away. He grinned. ' I heard there was a council of war under the auspices of Krishnan Nair. . .'

' What has Krishnan Nair got to do with it ?' Kesavan asked, incensed.

'No, no,' the assistant said. 'I meant, in the canteen... News spreads fast here,' he said in a sing-song falsetto. ' Another strike ?'

'Why?' Kesavan spoke tauntingly, 'You're itching for a holiday?' It was well-known that the man always grumbled about his low wages and high responsibilities—thieving students were his nightmare and he considered every student a potential thief. He could not afford to keep his family with him in town. He visited them once or so in a fortnight over the weekends. He was a man in his mid-fifties with seven children, and the boys used to make fun of him, asking him to cut short his visits to the village. A practical joker had even been once hauled up in front of the principal for trying to pass off contraceptives to the assistant telling the poor man that they were 'imported balloons' for his children.

The assistant's face changed colour slightly. 'You are all getting too smart for your age', he said morosely. 'That is the trouble with you. It doesn't take much cleverness to make fun of an old man.'

Kesavan laughed, put his hand through the opening in the grill and patted the other's arm. 'I was only joking ! How's the family?'

'Oh, they're all right,' the man replied, not quite appeased. He got on well with Kesavan normally. Both of them shared a passion, almost reverence, for books. 'Though with these rising prices, only I know how difficult it is to manage things, to send boys to school and college so that they will grow up into little revolutionaries and raise hell.' He thought he had now evened the score with Kesavan. He smiled. 'Keep away from trouble, boy. Don't break the heart of your parents!'

Kesavan nodded and looked round, anxious to get away. He pushed in his cards through the window and started walking towards the inner room where, in shelves lining the walls, the books were kept.

The place was lit, even in daytime, by electric bulbs which hung down, bare and faintly dust-coated, from wires coming down from the high ceiling. High up on the northern wall, a circular window of garishly coloured glass let in a diffused stream of light like an irregular prism. The interior smelled faintly of decaying leather and dust. Rows of high shelves in the middle dissected the room into narrow corridors. Kesavan felt his mind lifting a little, he was at home here, immune to the doings of the world outside.

With quick steps, he walked over to the mathematics section and began to scan the shelves . . . *Spherical Geometry* by Abelard. *Advanced Algebra* by Jarman . . . He noted with dismay that many of the volumes were upside down and out of the alphabetical order, put back on the shelf by careless students. Out of habit, he began to set right a few . . . then gave it up as a bad job. There were too many of them. He must, he decided vaguely, draw the attention of the assistant to this disorder.

He selected three books and moved over to the history section. He scanned the shelf and, aware that he was completely alone now, stopped in front of Gibbon's *Roman Empire*. The dust indicated that no one ever disturbed these volumes. He took one more quick look over his shoulder and then pulled out the third book in the series. He put his hand into the cavity that it revealed and . . . it was there. He was more or less certain that it would be. A piece of neatly folded paper. He replaced the volume and unfolded the paper with one hand to take a hasty look in the dim light.

'Dearest K,' it said. 'I must see you at once. Please forgive me for the trouble. It is very urgent—I've been frantic with worry. Can we meet in the usual place, tomorrow at 3? I shall miss practicals. I'll be there anyway. Please try— yours as ever, N.'

Tomorrow? He took a quick look at the date on the note. Thank God, it was written today! He stuck the paper in his pocket as he walked towards the exit.

The way things were going, he wondered, where would he be at 3 p.m. tomorrow. . .?

How easy life would have been if it had the orderliness of mathematics, Kesavan though, as he trudged towards home, the three fraying volumes under his arm. The problems were always specific, challenging, almost exalting . . . needing nothing more than cold logic and a little imagination to come to totally satisfying solutions. The figures, unlike people, were consistent and obeyed certain comprehensible laws. X and Y had an intriguing intransigence which could be, after a little struggle perhaps, contained within meaningful equations. The square on the hypotenuse remained predictable and friendly. And there was always the shortest distance between two points whether on a plane or a curved surface.

Life was too full of unknown quantities which, by and large, remained unknown. (Would there be a bus when he reached the stop? Would it be crowded? Would it start at all? And what would happen to it on the way?...) No solution was really final—if at all, it had only a temporary validity. Even friendships. Man and man were friends one moment, enemies the next. Bhai-bhai one day, bang-bang the next! It was that clown Vidyanathan who said that. Funny character, that one. 'I am a punster, but also a funster!'—Oh, that was the limit! A pain in the neck when he really got going! And yet, there you have a really brilliant student. He would clown his way through the toughest test paper. Always practising oneupmanship with the professors. 'China-swamy' was his nickname because he had pure Mongolian features! Hundred per cent South Indian Brahmin, poor as a churchmouse and Father Joshe's favourite. ... How would he tackle the problems of adult life? (Oh, God, I must remember to borrow his physics notes, Kesavan told himself.) Would he be able to find solutions to them with the same facility with which he treated mathematical equations? . . . Life was really strange. Somewhere, Kesavan remembered, he had read a joke about a puzzle specially designed to condition children to face the paradoxes of modern life. Whichever way you put it together, it always turned out to be wrong!

He knew that he was in the college on borrowed time, so to speak. But for the scholarship, he would probably have been at this very moment sitting in some dingy office, coughing among files, taking home a pittance at the end of the month like his own father . . . like thousands, perhaps millions, of others all over the country. With what ambitions had each one of them started life? Perhaps even they would not remember now. Life would have broken them in slowly, turning protest into heart-breaking acquiescence, demolishing dream castles, taking them along an unending road without milestones or landmarks. The only challenge was the one of making ends meet. The only adventure was the one of fighting fatigue and frustration. Plodding on and on . . . to what end?

Death was a certainty, the only certainty. Plants and trees grew up and decayed. Men fought their battles, sometimes heroically but more often ingloriously, and died. 'Some little talk of you and me. . .' That was all there was to it. Kesavan himself had seen one of them die, an uncle on his mother's side, senile, grumbling and petulant, greedy for the little comforts of life, petty still and quarrelling over money for which he had no conceivable use, with no achievement to speak of except the fact that he had lived on for eighty-five years. During the last few months of his life, he had been more than ever hungry for attention. He made things miserable for those near and dear to him. He was in turn beseeching and rude with visitors. It was his mother who, out of a sense of duty, made Kesavan visit the old man now and then... And yet, when the man lay dying, Kesavan had been moved by pity. He had stood with the others, with a vulgar and horrified curiosity, watching the final spasms of death as the shrivelled up figure lay on the bed, on unclean sheets and opened his toothless mouth to snap at the faint breath of life. 'It will be over in a few more minutes,' a bystander had said, in a tone that suggested he perhaps had a train to catch after this show ended. 'This is what the doctors call jaw-breathing!'

Jaw-breathing! Poor, miserable creature. Kesavan's eyes had suddenly misted with tears, not because he had felt any personal sense of loss, but merely because he was moved by the spectacle of this inglorious death. Standing there with the others, bound to them by the awe and awareness of the reality of their own being, conscious of his own loud and assertive heart-beats, Kesavan had understood, the dying man's loneliness and his isolation from life which had, in a few minutes, become irrevocably final . . .

He was feeling morbid today, Kesavan thought, as he saw the bus turn a corner and come towards the people waiting for it. In a second, the queue broke up and there was a scramble and scuffle at the door to get in, blocking those who wanted to get out. Kesavan elbowed his way in, resolutely and desperately, nearly losing the books in the process. But the bus was half-empty! Wonder of wonders! With a sigh of satisfaction, he settled himself in a corner.

The college was situated on high ground, almost a small hill, eight miles away from the heart of town, and the driver sped down the incline, taking the curves with skill, relying more on his reflexes than on the brakes. The surrounding countryside looked so peaceful in the tropical twilight hour. Far away, Kesavan could identify the sea as a black line on the horizon. As the bus turned, the landscape swung this side and that with it, like a toy town in a child's hand. Then a final curve and a bump brought the vehicle rushing down to plain surface...

'You neither kill, nor are you killed...', isn't that what the *Gita* said? (You only end up with statistics, Kesavan thought.) When he was younger and more tractable, his mother used to make him sit and read out the *Gita* to her. This was really the second phase of his religious instruction. The first was when he was very young, starting while he was just two or three. He would, like other children of his social class, wash his feet and face in the evening, put sacred ash on his forehead (in the morning it would be sandal paste), and sit on the floor of the puja room, cross-legged, before the framed pictures of the gods. He would recite a whole string of Sanskrit verses, understanding a word or phrase here and there, lulled into sleep by the drone of his own voice, watching the reflection on the glass surfaces of the flickering flame of the bell-metal lamp. His mother would be by his side, her eyes closed, palms pressed together in her lap, swaying a little to the rhythm

Abhimanyu

of the recitation. He had only to bend a little this way or that to make the flame sprout from the head of one deity or from the open hand of another. Vishnu, Siva and Subrahmanya seemed to watch his antics from within their glass frames with a faint smile of compassion. Now and then, his mother would open her eyes and catch him at it, or pause to correct his pronunciation and give instructions: Don't keep on pulling at your ears, and don't yawn, it is not polite . . . Recite the *slokas* clearly, like this. . .

The *Gita* phase, as he called it, began much later, when he had long ago got through the multiplication tables and was grappling with Euclid and Shelley and the precepts of Dandin. His mother would request him to read out the passages to her as her eyesight was bad—but he knew the readings were really for his benefit. Perhaps she thought that if Ajamila could get salvation by just calling out the name of his son Narayana, Kesavan had certainly a chance! But he had come to like the *Gita* in course of time and for a while was totally absorbed in it. He marvelled at the simplicity of the language, the crispness of the rhymes and the astonishing economy of words to imply such a wealth of meaning. It has appeared to give meaning to all life's paradoxes. The *Mahabharata* was truly a noble epic, a breath-taking canvas of human foibles and strength. And the eighteenth chapter really sounded like the voice of God—a divinity acceptable to the modern mind. Like mathematics, the *Gita* laid down certain axioms and proceeded to explain away life's complexities. To him, it spoke the language of logic. It had at that time filled him with a strange excitement and opened the way to many erudite metaphysical texts. Life was bearable, even challenging, if you could accept the reality of an afterlife. But could you?

With the uncompromising and unyielding zeal of youth, rather with a mathematician's distrust of imprecision, he had rejected the whole lot. The axioms of that spiritual life, on closer approach, had vanished like mirages and had left him again floundering in a desert. Life was here and now and it had an unpleasant face. It was real and demanding and apparently beyond the pale of justice and fair play. It was the mental contortions his father went through to make ends meet. It was the insatiable greed and pettiness of relatives and the phenomenon of 'dog eat dog.' It was the indignity of begging others for help, the difficulty of paying one's fees and the uncertainties of a job after one went so laboriously through college. The axioms were good enough only for a Buddha or a saint, for those who had—yes, perhaps overcome the lust for life. They were not for those who stood poised on the threshold of life, feeling the many urgent and irrepressible stirrings within, which sent mere men stumbling along the way of all flesh.

He would never marry, Kesavan had decided, until he was well established in life. That seemed to be the whole trouble with man, a vulgar eagerness to propagate the species. What point was there in bringing children into this world if you did not have the wherewithal to support them? What future did he himself have to look forward to? A clerk in a stuffy office? What did those axioms have to say about that! His father perhaps had fantastic ambitions for Kesavan: a first class from college, an IAS career, pomp and splendour as a District Collector dispensing justice, and permits, to the deserving. To think of an after-life in the context of ration-cards and tax returns! Revise your axioms and observe the rules of the game, so that you too would get an honourable place in the queue—for what?

For honourable disillusionment, that was what! Look at the mess the whole country was in! One moment the worship of swamis and the pursuit of nirvana, the next taking up cudgels and breaking your neighbour's head because he talks a different language. That was politics, adult politics. Buffoonery in the Assemblies and double-dealing before the electorate. Horse-trading of loyalties and principles, as someone had said. And such men are felicitated and feted! Chandran once called the Parliament the biggest cattle-market in the country and the boys had roared with laughter. 'They'll jail you for contempt,' someone had warned him ironically.

'Well,' the reply had come without hesitation, 'I am told the jails are the best places to be in these days! No ration cards, no taxes, no permits... They are turning them into health resorts with all that reforming and ballyhoo. We are a humane nation, you see. Go to jail—you'll at least be in lively company.'

Would they also—people like him and Chandran and the others—end up one day in jail? He did not baulk at the prospect, except that, he told himself sadly, it would break his mother's heart.

When he reached home, he found his mother on the verandah, combing her hair after the evening bath. She was clad in white, as usual, starched and crisp and clean. He thought that it somehow gave her an austere look and made her appear thinner than she really was. She used no comb, as her hair was still wet, and she was passing her fingers through it, stroke after stroke, thoughtfully. As he went by he got a faint aroma of sandal paste and tulsi leaves.

He threw down the books on the table in the central room and came out again. His mother was now engrossed in picking up strands of hair which had come loose and were sticking to her clothes, turning her body this side and that as she searched for them. When she was satisfied that she had gathered them all, she wound them round her fingers, made a tight ball of them and tucked it into the folds of the dhoti at her waist. She was fastidious about these things. Later she would go to the back of the house and throw those strands of hair away where no wind would blow them back into the house. Dead hair inside the house was unclean and inauspicious.

'There is not much left of it,' she said sadly, stroking her hair again. 'It is the water. The salt in it is bad for the hair.'

'It is not the water, Mother, and you know it,' Kesavan said in a bantering tone. 'It's your age. Why don't you admit it? How vain you are!' He laughed as he saw a look of dismay on her face.

'Vain?... Yes, I suppose you're right.' Her eyes became reflective, and Kesavan thought, here comes an aphorism.

'Vanity goes only when life goes.' She stopped suddenly and looked at him, knowing that he had somehow trapped her into making one of her philosophical statements which always seemed to amuse him. She smiled shyly and Kesavan thought how youthful she looked now, almost a girlish expression on her face obliterating all lines of worry. He watched her, feeling very close to her.

'Don't stand there and grin!' she exclaimed. 'It is nothing to be laughed at. At least it wasn't when I was young. I had a lot of hair then, thick and black, coming down almost to my knees. I was the envy of the other girls. And your father was proud of it—ask him!'

She checked herself, and looked at him, her face now serious. 'Your father had gone to see that man—Menon.'

'Raghava Menon?' Kesavan began to feel uneasy. 'What about?'

'About you.'

He wanted to change the subject, but did not know how to do it without rousing her suspicions.

'He said it is all right,' Kalyani Amma said.

'What is all right?'

'About the suspension. He promised to speak to your principal about it.'

This was a laugh, but the expression on his face did not change. His mother could, understandably, be naive about such things, but how could his father fall for a line like that from a smooth-talking politician! Or did he? He must have been really desperate. He need not have been, Kesavan thought. There was no real danger of losing the scholarship. There was no reason why Father Joshe should single him out for punishment. That would never happen. Kesavan was positive. This was not his individual struggle; too many students were involved. This would also blow over like so many other things had in the past . . . with some blows struck on behalf of Parkinsonpet perhaps.

But there was such an undertone of assurance and relief in her voice that for a moment Kesavan did not know how to break the news of the strike to her. Should he just keep silent now and let her find out when the time came? It would be difficult—impossible to make her see such things in the proper perspective. He looked at her helplessly.

'What is it, my son?' she asked. 'What is troubling you? Menon is a very influential man, you know, and he had been considerate to us before.'

'It's no use, Mother,' he said wearily. 'It doesn't matter now about the suspension. . .'

'What is it, Kesavan?' she repeated, a note of genuine alarm in her voice. 'Why doesn't it matter?' She was watching him closely.

He walked over to a chair and sat down. 'Well, you better know about it now than later . . . There's going to be a strike.'

'Again?'

'Yes, again.'

She did not say anything for a while, and Kesavan sat patiently waiting for the explosion. But when she spoke, her voice was almost a whisper, breaking a little. 'Your father doesn't have much luck, has he? He went early in the morning and hung around that house like a servant. I know it hurt his pride. But there was nothing else he could do. He wanted to help.'

Kesavan did not look at her. He did not want to see the tears in her eyes, and he knew they would be there; he could tell that from her voice. 'There is nothing to worry about, really, Mother,' he said. 'It was coming all the time; now it is here, that's all.'

'Yes. That's all. What else is there to be said?'

He waited for her mood to change, giving her time to get angry and shout at him, and get it over with. He waited in vain. She did not say anything further and he looked up at her in surprise.

She was sitting in his father's chair, staring into space. Why could she not say something? he thought.

'There is no point in talking about it now,' she said, almost reading his mind, but not looking at him. 'I have feared this. I knew it will come one day, the way you were going . . . talking with that Gopalan and the rest of them . . . Is there any use now asking you not to join it?'

His voice was also subdued. 'No, Mother . . . I have to join. It's a matter—a matter of principle.' He looked at her anxiously, expecting—expecting what? He was not sure. Impatience? Sarcasm? But her face seemed to be drained of all emotion. 'There are certain . . . loyalties . . . among students, too, Mother. I believe in what they believe, at least in this issue. I cannot hold back this time.'

She looked at him. 'Have you no loyalty towards your father?'

He paused, as though he wanted to consider the question dispassionately. 'Yes. And towards you. I have loyalty. This is not a denial of that. I owe myself something, too. It is loyalty to my own convictions. . . however illogical or far-fetched they might look to others. . . The strike is a different matter altogether. It is over an issue that concerns all of us; all the people in this State.'

'Do you children think that you have better ways of solving problems than the grown-ups?'

'We are not children, Mother,' he said sharply. 'We are old enough to understand things. They don't let us remain children in this country for long. They. . .'

'Who are they?'

Kesavan ignored the question. 'You must try to look at it from a man's point of view, mother ... remember, I'll be a man, too, soon enough. Our reactions and responsibilities have changed from what they were in your time, because times have changed. In judging us, it is foolish to apply norms which have become obsolete ... There are strikes all over the country—and by students, too—everywhere. It is not like fighting the British—this is a legitimate mode of protest. Ours is no different. . . .My studies won't be affected by that. There are too many of us in it.'

'I don't know,' she said slowly. 'There are things that I don't understand perhaps ... But somehow I don't think it is right. I'm afraid and there is no point in denying that. Last time there was all that trouble ... breaking chairs and things. When people get angry, they do things that they hadn't bargained for in the beginning.'

'There'll be no trouble of that nature this time, Mother. I assure you. The last time a few fellows got a little excited.'

'What guarantee was there that this time they would not get excited?' she wanted to ask him, but did not. She got up from the chair and stood looking down at him for some time. Then she put her hand on his head, almost possessively. When she spoke, it was about a different subject altogether:

'Today is the day of your birth-star, did you know that? I went to the temple and brought the prasadam. Times are bad. . .' She stopped, seeing him smile. 'All right, all right, horoscopes are all a pack of lies, isn't that what you were about to say? But your mother is old-fashioned and superstitious. I was worried. I had a special puja performed for you today.'

'That's very good,' he said solemnly. 'I hope it will help me pass in the examinations!'

She went inside and presently came with the prasadam— a piece of plantain leaf on which were some flowers and tulsi leaves, a piece of jaggery and copra peels. She picked out the flowers and leaves and put some of them on his head and rest behind his ears, ignoring the fact that he appeared to flinch and squirm a little. 'Have you had your bath today?' She asked suddenly.

'Oh, yes. Early in the morning. Go ahead. I'm not unclean, except that I've come walking through the bazaar.' He smiled at her.

She put her hand again on his head, her eyes closed, lips moving silently. Then she opened them and looked at him. Her eyes were troubled and bright with a touch of moisture.

'God keep you in good health and cheer, my son,' she uttered a benediction. 'And may you live in happiness and prosperity for many, many years to come. . .'

There was loud, metallic clang of a brass vessel, coming from the kitchen, reverberating and slowly subsiding into a whine on the hard cemented floor. His mother, startled out of her wits, put her hand again on his head, as though seeking support. She stood for a moment like that, transfixed, and then quickly turned and went inside the house.

It was time somebody did something to that cat, Kesavan thought. The way it startled his mother! It was really becoming a nuisance. He realized then that even his own heart was beating a little faster.

8

This was inconceivable, Raghava Menon said to himself. Irresponsible and impertinent! A student strike and at this time! And what about? Parkinsonpet! As though that obscure stretch of jungle land was any of their concern! He was not deceived by the fact that all this business was made to appear initially as a college affair. The boys were clever, or those who were behind them really knew the ropes. This was purely the lighting of the fuse. The explosion would come later, and in all probability it would be bigger than what anybody could foresee now. That was how these things went.

Oh, he had 'informers' in the college. He was after all a full-fledged member of the Board and it was his business to keep himself up to date with what was happening there, what was going on in those little delinquent minds. It would all start as a purely 'internal' affair. The public would be fooled as it perhaps deserved to be. Strikes in scholastic institutions were becoming almost part of the curriculum all over the land. Why look at this particular one in any other light? Even parents and responsible leaders in public life were taking them as a harmless—not harmless any more, perhaps—but still a legitimate extra-curricular activity to sharpen the student mind! They could then wash their hands off the business with a clear conscience. Let the college settle its own affairs—after all, they were paying the fees through their noses, weren't they? How many of them realized, how many of them would be honest enough to admit that their 'little boys' were also little arsonists and thugs? This was the comic-book generation they were dealing with!

Menon was not really blaming the boys. He himself had two sons, though, thank God, they were safely out of college now. Look at all the violence that was going on all around! No film was complete without a rape scene these days and the censors pass it if the heroine's skirt is not too short to offend their delicate taste! The foreign pictures were indeed more tolerable in this respect. At least they did not dish out nonsense on the one hand and assume a holier-than-thou attitude on the other. What happened on the screen was something that was happening in a different place and in a different culture, not on your doorstep! It was far worse if you were made to feel that your neighbour was a repressed rapist. . .

The strike must be stopped at any cost. . . but how? Was it already getting too late for that? Perhaps the college should have been closed for a fortnight as demanded by the students. The real hard cases would more than likely be found in the hostel. Away from parental restrictions and looking for excuses to shirk their studies. Once they were packed away home . . . but what guarantee was there that they would go even if the hostel was closed? They would all probably hang around and turn out to be a bigger nuisance than ever . . . No, that would be no solution. The Board decision was right. Menon had agreed with the majority view that closing the college would have had some effect if the issue was an internal one. With that idiotic Parkinsonpet hanging in the balance, even the closure of the college would be a victory for the students, which meant, really for the Opposition. It would be better to go through with it all and demonstrate beyond doubt to all concerned—students included—that the official line would be a tough one. At this crucial juncture it would be better not to leave any loose ends.

Only Father Joshe had expressed doubts. God, that man must be the incarnation of the original doubting Thomas! He did not want his 'boys' to be touched.

Good, Menon had said. We did not want the boys to be touched either. But who was asking them to stick their necks out? If the present younger generation was a tougher breed, they probably needed something tougher than the cane, that was the gist of it. Father Joshe had sat through the session as though he were in the docks!

He was getting senile, that was the trouble with that Father Joshe. Too indifferent for his own good . . . not indifferent, perhaps, but definitely soft. Incompetence was a better word. He could not control his students, that was abundantly clear. It was high time that the man was replaced. It would not be difficult to find a younger, abler principal—someone who would be more realistic, who would run the institution with common sense and not with outdated idealism. If this mess turned out to be something really ugly, Menon would see to it that it would be Father Joshe's funeral. The man must be made to resign.

He had nothing personally against the principal, of course. He had served the institution creditably. Few would dispute that. But the best of people could outlive their utility . . . it was better if they realized it themselves. Times were changing and if you did change your ways and attitudes with it, you deserved to be left behind.

What was the principal doing about the strike except voice a lot of Christian homilies? He must be tough with the students. That was far better and more natural than any outside forces being tough with them. It was his duty, did he realize that? He talked as though he were running an orphanage, not a college. As though charity were the prime virtue to be exercised! He should punish them! Threaten them! Weed out the incorrigibles ruthlessly, like that secretary of the Student Union, what was his name? Yes, Chandran. Arrogant fellow. Did not know how to speak to his betters. Raghava Menon had sent for him once, just to give the boy some good advice. If he were all that dynamic as some people had told him, perhaps Chandran should be found a place in the Youth Congress. The old party needed young blood. Why, Menon was really willing to take the boy under his wing, so to speak... And what did that firebrand do? He just ignored the request. Sent word that Menon was free to come, if Father Joshe permitted it, and see Chandran in the college. Impertinent cur! As though Menon needed anyone's permission to come to the college. They forgot that he was an active member of the Board.

Menon remembered the occasion well, and it still rankled. They—the students—had his sympathy, he had made it very clear when a reporter from *Motherland*, at his own request of course, had interviewed him. What was wrong with that? He was a public figure and it was in the public interest to let his views on such matters be known. Later he had moved the Assembly to reconsider the grant to private educational institutions. That was a good speech he made, hard-hitting, to the point, incisive, and sometimes, let him admit it, rising to magnificent heights. He had demolished the Opposition view that the grants were in any case inadequate. He had cited instances to disprove the charge that there were inordinate delays in payment. The bogey of corruption was raised, but he had challenged them to bring proof. The Government was really interested in rooting out malpractices. They would indeed appreciate help in this matter from other quarters.

Many members, some even from the Opposition, had shaken his hands. Even the Chief Minister was impressed. 'You made out a very convincing case, Mr Menon,' he had said.

Menon, a little carried away by the praise perhaps, had been bold enough to reply: 'There is still a lot of fight left in the old horses, sir.' The Chief Minister had nodded thoughtfully and looked away. He had taken the hint, Menon later told his wife. This horse was still good enough for a long run.

And now, a thing like this to happen before the elections! Father Joshe, it was clear, was an unreliable man. Who knew, he might even have a hand in this. He had been rather put out by Menon's speech in the Assembly. The missionaries were not spared. In fact, they had provided a good spring-board for Menon. There had already been questions raised about the advisability of taking over the college. Menon wanted to set at rest such retrograde thinking. The occasion came handy, and he had used it. He was not conducting a crusade against the missionaries. The take-over was really only a concession to local sentiment . . . There were always exceptions, he was gentleman enough to admit that, in private, of course. On the Assembly floor, you needed ammunition and you took it where you found it. You had to have a wider view of things, a historical perspective. The missionaries' days were numbered, and what if some newspaper had accused him of driving a nail into their coffin? In his honest opinion, some of them should be grateful that they were getting a decent burial. That all was not well in the missionary department was public knowledge.

The real mistake, of course, was on the part of the leaders of his own party, though he had told the reporter that he did not want to be quoted on this point. They had taught the boys all the mischief, fumbling step by step, when the student struggle represented another spoke in the wheel of the larger freedom movement. Today let them cry over the fact that they had sowed the wind and were reaping the whirlwind! The line dividing patriotism and plain delinquency was almost unrecognizable now.

That scum, those professional rabble-rousers like Gopalan were having their heyday. That man had the audacity to challenge him at the polls this time. Where was this Gopalan and men of his ilk when Menon was spending the best years of his life in prison? What had they done to free the country from alien rule? Now they talk, and they talk foul and big! Socialism, as though he had personally invented it! Militant socialism! Militant fiddlesticks! The police were too lenient, that was the trouble. Communists—all working under cover, of course—had infiltrated the rank and file of the police force. The fence itself ate the crop, as the saying went. You could shout yourself hoarse on the Assembly floor . . . to what purpose?

The rabble would support its like. That was the strength of people like Gopalan. But why blame the rabble? Even the middle class, people who should have more sense, were indulging in loose talk about the need for change. What change? To chaos? Some of them would probably turn against him when the time came. People of his own community. But what were the majority of them when you came down to brass tacks ? Tattered remnants of the old aristocracy. Too proud to do any honest work, too lazy to care whether the country was really going to the dogs. An aristocracy of petty officials and briefless lawyers!

Raghava Menon could still rely on some staunch supporters, thank God! They would rally round him in an emergency. After all, he represented their interests. Gratitude was surely not too big a return to ask for in view of the tribulations he had gone through on their behalf.

As he thought of them, Menon's confidence returned. They would not let him down. Whatever one said in the heat of the moment, they still represented a major force in his electorate. Hadn't he—wasn't he still manoeuvring the land-ceiling issue cleverly? Some concessions had to be made here and there, but one day they would be glad that they had supported him. There was no need for them to feel threatened by his stand on the Land Reforms Bill. He would soft-pedal it this time. People did not appreciate a politician's dilemma. He also had a job to do. Politics was no longer flag-waving and cheering; with all the rabble mixed up in it, it had become a question of survival—for a praiseworthy mission, of course. People judged him too hastily and sometimes too harshly.

Raghava Menon had been one of the leading lights in the land-to-the-tiller movement. He was convinced of its inevitability and necessity, though some of his detractors had charged him with trying to outdo the Communists. He was fallible but he was not an upholder of vested interests. They said he was a champion of the cause because he himself had no land to lose. The five acres he got from the Government, or in fact which he was allowed to retain, was outside the pale of the law. This was a malicious and false charge. He had lost in this deal more than most people had. But how many of them would have taken the trouble to actually come and verify the facts? He had made sacrifices in his own way. Only his close associates knew that. One thing was certain: he was certainly in a position to appreciate the problems of the land-owning class in his state. They were not zamindars, the majority of them, but they were not tillers either. If they had not been so vulgarly job-hungry under the British, would they have let out their lands to the equally anachronistic middle-men and landed themselves in their present predicament? No law could appease everyone. No law could be fair to all. The middle class was the backbone of society and they had to take the shocks. Then why blame Menon if the land-to-the-tiller movement hit some of the small landholders hard? Would they rather have straight-faced Communism or would they allow him to beat those visionaries at their own game? He himself had chosen the latter step. He had been outspoken on the land reforms issue. He was not trying to win votes, but how many people realized that?

Menon felt depressed. His was a thankless job. Everything was a double-edged sword. It had become the fashion to sling mud at politicians. Why, it was becoming a national pastime. The newspapers thrived on it. They were becoming experts in raking up a lot of muck and came up invariably with sizzling editorials, which did good only to their circulation! The public really had only one choice—whose pawns should they be?

Menon decided that before the student strike developed into anything big, he should have a talk with the editor of the *Motherland*. Later in the evening he was going to address the students. Father Joshe, though he did not appear quite convinced of its efficacy had been gracious enough to concede him that privilege. Menon wanted to make sure that the newspaper really understood what the score was.

'Of course, my reporter will be there,' the Editor said, looking myopically at Raghava Menon over his steel-rimmed glasses. 'Now, let me see...' He pushed aside an assortment of typed pages and galley proofs on his table, and from under the rubble, pulled out a black assignment book. 'Hmm... Ramdas. A good man. One of the best on the staff. Always dependable for turning in good copy.'

Raghava Menon sat back, suppressing an urge to sneeze brought on by the dust and the faintly pungent smell which seemed to be a feature of all newspaper offices. From somewhere beyond the door, the clicking of teleprinters came, jerkily, stopping and starting again... a neurotic instrument, Menon thought irritably. The building vibrated to the subdued hum of a rotary working somewhere. He looked up. It was a miracle that the old beams held. No wonder most of the journalists he had met had appeared to him slightly cranky.

The Editor would be co-operative, Menon was sure of

Abhimanyu

that. This was a give and take game. The *Motherland* was not doing all that well in spite of its respectable circulation, and Menon had been approached now and then for small favours. At the moment, his stock was fairly high with the paper. He had recently sorted out a small hitch in newsprint allocation and had persuaded some perennial permit-seekers to spend a little money on advertising.

'This proposed strike is all nonsense,' Menon said, making quite clear his own viewpoint. 'There is no justification for getting agitated over Parkinsonpet at this time. After all, the commission is coming and there is no virtue, no virtue whatsoever—in spoiling our case.'

The Editor blanched a little. One of his own subordinates, in a sudden seizure of patriotic, rather chauvinistic zeal, had asked in an editorial for the withdrawal of the commission. He had argued that Parkinsonpet had always been an integral part of this state under the British administration, and it was just political chicanery to try to do some hair-splitting over the origin of the dialect the tribals spoke. He had made the appointment of the commission look like a mere stalling move. The Assistant Editor was called up and reprimanded in no vague terms about this indiscretion. It would have been less reprehensible if it had been a by-lined article, not necessarily reflecting the newspaper's —and the Editor's—views on the matter. The paper's policy had to be maintained, whatever the feelings of individual members of the staff. And that policy had all along been to support the ruling party—as simple as that. There were two sides to any question, and those who, for private reasons, decided to choose the wrong side, were always free to seek other avenues of employment.

'I quite agree with what you say, Mr Menon,' the Editor said now firmly. 'The commission is to be supported, at least on principle. There is no denying that.'

There was no denying that! Menon muttered under his breath bitterly. The mischief had been wrought and there was no denying that, either ! 'Then,' he continued aloud, hardly hiding the sarcasm, 'your policy has undergone a sea-change in recent times, hasn't it ?'

The Editor fidgeted with a paperweight on his desk. He looked at it speculatively, as though he thought a heavy object like that could be put to better use than it was intended for. 'I am sorry about that editorial, Mr. Menon. Unfortunately, I do not see everything before it gets into print.' He waved a hand at the galleys in front of him. 'I have become wiser now ... Some of the younger men are a bit carried away by emotion at times, always a bad thing for a journalist, I tell them. Objectivity should be their aim. What is good in the long run for the state and the country as a whole...'

Menon cut him short. 'Let me be quite frank with you. I do not want to be quoted, but I shall explain my attittude to you, man to man.'

The Editor nodded solemnly and waited.

'I'm sure you realize that Parkinsonpet is a sensitive issue. You know what our stand on it is. There is no gold there—just a lot of crow-shit ! This is all mischievous propaganda. I don't want this thing to snowball at the time of the elections and embarrass our party. At other times ... well, if there is an agitation, there is an agitation, that's all. Frankly, I don't even mind if it comes up after the fever of the elections is over. We would all be able to use a lot more common sense then. This is not the time for the issue. I had no end of trouble persuading Delhi to appoint a commission to look into it. They thought the move would be misinterpreted. The Opposition was openly accusing them, as you yourself know, of stalling tactics.'

'Gopalan's fast was a big stunt,' the Editor said enthusiastically. 'It's a hoax. People like that can fast, they are used to starvation anyway !' He laughed. 'And God alone knows whether he really went without food.'

Menon looked around, impatiently, considering all this

irrelevant. The fast had done the mischief, that was all there was to it. It had been timed perfectly and was a tactical master-stroke. It had received wide publicity, and Gopalan had appropriated the issue as his own, his party's own. He had very cleverly whipped up local patriotism, knowing well that his opponents would have to look on helplessly from the other side of the fence. What more could a politician like that ask for ? ... What a fuss was made. Reporters and photographers dancing attendance on that pest ! He had clearly, and cleverly, wrested the initiative from Menon's party. And he had fired the imagination of the students. That was another big gain. Karl Marx should, if he had any decency, turn in his grave ! His revolution might have been devised for a highly industrialised community ... here, in this country, it was being initiated in the nurseries !

Menon shook his head. That Gopalan was a clever one. He had launched a ripple and come home riding a wave.

'The students are getting out of hand,' he continued. 'The college authorities are slack. And the police, when the boys come out in the streets, are indifferent.' He paused for a moment. 'I must have a talk with the Commissioner. The boys plan to take out a procession and picket the Collectorate, it seems.'

'That Father Joshe would not even see a reporter,' the Editor grumbled. ' "I have nothing to say to you"—that's the attitude he takes.'

Suddenly Menon had another bone to pick : 'You let him off lightly last time, didn't you ?'

'I had to. I had no choice. Those students of his would have wrecked this place. They are capable of anything. I can't see why, but he is very popular with them and those miscreants are looking for some excuse to go on the warpath ... You think he has anything to do with this ?'

'No, not Father Joshe ! He is too wrapped up in his own affairs... but he can be very obstinate. I had trouble convincing him that I should address the students today evening. He was very sceptical. Why, he even looked worried about it.'

'Why should he mind? After all, you are a board member. As I see it, it is a good step.'

'I hope so, too.'

Menon got up and shook hands with the Editor. 'I shall look for your account of it in tomorrow's newspaper.'

The Editor accompanied Menon to the door and held it open for him. When he came back to his desk, he banged on the calling bell impatiently.

'Get me Ramdas. Now.' He told the sepoy who came in response to the summons.

Menon arrived at the college thirty minutes earlier than the appointed time and he was received by Father Joshe and taken to the principal's office. He did feel a little nervous as he walked along the corridors and watched small groups of students deferentially moving aside to make way for him. One could never guess what the boys were thinking, or how they would take his efforts to guide them. But, Menon told himself as he settled into a chair in Father Joshe's office, he had a duty to perform, not entirely pleasant, but in the circumstances, absolutely necessary. There was still some hope. The students should be made to see reason. Someone should show them the right path, and the logic of taking it.

The professors were of no great help in this matter, like this man himself sitting in front of him, absorbed, or pretending to be absorbed in some paper. One never got the kind of teachers there used to be in the old days any more, eminently competent, a little tyrannical perhaps, but who could command the students' respect beyond question. Menon remembered his own old headmaster—Watson by name—a bellicose Scot who believed that a cane judiciously used was a cure-all for anything that ailed a student. He made a big show of it when occasion demanded—a boy would be tied to a three-legged blackboard stand placed in the quadrangle and flogged with great precision, which the whole college assembled to watch.

The physical instructor used to be the one chosen to execute the punishment. Old Gaffoor Khan, bald as an egg and with a toothbrush moustache, growling his commands at the boys in a clipped accent appropriated from his military service during the First World War. 'This hurts me more than it hurts you,' he would say as an impersonal preliminary while he flexed the cane with obvious relish. 'But you young rascals don't seem able to manage without it.' And then it would start. One. Swish. Two. Swish... Six or twelve strokes on the bare bottom depending on the gravity of the offence. Delivered without emotion or waste of movement. The congregation watched the proceedings without a stir. The boy who was punished seldom cried out, though the pain must have been excruciating. There was in fact a little prestige attached to it. Not all boys were incorrigible enough to earn it. But to weep or whine would have been a negation of the honour. The boys in those days were tough in spirit. They took their punishment without a word...

Father Joshe put down his pen and looked at Mr. Menon, and then at his watch. There was still some time left. He turned his eyes away and watched the stragglers in the quadrangle outside. He felt as diffident about what was to come as, he thought, probably Menon himself. The boys were in a bad mood. They could be volatile and unpredictable. What would happen if Menon rubbed them the wrong way?

He had earlier tried to reason with Menon, that the students were in a restless frame of mind and that Menon might find the experience unpleasant. They were not in the right mood for taking advice. It was better to leave them alone, to let them form their own judgment and perhaps with gentle persuasion convince them that they were harming themselves, their own interests, their own people, the college itself—something, anything that would touch their heart. But no ! Menon would have none of it. He was a seasoned campaigner. He would not be put off by a restive audience.

Father Joshe had sighed. What else was there to be done ? When he himself spoke to them these days, he had experienced that helpless feeling of not being able to reach them, that he no more understood them or knew how they felt, as though he were talking to them from behind a glass wall. He could only make gestures—and gestures could always be misunderstood. He had a depressing feeling that he was perhaps now a man too old for his job, an anachronism as Gopalan had called him, and that all the work he had done these past many years and all that he had so assiduously tried to build up was now turning to dust. At times, in weak moments, he had felt pride and this was perhaps his punishment. Menon was probably right in getting impatient and implying that it was time for him to retire.

'This is a new and different generation, Father,' he had said while they had been discussing the evening's meeting without either man being able to see the other's point of view. 'You can't take their obedience for granted. I have no doubt that they respect you...'

What was the definition of that respect ? What was its value ? Menon had the right to question. Was it vanity, Father Joshe wondered, which had prevented him, as principal, from squarely facing the facts ? Would he objectively vote for his own continuance ? That morning, in this very room, he had looked up at the crucifix and asked for guidance. He had found no succour—perhaps he deserved none.

'One can only do one's best,' he said, uncomfortably, sensing his own inadequacy. 'But sometimes, I suppose, one's best is not good enough.'

'You have to appeal to their reason,' Menon had replied, hardly paying attention to what the principal had said. 'More than that : you have to make them see reason. Sometimes you have to force it down their throats ! Discipline is rarely if ever voluntary, is it ? It has always to be enforced. Which means sternness. The Board is with me on this point, as you know. The time has come when we have to draw the line.'

Father Joshe felt a total alien to Menon's line of reasoning. Didn't anyone realize that what was really at stake was not anyone's prestige or wisdom but the future of the boys ? What cause was more worthy of championing than the cause of the young ? They were the country's wealth. Who could afford to squander it away through such shortsighted arguments ! Everyone condemned violence—he himself whole-heartedly — but no one seemed concerned with the students' motivation for violence ! People, all and sundry, were prescribing cures which were worse than the disease. He could sense the boys' sense of aimlessness and frustration. He did not know the reason, not completely anyway. They were growing up in an increasingly hostile world. Would anyone deny that ? Then, didn't they deserve more sympathy and understanding than this high-and-mighty talk about logic and discipline ? Father Joshe was not belittling the importance of discipline in the young as well as the old. He conceded that it was not voluntary. But lack of discipline was becoming a national malaise, not something confined to the student community. What was needed was to take measures to ensure that their minds were not distracted from their legitimate work—studies. To give scholarship the respect it deserved. It was ironical, it was the height of irony, he thought, that a nation which took so much pride in the wisdom of its ancients and the greatness of its culture should turn out in the final analysis to be so indifferent, unworthy of its intellectual wealth...

Oh, what was the use ? He was probably biased. As a teacher, maybe he was attaching too much importance to his own profession, and his own wards. He was really getting old and unsure of himself. It was time that he withdrew...

The hall was crowded when they entered it, and Father Joshe felt his misgivings of a moment ago receding into the background of his mind. This was indeed like any other meeting at which he had presided in the past—the inaugural session of the College Council or a prize distribution on Annual Day. In the quietness that prevailed, even orderliness, he would have said, he read the same air of expectancy, the same eagerness to listen and perhaps applaud. He wished some of his senior colleagues were with him on the dias. Or maybe even Chandran or any other officebearer of the council. He had decided against it. Menon might misinterpret it as an attempt on his part to get an alibi. He now felt isolated, sitting in Menon's company, a guest in his own house. Was that a manifestation of his own ego, Father Joshe wondered. Did he secretly resent the fact that he was in this case not the one to decide either the pace or the pattern of the proceedings to follow ?

He had no intention of making a speech. He would merely introduce the speaker for formality's sake, as Menon did not need an introduction, and leave to him to decide the course of events. From where he sat, he could see that only a few girl students had turned up, and they sat in the front row self-consciously and pretending to be very attentive. This was not a good sign—was a roughhouse expected ? There were too many boys standing near the doors, and Father Joshe was as usual dismayed. People who just stood around became as a rule restive and impatient. They would shuffle about and distract the others. Normally he would have discouraged the practice and sent someone round to make them either come in and sit down or leave the hall. He could see some lecturers at the

Abhimanyu

back of the hall and even they seemed to be having an eye on the exit. He began to feel genuinely apprehensive. There was certainly an air of tension inside the hall. He looked round and again felt that sense of isolation. He tried vainly to catch the eye of a lecturer; and if there were any student council members present, he could not see them from where he sat.

Menon was impatient. Father Joshe could see that. He looked at him and saw him nod, as though he was ready to start the meeting now. Father Joshe stood up and cleared his throat. He waited for the gentle murmur from the assembly to subside into silence.

'It had been my privilege to be the principal of this college of well over twenty years,' he began. His voice faltered a little and words did not seem to come very easily. This was very unusual for him. He braced himself and went on : 'It had not all been smooth going. We had our differences, though mostly, I am glad to say, these differences were on academic issues ...'

He heard himself speak, detached, as though he were another person who had no volition over what the speaker was saying. It was odd that much later, after the meeting was over, he could not recall clearly anything he had said. He was not aware at the time of the man who sat by his side. In a way, he was not even aware of the audience and there was no way of knowing how they felt and reacted. It was a fiasco, of that he was sure, judging from what followed. Only odd phrases remained in his memory, as out of place and isolated as he himself had felt... relevant only to a growing sense of departure that lay oppressively on his mind.

For the first time in his life, he felt detached—disassociated suddenly by a quirk of circumstance from this world of books and admissions and examinations, of debates and tournaments, of failures and achievements, of some beginnings and some endings, too. He was sometimes vaguely apologetic, but apologetic of what ? A man was never so old as when he began to forget the problems of youth, he had said. That was right. He did not know what agitated the minds of the younger generation. Perhaps he never quite knew in all these years... he had never been able to totally bridge the gulf between the generations. Shakespeare and Milton only helped to build a temporary one which had to be demolished at the end of every year and built again. And each year the task had become a little more difficult, taxing his patience and ingenuity, till a time had come when he feared the bridge existed only in his imagination, held up by little more than his own vanity.

That admission, clearly, was an admission of failure and there was nothing now to be done about it. A younger man would come, armed with the zeal and energy that he himself had known a long time ago, and the cycle would be repeated. He would be able to instill in them a respect for learning, an awareness and regard for fundamental values, a sense of purpose and a clear direction... for these were the foundations of the human spirit, the true objective of education, irrespective of the troubles of the times. Problems would come and go, people would come and go—but these alone would endure... What was he saying, where was he going ? Father Joshe checked himself. This was not what he had set out to say ! The hall was very quiet. The hangers-on at the door had not moved. Menon sat staring ahead and his fingers were tapping on the table restlessly, impatiently.

'You must forgive me if I have rambled on a bit,' he concluded, 'and said things which are not totally relevant to the occasion. I only wanted to impress upon you the need to look into your own minds and judge for yourself whether you know the significance of your actions and the responsibility attached to them. This is the only test of maturity. I would now request you to give a patient hearing to Mr Menon, as indeed you have given me.'

Abhimanyu

He sat down, his eyes still not focused on the audience. There was a hush, as he heard Menon get up from his chair at his side. There was clapping, at first tentative and then loud and prolonged—Father Joshe did not care to speculate whether the applause was for him or for the guest speaker.

'...Discipline will be enforced—at any cost!' Menon was saying. Who would enforce it? Who had the authority? Father Joshe listened.

'The Government had been lenient in the past... too lenient according to some people, I can tell you that! You are too young to interfere in matters that should concern older men...'

The audience had become very restive. Menon was too seasoned a speaker to be unaware of it. The stragglers at the door were moving about, and there were many boys now standing at the back of the hall. There was an ominous hum which threatened to encroach upon his own voice, muffling and distorting his words, and there was laughter from here and there as though at some joke expressed by a heckler, though it was not audible enough for him. Menon had the uncomfortable feeling of a man who found the current in the stream getting too strong for him. His temper was rising and he felt he was being carried away by it in spite of all attempts to keep calm.

'There is law and order is this country and we in power intend to keep it that way,' he said, anxious now to make his point clear before the audience became unruly. 'This time, I know, very clear instructions have been given to the police ... to maintain peace... at any cost. It is my duty to warn you now...'

The hum was rising and it began to take a discernible pattern. It sounded like a chant. Menon could not make out the words. The boys were pounding with their feet on the floor and on benches... thump, thump, thump ... Father Joshe stood up, banged on the table with his fist and shouted feebly for order. He looked apprehensively, apologetically as Menon shook his head helplessly and sat down. The chant rose in tempo and volume and Menon could tell that it was directed against him and the Government. He could make out a few words : Parkinsonpet. Police raj. And now, very clearly, 'Menon, go home... Menon, go home...'

His temper rose suddenly, meeting the challenge of the audience. They were taunting him ! Insulting him ! Insolent brats ! Tomorrow it would be all over town—he knew too well how some of the papers would play it up. They would quote his angry words, out of context and distorted, and justify the ire of the students. Menon felt trapped. He banged on the table angrily and began to shout threats, but it was a roar now that came from the hall and his words were carried away like dry leaves in a torrent. He looked at Father Joshe accusingly, and found him sitting with a dazed look on his face, helpless at the tidal wave of defiance, looking totally lost. Menon pushed back his chair and walked across the platform as the chant now turned into hooting and cat-calls. He climbed down the steps at the end of it and walked out through a door, ignoring the roar behind him, his face red and set in angry lines.

He did not turn round even once to look at the boys or the principal. Father Joshe still sat at the table, alone, his head bent, as though waiting in tense expectation for the wave to submerge him and wash him away out to sea.

9

'People's feelings are conditioned by what they have eaten the day before. Even patriotism cannot survive on an acid stomach,' Kesavan often said. In the three months she had known him, as an acquaintance and later as a friend, Nandini had learnt to accept such statements as characteristic of him. And also to realize now that she loved him. For some time she had been too timid to examine her own feelings, but now—this sense of loss and loneliness that she felt when he was not around—surely that was love!

Smiling and wondering if his statements really made sense, she went over to the dressing-table and examined herself for a while. This was how people saw her... how he saw her. Did he like what he saw? She was not sure. He never commented. The most he could manage was 'nice'. Well, he was reserved, shy. But rather that than the arrogance of the other boys. Nandini herself was rather naive, cautious on such subjects as sex, which her classmates, it seemed to her, discussed rather loudly and unashamedly.

She speculated on her features. Her face looked far from experienced. Confused, yes. She smiled. She had a rather good smile, everyone said so, and, well, pleasant features, large black eyes and soft hair. Flushing at the thought of such critical self-examination, she hastily went over to the bed and continued reading, though distractedly. Did Kesavan think her good-looking? Did he love her? He had never told her so, but she was sure he did. She felt it.

So, let it be friendship for the moment. It was a good feeling, being friends. It had also started very unpromisingly. The girls called him 'Cold fish'. He had a perpetual preoccupied look, always aloof. Even on the debating society platform, where she had first observed him. He sounded so reasonable, so different from his friend Chandran in every way, such a contradiction that they were friends.

What a way to meet! She laughed aloud even now, when she recalled that scene at the library, in front of the dusty volumes of Gibbon's *Roman Empire*. She banged into him accidentally, coming round the corner in a hurry and the next thing she knew, he was picking up the books scattered on the floor, his and hers. When he straightened, he looked mildly annoyed; she was too embarrassed for words.

'You should be more careful,' he said, 'You could have knocked over one of these shelves... and that would have been a catastrophe.'

Nandini thought there was no need for sarcasm. It was just an accident.

'I'm sorry,' she said, rather coldly. 'I didn't see you.'

'Obviously,' he chuckled. 'Otherwise I would have been flattered ... a little discomfited no doubt, but flattered...'

She turned round angrily.

'Just a minute,' he said, lifting a restraining hand.

'Yes?'

'Does this fountain-pen happen to be yours?' He was smiling broadly. 'I found it on the floor.'

She snatched it away from him without a word.

'Perhaps I shouldn't have returned it,' his voice was very soft. 'I shouldn't have missed a chance to meet you again...'

'You are very impertinent !'

'Tck, tck...' he clicked his tongue. '... and I thought I was being very pertinent ! Just see that you haven't got any of my books.'

Cold fish indeed ! He was still smiling. 'I hope you have not hurt yourself. Are you all right ?'

That was, she learnt later, the most exasperating thing about him. Sarcasm one moment, gentleness the next ! She had fretted and fumed during the next few days. He had been impossible and even arrogant, with such a catlike air of contentment. She would put him in place, the next time she saw him.

And when she did, she didn't have a chance to speak at all. He was canvassing for Chandran, during the Union elections, almost forgetting that he was also contesting for the Council Membership. But he had recognized her. She detected that by a twinkle in his eyes when he saw her. She had gone on, to campaign seriously for him.

Curiously she met him again in the library, again in front of the volumes of Gibbon. Was he waiting there ? She had wanted to see him, to be nasty to him. Instead she had smiled and congratulated him on a speech at the debating society that he had made a few days back. He had sounded genuinely pleased. 'Thank you,' he said. 'Were you there ? I looked around for you, but you were missing.' Rather eager, she felt shy and reddened. 'I was sitting on the side.'

He watched her wistfully. 'It's been days since I saw you...' What was that supposed to mean? She didn't have time to speculate, and moved away hastily when she heard some voices.

In the next few months, they did little more than exchange letters. Surreptitiously and at long intervals. The letters were formal, merely exchanging views on problems, on life...planning for the future diffidently. Gibbon was a safe and faithful ally to their correspondence. Kesavan had been doubtful at first, but well, it worked. The ruse had a clandestine air which pleased her. She wondered if her final note had reached him. She was desperate and worried. Would he be there at their usual meeting place?

They had met there only on two occasions before. A small bookshop she had discovered where she had purchased a gift for his birthday. She had posted it, and enclosed within it one of the longest letters she had ever written to him. She had been more personal and direct, and mentioned her future. Was she wrong to imply things? Had he understood what she felt? She wouldn't know, but soon they met at the shop for the first time by arrangement.

That was one of the happiest days of her life. She had been alone with him and thrilled. He had seemed embarrassed and nervous. When she asked him if it was because of her company, he had laughed, and replied, 'No, not that. Any man would be proud to be seen with you...I'm worried about you, for you, I mean. A lot of people know your father.'

'I don't care.' She had no intention of spoiling the evening. 'Let people say what they want.'

It was just after two. Nandini decided that it was time to start. With her father not at home, she could get out on some excuse on the other. Her mother never questioned, but Father, he was particular about everything, just everything from her choice of clothes to the college and subject that she chose.

She walked some distance away from home before boarding a bus, and took a seat, feeling rather self-conscious. Was she very elaborately dressed? Probably it was her chiffon sari; even her mother had looked at her questioningly when she saw her in it. She couldn't care less now. She was anxious to get things clarified, about the suspension, the strike and all the trouble. Would Kesavan take offence if she mentioned the subject? She had to be

Abhimanyu

away, she had no claim on his time or action, she realized. Kesavan did not care for violence, she was sure. Yet he defended his friends always. The students were in an angry mood... about Parkinsonpet. What would happen at today's meeting at College, that her father was addressing ? Her father was being unwise, she knew, but she had no courage to face him on that issue. He was adamant. She did not care for his political leanings. It hardly paid. Rather that he were a lawyer or an official. Yet, Nandini sympathized with him. He was genuinely sincere and felt he had to be in the midst of things to set them right. But he was growing old now ... old in age and values, banking a lot on prestige, horoscopes and the like. He had even disapproved of her sister and brother-in-law going out before their wedding. Would he approve of Kesavan, if he got through the IAS ?

Anyway, it was her life, and she didn't care for prosperity or for what people said, she decided. She would take up a job, be economically self-sufficient. Not for her to be dictated by a man's bank balance, or his social standing ...

The bookshop was practically deserted when she entered, but soon Kesavan joined her.

At this hour of the day, even the restaurant was empty, and business was slack. 'I'm so glad you could come,' she said. 'I was afraid you wouldn't get the note.'

'Sheer chance,' he smiled. He wasted no time on preliminaries. 'What's worrying you? The strike?' She nodded. 'And other things ... the tension in the air. What are you planning to do? I mean, the boys?'

'Oh nothing much. The usual stuff. Strike, I suppose.' Coffee arrived, and they fell silent. 'Anyway,' he said presently,' there is nothing to worry about really. It might turn out to be another storm in a tea cup.' He added speculatively,'A few tea-houses might get knocked up, of course ...'

'What if you were in one of them?' Her anxiety increased. 'What if ?' he shrugged. 'It's the cause that matters, isn't it ?'

She didn't feel amused in the least. 'It's nothing to be laughed at,' she said petulantly. 'You shouldn't get into trouble.'

He extended his hand and patted her gently. Coming from him it was like a sudden caress. She blushed selfconsciously.

'You look beautiful today,' he said softly, appraising her with very calm eyes. Was he trying to change the subject? Or was he being sincere? He noticed her confusion—a mixture of pleasure and consternation. 'I really mean it.'

'Oh, all right. Coming from you it's rather a surprise...', she smiled at him.

'Why do you say that? Coming from me.'

'You're supposed to be a cold fish. The girls say so. Did you know that?'

He burst out laughing. He looked at her critically. 'Yes, I like your sari, and the person who's wearing it too. Very much. I was not trying to change the subject ... Perhaps we really ought to have a change of scene.'

'Let's not go home so early. Father will be back only after six. God, I hope he does not get it into his head to look for me at college. Where shall we go?'

He shrugged, and paid the bill.

Outside, they boarded the first bus that came their way, and realized that it was a mofussil bus. She felt very adventurous, as if they were running away together. He bought tickets for the destination, thirty miles away, and sat down beside her. She looked at him, surprised, then giggled nervously and settled down to watch the passing scene. And yet she dared not look outside too much. What if somebody recognized her? Disaster to be seen in a mofussil bus! She let her eyes wander inside the bus.

Rustic types, her fellow passengers, they eyed her with

ill-concealed curiosity. She shifted uncomfortably in her seat, ill at ease, wondering if her sari was drawing attention. She shuddered on hearing the rhythmic beat and shriek of a train that sped by, and involuntarily sought Kesavan's hand.

The train sped away and the air cleared as they passed stretches of paddy fields, fringed with coconut palms. The countryside took on a peaceful air in the light of the setting sun. The bustle of the town was left far behind and the silence here was interrupted only by the warble of an occasional rivulet near the fields.

Nandini was suddenly conscious of Kesavan's hand resting on hers; she looked down at it and he made as if to withdraw it.

'Give me your hand, please,' she said softly. She held on to it for the rest of the journey; she liked the firmness of his grip. What would happen to the two of them? Did they have a future together?

At the moment she could not picture it otherwise. Did he too feel the same way, anxious? She glanced at him through the corner of an eye. He was looking ahead, absorbed in his own thoughts. What were they about? The college, or them? She was curious.

'Kesavan.' He looked slightly startled.

'What do you intend to do after college?'

'I don't know... Look for a job, I suppose.'

'What kind?'

'I haven't thought of it. My father would want me to try for the IAS.'

'Would you like that?'

'I don't really know. I would like to continue my studies, personally. But it's a question of economics, I'm afraid.'

'Economics?'

He looked at her and smiled. 'Not the subject, I mean the economics of day-to-day living. I don't come from a very affluent family, you know. I should think of helping my father very soon.'

She felt vaguely guilty. 'And after that? After you get a job?'

He shrugged 'Well . . . Marry, have children. Go through the middle-class routine. My mother would want that.' He looked at her speculatively.

'What's wrong with that?'

'Nothing! Nothing at all! . . . Will you marry me?'

'I might, too, at that! If you ask me seriously.'

He laughed and fell silent. The bus stopped near a crowded, noisy, suburban bazaar. She looked at the low tiled shops, with counters full of coloured glass bottles, coolies returning after work, or standing in groups, gossiping, vendors selling some sticky-looking sweets covered with flies. There was a faint smell of cowdung in the air. The sun had nearly set, and they had yet a long way to go, to reach their destination.

A furlong away, Kesavan signalled to the conductor to stop the bus, and they got down, watched by curious eyes from the bus.

'What is this place?' Nandini asked. He mentioned a name. 'There is an old temple here. We'll go there. In any case, it's getting late, do you realize?'

She looked hastily at her watch. It was five thirty. 'We'll be back in half an hour, won't we?' He nodded, took her hand and they began to walk.

Shadows lengthened across the paddy fields as they reached the temple, which stood on a slightly elevated ground. A narrow, pebble-strewn path, probably the bed of a river, led up to it. There was hardly anybody around; it was deserted and calm but for an occasional head of cattle here and there in the distance.

'I never thought you would be interested in going to the temple,' Nandini said, looking around. The granite outer wall of the temple was now in ruins, the blocks displaced, shrubs and grass growing among the crevices.

'I used to come here as a child,' he answered, 'with my mother. My ancestral village is nearby, but I haven't gone there for years.'

'It's beautiful here,' she said. 'I wonder why there are no people about.' The temple inside also seemed deserted.

'Oh, hardly anyone will be around at this time of day. The puja is only in the mornings. You see, the temple has fallen on bad days. The villagers come for a bath to the tank here only in the morning.'

They came around, and on the western side was an ancient tree, thick branches swooping low, almost touching the ground. On an impulse Nandini ran across and sat on a branch.

'Kesavan, why have we come here?' she asked. He looked across the landscape. 'I don't know. It just occurred to me. It's strange coming here after a long time. To think that I used to stand here, holding my mother's hand, believing everything with a simple faith...'

'Don't you believe any more?'

'I can't say. I don't know. Yet, I suppose the faith is ingrained in one. It's something that dies hard. I don't think about such things, that's all.'

He sat down next to her. She moved away self-consciously.

'Kesavan.'

'Yes?'

'Do you think this is wrong? I mean, our seeing each other, like this, unless...'

'Unless what?'

'Did you really mean it ... what you said about marriage? That you want to marry me?'

'Did I say that?' He smiled, tilting his head.

'Of course, you did . . . in the bus?'

'Ah, then you were holding my hand.'

'Oh, you're impossible . . .' She walked away, hurt and undecided.

Tears smarted in her eyes.

When he caught up with her, he tried to take her hand in his but she shook herself free. He noticed that her eyes were wet.

'I'm sorry. I'm really sorry. Please . . .'

'You're making fun of me . . .'

'No, I'm not. Come back. I want to talk to you. That's why I brought you here.' He took out a handkerchief and handed it to her. Still unsure, she smiled weakly at him. 'I'm all nerves today. I don't know why. . .'

'So am I,' he said softly. 'I suppose that's why I was talking like that.'

They walked back to the branch and sat on it. The sun had disappeared and a cool breeze had begun to blow. She wound her sari tightly round her.

'I shouldn't have worn this stupid sari.' she said. 'It was making me very conspicuous . . . in that bus.'

'I really meant what I said in the bus . . . You want me to swear it in front of the deity?'

She shook her head.

'But,' he went on, 'it's one thing to want something, quite another to . . . I have been asking myself a lot of questions lately.'

'So have I.'

'I love you very much. That's the only thing I'm sure of. Right now. But when I think of the future . . .'

The sky had now changed colour to a dull grey, and in the hazy dust of sunset looked like a shroud hanging over the atmosphere. It was very silent all around, except for an occasional group of crows noisily speeding home. Nandini was sitting with her head slightly bent, looking at the ground. He turned her face towards him and kissed her. He felt her shrink back and he let her go.

'Are you offended ?' he asked.

Abhimanyu

She shook her head, but did not look at him.

'I don't want to think of the future—now. It's full of questions . . . and not one that either of us can answer.' He put his hand tentatively around her waist.

'I want you to promise me one thing.' she said. 'Just *one* thing.'

'What is that?' his voice was almost a whisper.

'Promise me that you won't get into trouble. That Chandran and the rest of them are a rough lot.'

He got up and paced a bit, taking a short circle. He bent down and plucked a grass from the ground. It had a long stem, with narrow leaves, a common enough variety used for some kind of pujas. He looped it and wove it into the shape of a ring. He came back and sat next to her, took her hand and worked the ring gently up her third finger. She looked at it critically.

'It's not much,' he said with mock seriousness. 'But that is all I can find at the moment.'

She held her hand up against the fast-fading light and smiled. 'I shall take it that the green in it is supposed to be emeralds.'

'The best ever.'

He put his hands around her and kissed her again. This time her mouth opened a little and he felt the pressure of rose petals. His hand slid down her shoulder and softly enfolded her breast. She tensed, and then pushed his hand away.

'Do you know that we're in a temple.'

He was silent for a while.'Yes, you're right.' He laughed gently.'Our revered Hindu gods are notoriously jealous.'

She put her hand shyly round his waist, bent her head and rested it on his shoulder. 'Are you angry with me?'

'No.'

'Promise?'

'Yes, promise.'

After a while, she said, 'I don't know anything . . . I am

very—' she searched for an apropriate word. 'Very— ignorant.'

'I've never kissed a girl before. I'm not much of an expert either.'

'Do you think we'll have a lot of children . . . if we are married?'

'I don't doubt it. I love children.'

'So do I.'

They sat together in the dark, in silence. Presently she whispered, 'Give me your hand now.' He withdrew his arm around her waist and she said hastily : 'No, not that. The other one . . . Here.'

She held his hand in hers for a moment, and then placed it on her breast. He sat absolutely still, not quite trusting the pounding of his heart, as though he feared that it would break the spell. He kissed her ear softly. 'In case I haven't mentioned this before . . . I love you very, very much.'

His hand moved as though on its own volition, caressing, exploring the softness that it enfolded. He felt her tremble and pressed her close to him.

'Kesavan,' she whispered in the dark.

'Yes?'

'Do you—do you think—I am—promiscuous?'

He laughed softly. 'You are very sweet,' he said, kissing her again on the lips.

Sitting in the bus on the way home, holding on to his hand now with a vague sense of desperation, she wondered whether she was right in not yielding to him totally. The gods were jealous, he had said. Did he expect more than their—their closeness back there? Had she led him on, and then let him down? She was too confused to analyse her own feelings. She had been scared out of her wits... of the darkness, the loneliness... and, yes, even the tumult which she had felt within her as he touched her. Was she normal? Or was she just an ignorant girl? He had been kind and gentle, and understanding. He had disengaged himself when he had sensed her fear . . .

It was nearly eight o' clock when the bus brought them to the stop near her house. She got up hastily, moved to the exit and jumped down the steps. Her last glimpse of him was a blurred face at the window, a hand waving to her—then the dark night enveloped the bus.

10

Chandran felt pleased with the way things were going. This morning of the strike, he had left the hostel a little tired and sleepy, not quite sure of himself and diffident about his followers. Some of them had had a busy night, putting up posters. It had been hard work but fun, roaming the empty streets, carrying the heavy bundles and buckets of glue and brushes. They had climbed roofs and shinned up electric posts. They had shouted snatches of songs, thrown jokes around and squirted glue at each other till Chandran had irritably called them to order. They had virtually plastered the busy sections of the town with posters and had been particularly merciless with walls which displayed the stick-no-bills notices.

Few people had seen them at work—and fewer still had paid them much attention. Some lorries had passed by in the night and occasionally the boys had lustily cheered them on or exchanged abuse with the drivers. The beggars who slept on shop-fronts and pavements could have been dead bodies wrapped up in rags for all that the students cared. A boy had tripped over one of them and the sleeper had sat up and cursed and called them foul names. It was a cue for some lively action, to ward off sleep. The boys had gathered round and threatened not only to dump a bucket of glue on him but to make him eat part of it. That woke him up properly and he had immediately come to his senses. He had abjectly begged for forgiveness and Chandran, who alone seemed to be anxious about time being wasted, had called a halt to the racket.

'Nasty little monkeys!' the beggar had called out to them as they were walking away.

Gopalan had been extremely helpful. But for him, they would not have had the posters on time and that too at cost price; in fact the posters were virtually his idea.

'Let them know that you mean business this time,' he had said. 'no one would say that you are disorganized when they see your posters!'

Chandran had agreed with alacrity. The posters really did them credit—very striking and very professional. Yellow and red with black lettering. The illustration showed a powerful fist straining at a chain wound round it, with a few links shattering. The boys had been excited by the picture. It showed their new power and their determination to fight tyranny.

'Damn good, I say!' a boy had said,'but . . . '

'But what?'

'We should have had a handcuff instead of the chain. The chain is rather medieval. This is the police raj !'

'Oh, shut up ! you'll be the first to run when you see a lathi. . . This is all symbolism, my friend !'

The words on the poster called for the withdrawal of the one-man commission and appealed to the students for direct action. It also announced the date of the hartal and the grand procession which would culminate in a demonstration in front of the Collectorate.

'Police zulum, down, down,' a group of boys had cried, unable to contain their excitement.

'What is zulum, yaar ?' Mathew had asked a bystander.

'Ha, what d'you know? It means your grandfather's ass!'

Mathew shook his head nonplussed. 'Why don't you say

something which everybody can understand ! All this zulum rubbish!'

The town would wake up to realities tomorrow, Chandran had thought with pleasure, as he watched the boys tear away old cinema and election posters and paste the new ones on the walls. Tomorrow will be the great day!

Gopalan and some of his friends had come, some time in the middle of the night, to encourage and approve. When he nodded his head in appreciation, Chandran had shared with his friends a genuine sense of pride. Even Kesavan was enthusiastic. He was no longer moody and had roamed the streets, looking for strategic places to put up the posters. He had pulled up the boys who had skimped their work—in one or two cases he had actually peeled off some badly pasted posters and redone them himself. 'Brutus' was all right, Chandran had thought. He was a friend you could trust. He was no chicken . . .

Early in the morning, when they had begun to hear the sleepy stirrings in the milkmen's colonies and seen lights glowing a little bleary-eyed from restaurants, they had wound their way home, tired but happy, with the satisfaction of a good job done well, pausing only at a small tea-shop near the railway station to take refreshments. The man in the shop had looked at them with surprise—and some distrust—and then told them rather rudely that they would have to wait awhile before the water was boiled. He had no milk and had served them black coffee and slightly soggy buns as they sat at the tables, talking softly, while one or two of them lit cigarettes and watched their companions through the smoke with a new sense of camaraderie.

It was when the coffee was finished that Chandran discovered that no one had any money. They had all filed out of the shop laughing, with the manager shouting abuses at them.

'It is for a good cause, friend,' Chandran had flung back at him.

'Good cause!' the man was outraged. 'You bums ! I will hand you over to the police ! Don't think I won't be able to recognize you ! Tomorrow I'll speak to your principal.'

Chandran retraced his steps and came up to the angry man. 'You will do nothing of the kind,' he assured him coldly. 'These boys appreciate your hospitality.'

'In that case,' the man persisted, 'let them show their appreciation by paying cash!'

It was apparent to Chandran and his friends that the man was singularly lacking in common sense. 'Wouldn't it be worse if you had to spend money to replace the glass cases and furniture in your shop?' Chandran looked round speculatively. 'You must never, never reject an expression of genuine gratitude. People have come to grief that way.'

The man glared at Chandran, who was now looking at him with a smile. After a moment, he shifted his eyes and muttering something inaudible, went back into the shop. The man had sense after all! It only needed a little persuasion to make him use it. At one signal from Chandran, the boys would have wrecked the place in seconds. . .

Chandran felt the same surge of pride, the same tense excitement as he stood with a group of boys at the gate of the college, under the shade of an arch of brick and mortar built some years ago to commemorate a local patriot. The wall were resplendent in the morning sun with the red-and-yellow posters. The boys were scattered around in groups of three and four, talking and gesticulating excitedly. Some of them were being regaled with stories about the experiences of the night before. If anyone felt guilty or left out of the poster-sticking session, he more than made up for it by actively canvassing for the strike or explaining, if any explanation was required, the students' justification for it. Chandran himself was in a conciliatory mood—the hard core was stoutly behind him and he knew he would not lack support if some kind of a crisis developed.

There would be blacklegs, he was sure, and he had not

decided how to deal with them. Rumours had reached him that there would be a determined attempt to disrupt the strike—but when and in what form, he had no idea. There was a strong student faction, possibly motivated by the ruling party, who would try to block his path. Gopalan himself had warned him of this. This was not unexpected, but what would be their tactics? Would the police be standing by—or had they already been alerted? There could be no interference as long as the picketing was peaceful. But would it remain that way the whole day? There were the volatile ones on his own side. Real roughnecks, some of them, who hankered for action. It would not be possible to restrain them for long. Chandran had understood their psychology during his past association with them. If you held them on leash too much, they would either lose interest or turn rebels. A leader had to play it cool with his followers; sense their mood, sometimes anticipate them and always demonstrate that he was one step ahead of them in thinking and planning. Chandran had no intention of surrendering his initiative.

He had listened to Kesavan's arguments with patience, though some of the boys were less tolerant. 'Brutus' as usual had favoured logic and restraint. He had been for treating the blacklegs with silent censure and coldness. The strike must be peaceful throughout, he had argued. That was the best way to discountenance the authorities. No one should take them as a bunch of impulsive youngsters venting their exuberance and energy on any ready target. The public must sense—they should concede that the boys could handle adult problems in a mature way. Why, sometimes in a more mature way than the adults themselves! The boys had a better chance of being taken seriously if they established their credentials well.

Chandran had silenced a murmur of dissent from the gathering with a wave of his hand. It was not necessary at this stage to take an unwavering stand. They would have

Abhimanyu

to deal firmly with the blacklegs and the saboteurs—there was no question of it. Any eventuality would have to be treated on merit. He should leave it to the circumstances to dictate the methods of operation. Cajolery, and if necessary threats, there could be no harm in that. The point was that the strike must be an unqualified success. Victory always drew sympathy, failure never! That was a lesson he had learnt the hard way.

He knew that the morning would be the real time of test. If he could hold up things till lunch time, quite a few professors would have gone home. He had verified that surreptitiously. They were not unsympathetic to the students' cause. And those boys who did not care either way would be glad to go home anyway—as long as they had a good excuse. No movement could boast of hundred per cent unqualified support—there would be a lot of fringe hangers. But what of that? There was a saying in his own language that even if one beat up one's mother, there would be two sides, for and against. Gopalan had drilled him well in the philosophy of leadership. A good general should be able to make some use of even his worst reverses!

The crowd at the gate was slowly getting larger. The students exchanged pleasantries and laughed a lot. There was a holiday mood and even the slogan-shouters sounded as though they were cheering a football team . . . their voices trailed off every now and then into a cacophony of sounds which made Chandran laugh at times, in spite of himself. There was no harm in feeling a little light-hearted. The situation, as the police would have said, was well under control. 'Students unite!' . . . that was it! That was the spirit! In unity lay strength. United, no one could break them.

There was a commotion at the gate and Chandran quickly moved over. An argument was in progress, and he tensed at his first sign of resistance. He had anticipated it, after all. As a matter of fact, he had been awaiting it with some impatience so that he could test his strategy and settle things once and for all.

'What is the argument here?' he asked as he elbowed his way into the group.

"These fellows want to go in,' a volunteer said, contemptuously.

Chandran looked at the dissenters without anger. They were trying to hide their nervousness behind a facade of defiance. 'We have got the chemistry test today. We cannot miss it,' one of them said.

'There will be no chemistry test today,' Chandran assured them pleasantly. The three boys who faced him did not look like trouble-makers.

They looked around, trying to assess the strike's chances of success, and then at each other doubtfully. 'We'll go in and find out,' one of them ventured hesitantly, not glancing in Chandran's direction. 'If there's no test, we'll come out.'

Some of the boys standing around laughed and Chandran raised his hand to silence them. 'Why, you don't believe us?' he asked, still smiling, still reasonable.

The three students stood there undecided for a moment, and then cautiously moved over to a side. Someone standing by patted them rather lustily on their backs. 'That's the spirit, boys!'

'Students unite!' the cry arose all around with renewed vigour. 'Hands off Parkinsonpet!'

That was easy, too easy, Chandran thought. There was no conviction in them, and not much fight either, when you came to think of it. This was too mild even for a feeler!

He saw Gopalan on the periphery of the crowd and he edged his way towards him.

Gopalan raised his hand in greeting. 'How does it go?' he asked, at the same time looking around to make an assessment for himself.

'Quite well, I think,' Chandran said, feeling pleased. 'Not a single student has gone in yet.' He looked beyond the college gate into the quadrangle and noticed that it was quite deserted except for a few lecturers and some peons who had apparently gathered there to watch the fun. There was no sign of Father Joshe.

'It could be the calm before the storm,' Gopalan said. 'I know for certain that a group of students are determined to go in—I don't know under whose prompting, but I can guess. They will try to create trouble.'

Chandran shrugged, but he felt uneasy. He could see the tower clock from where he stood and the dial showed the time as 10.45. He had his own spies and he was well aware of the Board's strategy. Father Joshe personally had been for ignoring the strike. What would be achieved by declaring a holiday? The students would just postpone the strike. 'If they must have their tamasha, let them have it!' he was reported to have said. 'You only give it a new importance by opposing it.' (That we would see, Father, Chandran had said to himself.) Did the principal know that there would be a group to disrupt the strike? Perhaps he did not. And even if he did, what could he do? It was better that he was confining himself to his office, Chandran decided. There has been desultory talk about gheraoing him. In a certain northern university, Chandran had heard, students had stuffed a burning cigarette in a Vice-Chancellor's ear when he tried to interfere in a demonstration! Boys could be very unpredictable.

Gopalan was calmly watching Chandran. 'If you let in one, you'll let in a hundred! There will be no stopping them. Then before you know, there'll be a crowd inside as large as the one outside.'

'No no, no,' Chandran said determinedly. 'I quite understand what you mean. I was only wondering how we'll deal with the situation.'

'Hey, what is the ruckus about?' a man pushing a bicycle stopped to ask.

Gopalan ignored him. 'There is only one way to deal

with such situations,' he told Chandran soberly. 'Persuasion first. Though I do not think it will work in this case. They are coming to break the strike. They will not listen to any arguments. And that leaves only one way out, doesn't it?'

Chandran looked at Gopalan but did not say anything.

The bicycle owner again repeated his question, not addressing anyone in particular. 'What's going on?'

'Oh, get lost,' Chandran said.

Gopalan bent closer and virtually hissed in his ears: 'Force! Resist them. Don't let them pass. Threaten them.' He looked around again, squint-eyed at the student crowd, trying to sense their mood and strength. 'Hold them back at any cost. Frighten them a little. You will realize that that's the only way to deal with them. They have people behind them inside and outside the college. . . Don't be frightened if you see a few police uniforms around.'

'Of course, we're not afraid of the police,' Chandran said quickly. 'What have they got to do with this? We are not breaking any law, are we?'

'No, you're not . . . But still—after all they make the law in such cases, and they have a habit of making those very flimsy!' Gopalan laughed. He glanced over his shoulder and waved at a small group of onlookers on the other side of the road. 'I will be around,' he told Chandran. 'With them, I have friends there. We will be keeping an eye on the proceedings. You have nothing to fear. He smiled and patted Chandran reassuringly on the back. Then he walked away.

For some reason, Chandran felt a little alone and abandoned. He felt a stir of misgiving and hoped that it did not show on his face. This was a time of test for any leader. The lull before things began to happen. The slogan-shouting was going on sporadically. The crowd at the gate was very large now and was overflowing onto the road, blocking the traffic. But passers-by were not giving them much attention. This was a common enough sight these days.

How did a general feel before a battle ? Chandran wondered. As nervous as this ? His mind was troubled by vague forebodings, not frightening really, but disturbing. Did he clearly understand his enemy's mood and strategy? Who was his enemy, anyway? He could make a guess about one or two students—but who would be masterminding their moves? He felt a surge of anger—no one was going to thwart him this time! Why could not the bastards show up? . . . This waiting was getting on his nerves. He looked at his companions. They did not seem worried about anything. They were still indulging in some horseplay. Chandran felt an urge for action, to do something, to shout something—to pin his mind on this moment and not on the next or the ones thereafter. He spotted Kesavan and with a sense of relief beckoned to him.

'We can expect some trouble soon,' he said as his friend approached him. 'The blacklegs.'

'Who will be leading them? Sekharan?'

'I think so. That son of a bitch has been gunning for me for some time. But I don't expect him to be anything more than a nuisance. That fool can't organize even a children's picnic!'

Kesavan looked at the boys around speculatively. 'What do we do?'

Oh, God, Chandran thought impatiently. What do we do indeed! Why could not Kesavan be more helpful instead of just asking an obvious question. 'What do we do?' he exclaimed. 'Stop them, of course. What else?'

'We can always talk to them,' Kesavan said.

'Talk with them! About what? About the weather?... Don't be so naive ! They're coming to break the strike. And I'm not going to let them!'

'I think it will be far more advisable to let them go in. We'll protest, but we will refuse to use force. Isn't that what everybody is waiting for . . . for us to use force?'

Chandran scratched his head, perplexed. 'I don't know. What will we gain by letting them go? Demoralize these boys here? Give up the strike? You tell me!'

Kesavan looked at his friend and made a face. 'I see what you mean, of course . . . but still. . .'

'Hey, you keep out of this!' Mathew who had joined them spoke sharply to Kesavan. 'What are you worried about? Getting hurt?'

'Oh, cut it out, Mathew!' Chandran exploded. 'You people don't start an argument now . . .'

He was interrupted by voices raised in anger coming from the gate.

'There they are, I think,' he said, suddenly alert, his voice no more diffident but quivering with a strange excitement. 'Our little busybody friends are here. Let us go and receive them!'

There were about twenty of them, Chandran estimated—and they looked peaceful, confident and determined. Gopalan must be right. He could recognize a few who were avowed supporters of the ruling party. They had often criticized the Student Council's actions and had tried in vain to infiltrate their ranks. It had taken all of Chandran's organizational skill and resources to keep them at bay during the college election.

They had an air of assurance about them, which meant they were well prepared and were certain of official support. Chandran decided to be tactful.

The conversation petered into silence as he approached. He had been right about Sekharan, too. The boy was apparently their spokesman. He was a senior B.A. student reputed to be good at his studies.

Sekharan turned round and faced Chandran calmly, while some of his companions moved away towards the

Abhimanyu

college gate. They were stopped by a ring of volunteers holding hands. They looked back at their leader for guidance on what they should do next.

Sekharan was shorter than Chandran, but stockier, and he did not betray any sign of nervousness. He was wearing a dhoti, as he always did, unlike most of the other boys who wore trousers. He was an outspoken critic of people who 'aped the West.' He called himself a rabid nationalist.

'You have no right to stop anyone from going to the college,' he said, a little louder than necessary, to Chandran. 'This is a free country!'

'Sure, sure,' Chandran said amiably, 'and let us all try to keep it that way.'

'This is your way of doing it?'

'It is not my way. It is the majority way ... the students' way. We are all in it together. We are all students, you must not forget that. We must stand together, irrespective of—of individual differences. That is the way a democracy works, isn't it?' Well, Chandran thought, if Sekharan had prepared his lines, so had he! 'You are in disagreement with this strike?'

'Yes, I am. So are these boys. We will attend college today and nobody can prevent that.'

Chandran sighed, rather theatrically. 'Of course, of course, I do not dispute that you'll have your own views about the matter. But can't you stay away from college, at least for one day, to demonstrate the solidarity of the students?'

'Look, don't give us all that crap! You are wasting our time. Ask your volunteers to move over.'

'They are not my volunteers ... they are our friends. You must not misunderstand their motives.'

'That is for us to decide! Who are you to tell us how we should act—and feel?'

'I am nobody ... Correct. But have you no feelings for Parkinsonpet?'

'That's not your concern—our feelings about it. And in any case, right at the moment, we think there are people more competent than you to settle it. . .'

'Sekharan,' Kesavan cut in placatingly, 'why don't you listen to sense. . .'

'Oh, you mind your own business!' Sekharan exploded. 'I don't care for him—you think I care for his side-kicks?'

Mathew pushed forward angrily. 'What d'you mean by that, you boot-licker?'

'You better watch your language, Mathew!' Sekharan said menacingly.

Chandran clapped his hands impatiently. 'Let us not get agitated over nothing. I think we should spare our energy and words for Parkinsonpet.'

'I told you,' Sekharan repeated coolly, 'there are better people than all of us to settle it.'

'Let us settle it here and now, Chandran,' someone in the crowd shouted angrily. 'We'll just give him the first lesson.' More shouts followed this, but Sekharan did not even take his eyes away from Chandran's face.

Chandran turned and snapped over his shoulder at his followers: 'Quiet!' Then he looked again at Sekharan as though they had not been interrupted. 'All right. I am prepared to concede even that. But have you no concern for students' unity? If you were in disagreement, why didn't you raise the issue at the last meeting?'

Sekharan laughed mirthlessly. 'You think everybody in the college attends your meetings? You are overestimating your own importance.'

Chandran's face flushed, but he kept his cool. 'Why are you opposed to the strike?'

'Now you are asking a real question, my friend!' Sekharan said. 'I am opposed to all strikes. How many of them did we have in the course of a year—two or twenty? We have lost count. I can't afford to miss classes. I am in college for a specific purpose—and Parkinsonpet can go to hell!'

'You think we don't care for our studies? But we have to make some sacrifices. We're working for the country's good.'

'By the time you people finish, there'll be no good left to work for!'

'Who taught you to say that?' Mathew exploded again.

Sekharan ignored him.

Chandran changed his tactics. One last effort, he told himself. He put on a broad smile. 'Look we humbly request you not to go to college today.' He looked over his shoulder and winked at his companions. 'We are prepared to fall at your feet . . .'

Sekharan stepped back angrily. 'Don't think you can win us over with histrionics! You reserve you buffoonery for the stage. I am requesting you for the last time: ask your volunteers to step aside!'

'We know who's behind you,' Chandran said, his voice now cold. 'We don't want any trouble. But don't push us. We've nothing against you . . . Maybe you will win your way through today. But tomorrow, and the day after, you will have to come to college. Do you think it is wise to make enemies among the boys unnecessarily?'

Sekharan laughed. 'Oh, now you are threatening us! We are quite capable of looking after ourselves, I can assure you. We are not afraid of your gang . . .'

Chandran shrugged. 'If that's the way you want it. . . You are not going in today,' he said firmly. 'Any objections?'

Sekharan looked at the cordon of volunteers speculatively and then glanced meaningfully at his group. He folded his dhoti knee-length and tied it securely in front. Then slowly he began to advance towards the gate.

Someone near to him made a sudden lunge and caught hold of his books. Sekharan swirled round and swung his free hand wildly, but it was too late. The boy held the books aloft and cried: 'If you take one step forward, I'll tear them . . . throw them . . .!'

Sekharan looked at him in fury, but hesitated for a fraction of a second. Then he changed his mind and started towards the cordon. 'Charge them!' he shouted, above the screams and curses that arose from a score of throats around him.

Three books shot up into the air and making a wide curve fell among the crowd. The next instant torn paper was flying about like the feathers of a dismembered bird.

One of his own books hit Sekharan squarely on the back of his head as he fought his way forward. Hands, shoulders and heads barred his way, but he flailed his arms left and right, listening to angry grunts and howls. There was the noise of loud slaps and of clothes tearing. Chandran now entered the fray, his long arms swinging wildly like a windmill gone berserk, meeting flesh and bone and not bothering whether they belonged to friend or foe. Groups of boys came running in from all sides, shouting and some of them still laughing, and began to push and heave, trying to find an opening into the closely knit group of struggling bodies. Sekharan was on his knees, his hair in disarray, his shirt torn from shoulder to hip. Two hands held him down tenaciously and in desperation he whirled round and bit one of them viciously. The answer was a sharp slap in his face, but he had managed to free himself and jump up, and he began to kick wildly, his dhoti coming loose at the hips. 'Communist bastards!' he shouted, now using his elbows with good effect and a boy next to him screamed in agony.

The dissidents suddenly changed their tactics. They tried to beak away and in a single phalanx charged the gate. Chandran's long leg shot out and tripped Sekharan, and all of them fell in a heap, rolling in the dust . . .

A screech of brakes and a whistle announced the arrival of the police. Khaki-clad men jumped down from a jeep and advanced towards the fighting boys, waving lathis in the air above their heads. The Inspector, who stood up in the jeep, blew his whistle again and again while the constables, keeping their distance, surrounded the fighting boys.

'Stop it! Stop it!' the Inspector cried, blowing on his whistle in between. Gradually the turmoil subsided. The boys stood up and instinctively separated into two groups. Sekharan had a cut lip but he still looked full of fight. Chandran was calmly tucking his shirt into his pants and searching at the waist for buttons which no longer were there.

'What do you people think you are doing?' the Inspector snapped at them angrily, looking from Sekharan to Chandran and then over their head at the other boys. 'Fighting in the streets! I'm taking the whole lot of you to the station!'

'We had a little disagreement on a personal matter,' Chandran said lightly, smiling at the Inspector. 'We were not fighting really. And not on the streets . . .' He looked down. They were technically still on college ground.

The Inspector watched a boy wipe his nose with a handkerchief. There were bright red stains on it.

'So you're the ringleader, are you?' he turned to Chandran. 'You're coming to the station with me!'

'What for?'

'I'll tell you that in due course,' the Inspector said contemptuously. He turned to the other boys. 'You fellows go home—or to the college. Unless some of you also would like to visit the station.'

'Is it a nice place,' Mathew asked, 'this station you are talking of? You make it sound like one of the town's beauty spots.'

Loud laughter followed this remark.

'Smart alec, eh?' the Inspector retorted angrily. 'It is a spot all right, for scoun—for roughnecks like you.'

'You have no authority to take us anywhere!' Chandran said.

'Oh, don't I? We'll see about that, young fellow. Now get

into the jeep.'

Chandran suppressed an urge to step back. The Inspector looked pretty tough. 'You cannot arrest anyone without a warrant!' he said defiantly.

The police officer threw back his head and laughed. 'Who told you that? I will go over the police rules with you at the station.'

A constable guffawed—but instantly fell silent at a look from the officer.

'I will not budge from here,' Chandran said. 'Nor will any of these boys. We are standing on college property. Your bluff won't work with us.'

The Inspector's face became very stern. 'I am asking you to get into the jeep.'

'And I am asking you to go to hell!' Chandran spat back, and as though on a cue, a crowd of boys gathered round him in a second, cutting him away from the Inspector.

The police officer sighed and threw up his hands. He snapped his fingers imperiously at the constable. Then he turned round and walked unconcerned towards the jeep.

Only four policemen, counting the driver, had come with the officer. They now closed in on the boys cautiously. They looked half-amused and half-frightened. These young rascals—and there was quite a crowd of them—could be unpredictable. 'Step back,' they shouted warningly as they came closer.

The boys looked at them challengingly, pushing Chandran further and further back. Head Constable Raman took hold of the nearest boy, who suddenly began to kick wildly. In a quick move, the policeman caught the boy by the neck and pushed him aside. That was the green signal for another scuffle. The boys again closed in from all sides, trying to latch on to the khaki uniforms, knocking over the cap of one of the constables.

The Inspector watched the scene with mild distaste from the driver's seat of the jeep. He turned aside and fished in his pocket—perhaps for a cigarette—when the constables began to hit the boys deftly with the flat of their hands. They had skill and experience on their side and would have made short shrift of the whole business, except that they had been warned to use restraint. There was a tug-of-war going on for the displaced cap when one of the boys bent down and gave the constable's hand a sharp bite. There was a howl of pain and the Inspector jumped out of the jeep. He knew his men. They were also human. If they lost their head, there would be hell to pay later—from the higher-ups!

They had almost got to Chandran, whom the boys were trying desperately to push through the gate into the college compound, when a shout was heard above the din.

'Stop this! Not in front of my college! Stop this!'

It was a man's voice, urgent, almost imperious, and the scuffle quickly subsided. Father Joshe stepped forward through the crowd, his eyes blazing, and spotting the Inspector, asked him sharply: 'What is the meaning of this?'

The constables withdrew and sidled up to the jeep, not knowing what do to. Chandran had vanished from view. The Inspector stepped forward. 'There was trouble here, sir—Father.' After a moment's hesitation, he saluted the principal. 'There was fighting and when we tried to break it up, they resisted.'

'I saw your men hitting the boys.' Father Joshe said angrily. 'There was no need for that, Inspector. They are students—not criminals!'

The Inspector took a deep breath. 'They were resisting arrest.'

'Oh, I've heard that line before!' Father Joshe raised his hand as though to wave away an unpleasant odour. 'I've heard that line before you ever got into the police force! Why do you want to arrest them?'

'They were fighting in the streets.' He searched again for Chandran in the crowd. 'There was one chap here—I asked him to come to the station.'

'What for?'

'Well he was obviously the ring-leader. I know him. Chandran...'

'You will not take any of my boys to the station,' Father Joshe said firmly. 'What is your name?'

'Rangaswamy. Sub-Inspector Rangaswamy of the Town Police, Father.'

Father Joshe nodded. 'The trouble is over now, isn't it? Don't you think the college authorities are capable of settling these... these skirmishes on our premises?'

The Inspector shrugged. 'They were fighting when we came here. And I have my orders...'

'Orders? Orders from whom?'

'It's my duty to maintain the peace, Father,' the officer said, a faint note of sarcasm in his voice.

'You have done your duty, Inspector,' Father Joshe said. 'I congratulate you. You have stopped the fighting, haven't you? Good morning, Inspector,' Father Joshe turned round and without haste walked past the gate, towards the college buildings.

The Inspector stood there, watching the receding back for a while. He noticed that the crowd had thinned considerably and most of the boys were behind the gate, and they watched his movements, while one or two laughed derisively.

He beckoned to his constables, got into the jeep and drove away, leaving behind a quivering cloud of dust.

At about 6.30 p.m. the same day, Kesavan sprinted down the hostel corridor, took the flight of steps to the first floor two at a time, wheeled left and came to a stop in front of Chandran's door. He paused for a moment, trying to catch his breath.

Voices and laughter came from the other side. He had expected it—that there would be a crowd in Chandran's

Abhimanyu

room to hold a review of the day's events. He knocked sharply.

A bolt scraped, the door opened an inch or two and a face peered at him from within. Without further ado, Kesavan pushed his way in. The door immediately closed behind him.

Chandran was sitting on the cot, stripped to the waist, a bottle of liniment on the floor. A dark patch showed under his eyes and there were bruises on his body. He was grinning widely and applying the lotion on one hand almost lovingly.

'Hah!' he exclaimed on seeing Kesavan. 'Where were you all this time? I was wondering what happened to you! One fellow here hinted that you might have been arrested.' He laughed.

Kesavan moved over to the table. There was a bottle on it and he picked it up and looked at the label. It was a popular brand of rum. He put it down without a word.

'Want a swig?' Someone asked. 'We are celebrating. Good show, wasn't it?'

Kesavan shook his head negatively. 'It was a good show all right.'

Chandran laughed. He rubbed his hand again fondly. 'Not bad for a man long out of practice . . . Where were you anyway?'

'I went home for a while,' Kesavan said without smiling. He avoided Chandran's eyes. 'I thought I'd show my face there before the report of the strike reached my—my people.'

He sat down on the cot next to Chandran.

'Anything on your mind, Kesavan?' Chandran asked. His breath smelt faintly of liquor.

Kesavan nodded. 'But I don't want to talk here.' He kept his voice low so that the others would not hear. He need not have bothered. Everybody was talking at the top of their voices.

Chandran looked at him anxiously for a second, then got up from the cot. He wiped his hands on a towel and picked up a shirt from a chair.

'Excuse us, fellows!' he shouted above the noise. 'We'll be back in a minute. You chaps help yourself to the bottle.' He picked up a half-full glass from the table and drained it in a gulp. 'Come on!'

The moment they were in the corridor, Kesavan started to speak, but Chandran put a restraining hand on him. 'Not here. Let's go down.'

A few boys were hanging around the corridor and one or two greeted Chandran. The two of them walked quickly, went down the steps and walked over to the lawn.

'Okay, now. What is it?' Chandran asked. 'Something worrying you?'

Kesavan hesitated. Then his words came out in a hiss. 'What's this I hear about Sekharan?'

'What about him?'

'Oh, don't act innocent, Chandran! Where is Mathew and the rest of them?'

'I have no idea! I don't know what you're driving at...'

'Don't lie to me,' Kesavan said softly. 'The boys said they had gone to finish what they started this morning...'

Chandran did not speak for a while.

'Well?'

'Well what? Why don't you sit down? . . . I had nothing to do with it. I couldn't stop them. Kesavan. I swear. I swear on my mother.'

Kesavan started walking away. Chandran jumped up and followed him. 'Hey! Where are you going? Wait a minute . . . Listen to me!'

He caught up with his friend and took hold of his hand firmly. 'Don't run away like that! Give me a chance to explain.'

'I'm not running away. I have a bicycle outside. I know where they'll catch him. I am going to warn him.' He shook himself free and began to walk.

'Don't be a bloody fool, Kesavan! You want to get hurt?'

The other boy stopped in his tracks. He turned round and retraced a few steps towards Chandran.

'You think I'm afraid of getting hurt? You think I'm afraid of your thugs?'

'Oh, don't be melodramatic, please! . . . It will be too late now, Kesavan. They would have—seen him by this time.'

The two of them stood in the dark for minutes, without speaking.

'Come back,' Chandran pleaded. 'Give me a chance.'

They sat down. Chandran took out a packet of cigarettes and offered it to Kesavan. Then he lit one for himself and said, his voice very low and gentle. 'I couldn't do a thing about it. I swear. The boys. . .'

'Who put the idea into their heads?'

'I didn't. You don't believe me? Ask Mathew. Why should I lie to you?'

'But you gave them the green signal.'

'I had to.'

'Oh, forget it. It's too late to do anything about it now, as you say.' His voice was very grim. 'What are they going to do to him?'

Chandran puffed silently on the cigarette. 'Don't worry. I have asked them not to be too rough. . .'

Kesavan did not go back with Chandran to the room. For one thing, he had to return the bicycle he had borrowed. As he got on to the road, he remembered what his mother had said: when people get angry, they do more than what they had bargained for. He himself felt drained of all emotion.

11

Inspector Rangaswamy tossed away the copy of the *People's Voice* with contempt. Its lead story was embellished with a headline in 24-point bold : 'Police manhandle students—given marching orders by Principal.' In contrast the *Motherland* had covered the incident in three short paragraphs with a single-column headline tucked away on the local page. Ironically—was it deliberate ?—the item appeared next to 'Today's Entertainment.' Rangaswamy was neither amused nor dismayed. Reporters were a breed that he treated with respect, but at arm's length. As a habit, they wielded double-edged swords.

The station room in which he sat presented a dismal picture. Rangaswamy looked without emotion at the old, rickety furniture, all numbered in white with flowery letters. An utter waste of effort, all that trouble taken to shape an 'A' or put a whorl on the tail of a 7—the signwriter they hired for the purpose was servile and ingratiating and wanted to be in the good books of the police. On the tables and shelves were tattered old files. Bundles of cheap Government stationery, useless pens and dried-up ink-pots lay all over the place. The floor was a mosaic of stains in red and blue. All this furniture and stuff should be collected and made into a bonfire, Rangaswamy thought. Just plain junk—dried up, moth-eaten, repaired crudely with bits of tarnished metal and screws! They reflected the condition of the police force itself!

He had no tact, it seemed! The DSP had no need for it either, except when he was hauled up before the IG or one of those meddling members of the Assembly. Rangaswamy felt dispirited and abandoned. The students were a nuisance, every officer in the police force knew that. The community always became conscience-stricken after the boys got pushed around a bit ... but only after, mark that, Rangaswamy said viciously to the greying wall in front of him. If they threw stones at you, should you gingerly pick them up and put them in your pockets ? That was tact. Constable Raman was going round with a bandage on his hand. He was a past master at the Third Degree, and yet how he howled when the doctor poured iodine on the spot where the student had bitten him! The man had no tact!

The Inspector got up from his chair and went over to the window. He could see, from where he stood, a part of the station compound and the whole length of the verandah with the regulation brick-red wall. Some men were sitting on straight-backed benches in various attitudes of gloom, despair, hope, defiance ... petty thieves and pick-pockets, pimps and small-time gamblers, watched over by a disdainful constable holding a rifle with a bayonet fixed. He would have spat at them as unfeelingly and unthinkingly as he would spit into the gutter! Rangaswamy smiled bitterly. Take that wretch on the bench nearest to the constable, for instance. Dust-coloured dhoti, soiled ink-blue shirt frayed beyond repair, hollow cheeks, sunken eyes and fibre-dry hair looking like the stuffing out of an old sofa! The man sat with his head bent, staring at the coarse brick floor, his spine curved like a bow. The look of despair was deceptive—to Rangaswamy's expert eyes, the man appeared to be one who had taken and who could take a lot of punishment. And yet leave that gutless Constable Raman with him to work on for five minutes in a room—and he would confess to the assassination of Kennedy himself! This was not an example of tact either. This was how the police force functioned—and got results.

Inspector Rangaswamy sighed and went back to his desk. It was some consolation that he would not have to deal with those petty crooks today. He would finish the report on the student unrest and go home. With distaste, he picked up the sheets of paper in front of him and began to read :

'At 11 a.m. or thereabouts a telephone call was received at the station from a person who refused to reveal his identity. The gist of the message was this: There was a strike at the Missionary College and a fight was in progress between the students who wanted to attend college and those who would not let them in. As we had been told to expect trouble, (he scored this out and wrote instead: As we had reason to expect trouble) of this nature, I took three constables with me and proceeded forthwith in a jeep to the above-mentioned scene. The situation was getting very serious and an outbreak of violence could be expected any moment . . .'

Enter hand-picked members of the town police force, armed with tact, Rangaswamy said to himself as he tossed the report back on to the table. They were not to use force in any circumstances, he had been warned the evening before. Trouble was expected—nothing big, but just enough to justify their presence on the scene and if necessary round up the ringleaders of the strike who should be taken to the station and let go before evening at the latest. He had been given names and this was a small enough town for him to be able to recognize the boys on sight—at least most of them. Constable Raman had excercised tact and was bitten for his troubles, Rangaswamy said to himself, bitterly. And the Principal himself came on the scene and made the dutiful members of the police force a laughing-stock for the students! That was not expected. The Principal, if at all he figured in the proceedings, was expected to play ball with the custodians of law and order. He did not. You could never count on these missionaries. They were unpredictable. Inspector Rangaswamy, according to the DSP, had not handled the situation very creditably. The students exhibited bruises on their faces and bodies which were alleged to have been inflicted by the police. Those lying bastards, Rangaswamy thought.

But who would listen to *him*? If the DSP thought otherwise, he did not give any indication. He had clearly implied that he had had no end of trouble persuading the newspapers not to publish the photographs—how would the police force look then? Who would speak up for them?

The net result of all that? Exit police and proclaim victory for the students—but, in point of fact, Rangaswamy thought, picking up the *People's Voice* again for reference, it was not much of a victory for the striking students. After the 'brutal manhandling' by the police and the 'marching orders from a shocked and disgusted Principal', the student crowd probably disintegrated. Perhaps some of them went back to their classes, though there was no mention of it in the paper. Perhaps they got bored and went home. Boys were very fickle in this respect. Political agitations for them should last only as long as football matches.

The Inspector pressed a bell on his desk and a constable entered and saluted.

'Get me a cup of tea,' Rangaswamy said. The constable was walking away when the Inspector flung a coin at him disgustedly.

'That is for the tea,' he said, and paused while the constable groped on the floor for the coin. He looked sternly at his subordinate when the man straightened up: 'Pay for the tea!'

It was no great fun being a police officer these days, Rangaswamy ruminated, as the constable went out through the door. That man was probably calling him names under his breath at this moment! Even small fish were becoming indigestible. Everybody was talking of rights and privileges. Very few talked of responsibilities. People were so busy defining and redefining rules that no one had the time to enforce them. The police force was becoming redundant. They had been reduced to the state of merely serving as subjects for judicial enquiries.

The trouble was that you never knew on whose side you stood—or who was the culprit and who the victim. If a man threw a bomb in the street, you never knew whether you should clap him in jail or hail him as a hero. Anyone, even that wretch sitting on the bench outside, could be related to an influential politician these days. Everything had shuffled up like a pack of cards and the knaves consorted with the kings. The police could quote neither rule nor precedent. The only thing they could be sure of was that they would invariably end up on the losing side, for things committed or not committed, for exercising restraint or exhibiting a lack of it, for using the lathi or not using it to best effect!

It was always police excesses! Excesses of what? Tact or sternness? No one was quite sure—and no one probably cared. Why could they not look for recruits in the diplomatic corps? If he did not have a family to support, Inspector Rangaswamy would have said goodbye to the police force long ago. He no more felt the old zest for the job. He found no excitement or reward in chasing offenders or pushing round demonstrators while under the eerie feeling that he himself, in turn and in all probability, would be chased and caught one day and accounted for without mercy.

He picked up the pen and again began to write furiously: 'A serious breach of peace can be expected the day after tomorrow, when the students, it is reliably learnt from various sources including newspapers, intend to call for a general hartal, take out a procession and picket the Collectorate. It is further learnt that the other colleges in the city will also take part in the demonstrations and a high percentage of the student community will turn out. A proper assessment of the situation has been made and adequate precautions are being taken to prevent any outbreak of violence.'

With this last part, of course, he was not directly concerned. That would be the DSP's headache. The report he had been asked to make was a semi-official one. It would be filed away and kept for future reference—if such reference was called for by coming events. Rangaswamy's own responsibilities would be confined to a particular area. While he was anxious not to commit himself too much, he did not want to sound out of touch with the realities of the situation either.

'Precautionary measures have been planned especially in view of the feelings roused on the Parkinsonpet issue, the divided public opinion regarding the matter and the active, if surreptitious, interest taken by certain leftist political parties in what might otherwise have been a purely student demonstration. The police are particularly watchful over the last aspect and some known goondas are being rounded up. The student procession is not likely to contain students alone. All the concerned police staff have been apprised of the official assessment of the situation and have been instructed that violence should be prevented at any cost and should be met with sternness.' Inspector Rangaswamy crossed out the word 'sternness' and instead wrote 'extreme sternness'. That was the set-up as he understood it. The Government was in no mood for half-measures.

The only thing left unsaid, Rangaswamy thought gloomily, was how far the police could go. The cliches dished out by people in authority were, as far as he could see, potentially more dangerous than bombs. With a cynical smile he contributed his bit: 'But, irrespective of all that has been said above, the police have been clearly made to understand that force should be used only under extreme provocation.'

He began to re-read the report before sending it for typing. Perhaps, he said to himself, a dictionary should be included with it to help define the work 'provocation'!

Gopalan's party office was located in the first floor of a ramshackle two-storeyed building, away from the main bazaar road and facing a large empty plot which was used by dhobis round the year and occasionally by circus companies and other travelling shows. It was an uneven stretch of grassy ground, the vegetation sprouting into shrubbery on the eastern corner, where an open well with a perennial supply of moss-covered water was situated. Its most distinguishing feature was the row upon row of clothes lines, strung over scissor-shaped bamboo poles, from which clothes of all shapes and hues fluttered in the breeze like streamers. If the dhobis could be persuaded, either through appeals, threats or bribes, the lines would be temporarily removed and the area cleared for meetings, mostly of the smaller political parties. The ground, like some battle-fields of old, was remembered by the townsfolk as the scene of many encounters between rival parties, or between the police and flag-waving hooligans.

The ground floor of the building was occupied by a laundry and general store which sold among other things, articles tacitly understood to be contraband. The shopkeeper also sold tea, from a boiling cauldron on a charcoal stove, to people standing on the road. It was reputed that while no 'hot' stuff was on display in the shop, deals for anything from a transistor radio to gold 'biscuits' could be negotiated while sipping a cup of tea. Friendly policemen also called occasionally; the tea was considered justly famous for its rich aroma and taste. And so was the proprietor, clad always in a clean, starched shirt and dhoti and stroking his moustache which would have done credit to a film actor in a mythological role. The place, lined with good teak cases and glass panels, looked prosperous.

Gopalan knew him, and therefore perhaps vicariously liked him, as the only man is town who had neither respect, nor awe, nor indeed any emotion for any political leader, whatever his party or creed. The whole day the man sat in his shop like a fat Chinese figurine, a faint smile on his lips, attentive to customers but not too friendly, contemplating the world as though he knew its secrets and in that knowledge found the key to his own safety and survival. Gopalan considered him slightly sinister and would have gladly shifted his office if only he could find cheaper premises.

The access to the party office was up a wooden staircase, so narrow and flimsy that no two men could stand on the same step at the same time without feeling uncomfortably jammed together. The entrance from the road was through a door between the laundry and the shop.

Upstairs was a large room filled with old benches and a smaller one which was the 'office'—with a table and chair and a typewriter in the corner. The walls were hung with pictures of leftist political leaders, including Lenin and a thickly bearded man who, according to the wayside vendor who had sold it to Gopalan, was Karl Marx. Prominently displayed were posters depicting various political highlights in the comparatively short history of the party. The overall effect was confusing but impressive. Today they did inspire a certain awe and confidence in the students who had gathered there along with a few party workers—all perched on available chairs and on window sills. Gopalan alone was standing, leaning against the table as though presiding over the proceedings.

'All things considered,' he was saying to his attentive

listeners,'you must look upon the strike as a success. The classes were disrupted and the college did not function that day, for all practical purposes. That was all that the strike was intended to do, and could do. And you must not look upon the arrival of the police as an interference or even a challenge.' Gopalan looked up at the ceiling. 'It is not known—and it is immaterial really—who summoned the police, but if you had been in this business as long as some of us here have been,' he looked around at his lieutenants with a smile, 'you will realize that khaki lends a certain dignity to such occasions.' Some of his listeners laughed and Gopalan nodded his head as though to underscore the point. 'Any kind of publicity strengthens the cause of political movements. Your struggle is futile only if you fail to draw public attention to it. And in this respect, I think you have succeeded quite spectacularly—yes, I repeat it, quite spectacularly.' He looked at Chandran encouragingly and himself led the applause that followed.

'Personally,' he continued, 'I think the decision of the authorities to close all educational institutions for a fortnight from now was a singular victory for my friend here. No action was taken when the demand was made in the original memorandum, but now the strike has forced their hands. That was its main purpose. The hartal and the demonstration will not in the least be affected by this belated move on the officials' part. But by far the most singular gain of the strike was the sympathy it aroused in the entire student community, and the decision of other college unions to join hands in this final showdown. All of us are pleased to see their representatives here today among our midst.'

(Actually, Gopalan thought, as some clapping of hands went on, that was a bonus. The hartal would be something to watch now!)

'Have you seen the posters calling for the hartal?' he asked the room in general, and paused while words of approval came from here and there. 'The student procession will start from the college at . . .' He looked enquiringly at Chandran.

'Ten o'clock ... the day after tomorrow,' Chandran replied.

'Are all your arrangements pakka?' Gopalan asked.

'Oh, yes. Of course, we can't predict now exactly how many will take part, but we expect quite a large number to turn up.'

'Yes, yes, the point is that the students must lead the procession. There will be enough people to make up the bulk,' Gopalan said, and looked significantly at his lieutenants.

'I suppose,' Chandran said hesitantly, 'we can expect some resistance from shopkeepers.'

'Oh, yes, that's inevitable,' Gopalan said. 'Here again, you must remember that it is the percentage that really matters. You cannot expect hundred per cent success. Some shopkeepers will have to be persuaded.'

'Only persuaded?'

Gopalan looked up at this interruption. He knew who had asked that. That Kesavan was all along harping about a peaceful demonstration. Always setting forth terms and conditions, a bad influence on Chandran.

'Yes,' Gopalan said, looking pointedly at Kesavan. 'Only persuasion. What else ? The police cannot object to your making any requests to shopkeepers, can they?... you are not intimidated by the police, are you?'

It was Chandran who answered the question. 'Why should we be ?'

There was a note of challenge in his tone, and Gopalan decided it wise to ignore it. 'Yes, that is the spirit ! Why should you be bothered about the police ? Refuse to be provoked by them, that is all... Ten o'clock then, shall we leave it at that ? The day after tomorrow.'

'One point,' a student from another college raised his hand. 'Why should we all meet in front of the Missionary College ?' Apparently he was not keen on surrendering all the initiative to an otherwise rival student body.

Chandran was the one who answered. 'We quite understand. We can choose some other place.' He thought for a moment and suggested a playground owned by the municipality in the centre of town.

Gopalan looked appreciatively at him. 'Good idea! You would then be able to organize things better. Are we all then agreed on that?'

On a general note of assent, the student leaders got up. They stood around for a while, not knowing what to do next, gazing idly around or at the pictures on the wall. Chandran shook hands with some of the people present, and then, nodding his farewell at Gopalan, walked out of the door and down the staircase. The other students followed him, one by one, shuffling about at the head of the stairs, and then going down in an orderly single file.

When they had all left, Gopalan came over to the window on the roadside and looked down. The students were gathered in a group on a side, while one or two were in front of the shop, apparently buying cigarettes. He watched them reflectively till they all began to walk down the road and presently disappeared from view.

He turned round, came back to the desk and sat on it, dangling his legs. He took a beedi from a side pocket of his kurta and lit it. He sent up a cloud of smoke to the bare electric bulb hanging down from the ceiling.

'I don't want any trouble till they reach the Collectorate,' he said, still looking at the electric bulb round which the smoke was slowly coiling like a luminous snake. 'After that, we'll see what happens.' He suddenly looked down at the faces turned expectantly towards him. 'I want you to be discreet. Very discreet. No one should connect us with it, or accuse us of fomenting trouble, is that clear to all? Remember, this is a students' struggle, and I want it to remain that way . . . all the way.'

'What if the students get—get out of hand?' someone asked.

'Nothing. That possibility is certainly there, and I want you to use your judgement. In a thing like this, no one can foresee every detail that might develop. Help them along, if you can do so without drawing attention to yourselves. In the front of the Collectorate, it will be a different matter. The crowd will be thick. Hold your hand back till then. I do not want this to have a political colouring just yet. I have my own reasons. The time for that will be later.'

His face relaxed, and he suddenly broke into a laugh. 'I wonder what that man Raghava Menon is up to at this moment,' he said as he stubbed out the beedi and flicked it expertly out through the window.

Raghava Menon listened with impatience to the dial tone coming from the instrument pressed to his ear. The high, piping note, jabbing his nerves agonizingly at spaced intervals as though in a newly-invented method of torture, seemed faintly diabolic and mocking. With his other hand. Menon clutched the cradle of the telephone, his knuckles standing out white out of the wads of flesh, squeezing the life out of it, coaxing it to respond to his own sense of urgency. Beep ... beep... it could have been an undecipherable message coming from outer space!

Menon banged the telephone back in its place with a grunt of despair. This whole town was run by nincompoops, he thought, as he went back to an easy chair by the side of the table. Where was the Collector gone at this crucial hour? Touring. Always touring. Burning up public money! It was time someone raised the point in the Assembly. No doubt that would stir up a big scandal. The Collectors, youngsters, most of them not long out of training institutions, trailing clouds of glory which were really anachronistic in independent India. What were they? Nothing but caretakers of a bureaucratic edifice left in ruins by the old sahibs of the British days! And the one who administered this district, Menon thought, was one of the worst. It was time he was shunted to some other town—or state.

Raghava Menon had tried in the past week, with all the influence he could muster, to get a ban order issued against processions and assemblies. That would strengthen the official position—and also the hand of the police. The people of this town respected officialdom, if not authority. They might dispute the need for a ban—but not its potency once it had been formally issued.

Oddly, the resources available to him had in the end turned out to be his undoing. The Collector had politely hinted that quite apart from his personal feelings or convictions, he had to go by the book. In a democratic country, could he honestly ban a purportedly peaceful procession? After all he did not draft the Constitution. It was people like Raghava Menon who were the architects of it. He knew fully well what political pressure was, but he did not know, no one really did, from which side it would come. And one had to be specially careful in dealing with students. In all probability they would create trouble. But speculation was one thing, facts quite another. He was not by any means ruling out the justification for a ban. He was only concerned with procedures. That was the only thing for people like him to go by. He needed time to think over, and possibly refer the matter to the higher authorities.

Stupid, strait-laced bureaucrat! Raghava Menon knew the kind. Never prepared to make a decision, never courageous enough to take responsiblility. What was happening to this country? And now that man was conveniently away on tour! Was that really necessary?

His daughter Nandini, all dressed up and smelling of talcum powder and sandalwood soap, breezed in and made straight for the telephone.

'Leave it alone,' Menon snapped. 'I'm expecting an

important call.'

'I just want to phone a friend. I wanted to ask her whether she is going to college tomorrow.'

'What college?' he asked. 'Don't you and your friends know it is closed?'

'Yes we do. It's officially closed. But we are all in the dark about what is going to happen. We have decided to see Father Joshe and ask him. There will be no classes but we'll be able to meet some professors. . . '

Menon's mouth was closed in tight line, and he did not reply. She hesitated, looked at him uncertainly, and said: 'Everything is in such confusion. I have overdue library books, and if possible I want to borrow some. I can't think of sitting at home for two weeks doing nothing.'

'Forget about library books. If you want I'll ring up Father Joshe later myself.'

'No, Daddy,' she was insistent. 'I must go to college tomorrow.'

'What do you mean, I must?' he asked angrily. 'I am telling you : stay at home.'

'But . . . please.'

He looked up sharply at her tone, and then became more adamant. 'There is no but to it. Don't go to college till this trouble is settled one way or another, do you hear ?'

'Yes, Daddy,' she said weakly and went out of the room.

He was incensed by her manner. What was worrying her? One never knew what these girls were up to these days. They were also getting undisciplined. They were a headache till one got them married and packed them off with their husbands. He had been somewhat indulgent with her. Given her more freedom than he had done in the case of his other children. 'Daddy' indeed! It made him wince now to hear her calling him 'Daddy' in that mincing tone. Stupid Anglo-Indian customs! That was the result of sending your children to those convents. You paid through your nose and they came back and called you 'Daddy'. They lolled in easy chairs, putting up their feet like boys, ate chocolates and listened to jazz music on the radio ... and they thought they were all civilized! There was indeed a case for doing away with English education in the country. Menon himself had pleaded for it from many a public platform in recent years. Not that he had anything against English, he had the highest respect for the language and the culture it represented. He himself would have liked to send his children to a vernacular medium school. But what was a parent to do if he wanted to give his children a decent education? He really had no choice. Not yet, anyway. The convents, when all was said and done, still maintained a reasonably high standard. Menon's detractors could say what they wanted, that he was not prepared to practise what he preached. When even Ministers were cadging for scholarships for their sons to go abroad, he could surely be forgiven for sending his own children to the only decently run schools and colleges in the country! His daughter could read Harold Robbins or even Henry Miller for all he cared, or listen to that cacophony they called pop music, but next time she called him 'Daddy' he was going to give her a good talking-to.

Menon got up and tried the telephone once again. This time it was not engaged but the ringing went on for some minutes before someone at the other end picked it up and said 'Hello'.

'Hello,' Menon said. (Why had they not yet invented a vernacular equivalent for that !—Menon wondered as he waited.)

'Yes, please ?' said a female voice.

'Is that the Collector's residence?'

'Yes.'

'Is he home ?'

'No...May I know who's calling ?'

'Raghava Menon.'

'Oh !' There was a pause. 'He's expected back today,

but I don't know when he will be back.'

'Could you ask him to ring me back as soon as he returns?'

'Yes, of course.'

Menon replaced the receiver without further ado. He always found it awkward to maintain a formal dialogue with women. Probably the Collector's wife knew very well why he had called. And to continue some pleasantries would have made him sound clumsy and false. He had no intention of sounding either way at the moment. A certain brusqueness, in fact, was called for. That would perhaps convey the sense of urgency better than words. Let the Collector realize that Menon was nearing the end of his patience.

His wife entered the room and stood by a side, looking at him a little anxiously. 'Nandini is in tears...' she said. 'What is the matter? Did you say something to her? I've noticed that she gets easily upset these days.'

Menon felt a female conspiracy closing in on him and he fought against it weakly. 'I told her not to use the telephone, that is all. I am trying to get in touch with the Collector—urgently.'

She went over to a bookshelf and rearranged some volumes there absent-mindedly. 'You didn't want her to go anywhere for a while,' he said fretfully. 'You yourself have complained about her coming home late...'

'Oh, it was not a complaint. I just mentioned it, that was all. That night she was with a friend, it seems. I was worried because you yourself had not returned, and Nandini had said nothing about going anywhere...'

'Friends! The girls have all kinds of friends these days,' he remarked cynically.

'Oh, this I checked! She made me . . .'

'She did, eh? Anyway, I told her not to go to college. I don't think it will be advisable. There might be some kind of trouble, you see. You never know what the boys will be up to.'

His wife glanced at him in alarm. 'Is there going to be trouble again?'

Menon looked away evasively. Any pre-knowledge of it, he feared, might imply some complicity on his part. Female logic was peculiar. 'The students are always up to some trouble these days. Day after tomorrow, I think, they want to take out a procession and stage a demonstration before the collectorate.'

She did not reply to this. Trouble of this nature was too frequent to merit comment. She personally had not been too pleased with Menon's interest in college affairs. Thank God, she did not have a college-going son at this moment.

'Is that why you wanted to speak to the Collector?'

'Yes. Prevention is better than cure, you know. If something could be done to avert it, all of us would have reason to be grateful.'

'Can the Collector stop it?'

Menon laughed. 'He can't stop it. The man can't stop anything, not even his own nervousness! . . . But I want him to issue a ban order and he is not available at his house. The police would have to just look on if there is no official ban.'

'The police?'

'Yes, police.' That word invariably frightened women! 'Why?'

'Why do they want to turn the police on the students?'

Menon felt his earlier irritation coming back. 'Why not the police? The boys have to be taught a lesson, or at least they should learn that they cannot fool around with this kind of nonsense. Otherwise there'll be no end to trouble like this.'

'Well, I was thinking. . .' she paused.

'Thinking what?'

'No, I was thinking how fortunate it is that we have no son in college now.'

'If we had one,' Menon said, 'I would have put him in his

place, have no doubt of it! You know what I think? The real culprits are the parents. There is no discipline at home. Where do you think the boys will learn it? In schools? Colleges? They are all so overcrowded and disorganized that the boys have no time to even learn their lessons.'

'Then what are the professors there for?'

'Ha, professors! It is all a big mess ... That's why I say, the parents should pay more attention to their children. If they did, the boys wouldn't be fraternizing today with the riff-raff.'

She looked at him uncertainly. 'Yes... And still... they are boys and the police...'

'Oh, you won't understand these things,' Menon exploded, his patience at an end. It had been a tiring day even without this pointless exchange! 'You are as bad as anyone else in this town. All soft where boys are concerned. You don't understand politics.'

Seeing his anger, she immediately became submissive. 'That is true, that is true... I don't understand politics.'

She paused, not too certain that her answer was satisfactory. But at that moment she was saved from making a further attempt by an interruption.

The telephone began to ring.

12

With a mechanical precision acquired from long experience, Inspector Rangaswamy's brain recorded the events of the day, not realizing then that many days and agonizing moments later, he would have to recall in correct sequence and detail everything he did on that day of the hartal, and give a reason for each.

But today, it was virtually like any other day for him, though the thought of the hartal, merely another of those routine things which made up a good part of a police officer's hours of conscious thought, was uppermost in his mind. He had left home early, gulping down his breakfast, grumbling to his wife about the uneven starching of his uniform, listening to the dull drone that his children made as they read their day's lessons in the spare room. Standing on the verandah, with the early morning sunlight slanting in through the trellised front, he had noticed the cobwebs on the electric light bracket and had pointed them out to his wife. In a small mirror below it, hanging from a nail driven at head level into the wall, he had studied his face critically as he adjusted his cap, and the man who stared back at him was known in the police force as honest and sincere, proud of his uniform in spite of occasional moods of disillusionment, a stickler for details and virtually incorruptible.

Rangaswamy smiled sadly at his reflection. Contrary to what the public might think, these were not rare qualities in the police force. Corrupt officers and men were there, of course, but their percentage was not alarming in comparison with other public service departments, if one took into consideration the temptations that a policeman was exposed to in his normal line of duty.

He came out of the house and briefly inspected his bicycle which the servant boy had cleaned and oiled, as he had been instructed to do every morning. Rangaswamy could easily have arranged for the jeep to pick him up, but he liked cycling. It was the only exercise he had time for nowadays. It relaxed his muscles and conditioned his mind to face the dreariness of a police officer's normal day : dealings with the dregs of society and exposure to human nature at its worst. One got immune to it in course of time, like hospital staff to disease, but still....

He was at the gate when his wife called out to him. He had a superstitious dread of such interruptions and he got off the bicycle irritably. She wanted some money for marketing, which he did not have, and one of his children, who had come running out to join his wife, apparently wanted a new notebook. He left the bicycle leaning against the gate-post and walked back to the house. It could well be that he was probably the poorest officer in the police force this morning, but there was no need to advertise the fact !

'Don't you realize it is the end of the month ? Can't you manage for a few more days?' he asked.

She started to speak, but knowing what she would say, he cut her short. 'Let me see by lunchtime,' he said, 'or by evening if you don't see me for lunch...Can't you borrow from someone ?' (With prices spiralling up, his meagre post-office savings were dwindling very fast.)

He pedalled at a steady pace through the morning traffic. Here and there a constable on duty at an intersection saluted him and he nodded with curt politeness. The bazaar area had not yet come fully to life, or was it an advance symptom of the hartal ? He knew shopkeepers: not necessarily an unpatriotic lot but greed was an uncompromising taskmaster. Unless there was real danger in the air, business would go on as usual.

Routine awaited him at the station, and he was almost in a cheerful mood, regretting now his irritation at his wife's legitimate request, when he got down from the bicycle and handed it to a constable standing at the gate. He acknowledged salutes as he briskly climbed the steps. The hartal might after all turn out to be nothing more than a nuisance. Politicians had a habit of blowing a lot of hot air around ! If all went well, the procession itself would not concern him much. Another detail had been assigned to that, and Rangaswamy personally would be involved only with any action at the Collectorate. The day before, he had properly briefed the riot squad. They might never be called out, but they had to be ready for any emergency. He had good, experienced men there, and the matter did not occupy his thoughts much. Perhaps, Rangaswamy smiled at the idea, he would be called upon to draw the fine line between sternness and 'excess'. He wished he could use the water hose as it was done in many other places. A very practical and effective technique. But not in this town—never! You could trust the municipal water supply to dry up into a trickle at crucial moments !

He knew vaguely of the proposed ban, but as yet no official communication had come to him. He had checked that the moment he entered. He knew from experience that a thing like this could sometimes change the whole aspect of the affair. It was resistance that developed and channelled force. He had seen cowering crowds change in a flash to fighting mobs. No one could say precisely what triggered off riots. The provocations were often evident and minor, but how the spark scaled the gap from the few initiators to a mass of otherwise normal, peace-loving citizens was a problem for psychologists. In college, Rangaswamy had been interested in subjects dealing with human behaviour. He had never imagined then that one day he would have to watch it in action through the fumes of a tear-gas shell!

Later in the day, he would most probably have to make a trip through the 'scenes of action' with senior officials. That would again be routine—bothersome but unavoidable. Rangaswamy smiled to himself. That would not require much tact or competence, sitting in a jeep and surveying the debris of a riot, if there indeed was some action going today. He hoped that no 'situation' would develop. He was not feeling in the least aggressive.

Gopalan was out of town, according to reports, and that was a feature he found vaguely disturbing. The man had been under surveillance for quite some time, that fat shopkeeper under the party office was a valuable contact. Rangaswamy had never shown himself anywhere near the place, as an officer's presence would rouse suspicion. Some constables on the beat frequented the place, and he knew, rather he imagined, that it must be a two-way deal. One had little choice in such matters. There was a price for everything and it was better to pay up without a grudge. He had a distaste for informers, but they were an essential evil in his line of work. Gopalan was a dangerous man, even deadly. Suave, slippery beyond belief, and unscrupulous. Just when one thought he was in the net, he emerged somewhere else, smiling and with an irreproachable alibi. If the students had any truck with him, Rangaswamy personally felt sorry for them. Gopalan would make them bite off more than they could chew. The Militant Socialist Party professed democratic methods, in spite of the contradiction in the name, but of late there had been quite a few unsolved cases of arson and violence which had set a lot of people speculating. The law really had a long arm. Even if it took some time, it often had the habit of closing in on the target in the long run.

Gopalan's absence was really suspicious. It was common knowledge that he had been ministering the 'students' struggle' for some time and Rangaswamy was fully aware of the meeting that had taken place in the party office. Then why was he away on a day like this ? Was there going to be something in which he did not care to be implicated even in a remote way ?

After a moment's reflection, Rangaswamy dismissed the idea. Gopalan did not have to leave town for that. Far more likely, he would be around, out of sight of course, but near enough to be in close touch with happenings and ready to make or mend plans if necessary. This could be a coincidence. Probably he would be saving his masterstrokes for the elections.

Rangaswamy pushed aside these speculations and turned back to some immediate things on the table. Routine again : papers to sign, charges to be drafted—but thank God, he did not have to attend court today. Or rather thank the Magistrate in fact—he had been very accommodating. Rangaswamy had little patience for those petty cases; such a waste of time and energy to bring some petty crooks to book! Unpleasant squabbles with the prosecutor and pointless apologies for police procedures! No system was one hundred per cent foolproof. After all, one was dealing with situations where the common denominator was human weakness. Those lawyers bungled a case and jumped at a chance to blame the police!

Rangaswamy settled back in the chair and sent a constable out for a cup of tea. The time was 10.30 a.m. The sun was bright outside and he could see part of the quadrangle from where he sat, the shadow of the tiled roof tracing a ragged line across the gravelled path. The benches on the verandah would be filling up and the station clerk, dipping his pen-holder in the crusted inkpots and cursing regulation stationery, would be kept busy writing dull and stale accounts of petty thefts and street brawls. Even crime was getting so predictable!

With nothing special to hold his interest here, his mind was going back to the morning and the exchange with his wife when the telephone suddenly came to life.

The lines on Rangaswamy's face hardened as he listened to the excited voice at the other end. His body straightened out from a slouch into stiff-backed attention. He replaced the receiver with a curt 'All right, we'll be there,' and stood up, ringing the bell on his desk sharply.

'Ask the driver to get the jeep ready,' he barked at the constable who came running in response to his summons. 'On the double!' He reeled off the names of six of the men in the station. 'Ask them to be ready in two minutes to come with me in the jeep.'

The constable made a skimpy salute and vanished.

Rangaswamy put on his cap and tightened his belt.

On the right side, against his lean hip, hung the revolver holster of heavy woven canvas. He patted it once, a decoration it was, more or less, meant for intimidation rather than offence.

When he came out, the jeep with the men was ready, waiting for him on the road.

He slid quickly into the front seat by the side of the driver and felt the vehicle jump forward as the gears engaged. He glanced at the driver in annoyance. As they rounded a corner he saw the rest of his men getting into a larger police van parked in front of the station.

He spoke above the drone of the engine. 'There seems to be trouble. . . in the big bazaar area. Nothing much from what I could make out on the phone. But it is off the approved route of the procession, which means, either a last-minute change of plans, or worse, and more likely, independent groups 'enforcing' the hartal. That kind of thing can be bad ... Right now, some shopkeeper is having a tussle with a crowd. Well,' he paused as the jeep swerved sharply to avoid a cart, 'we'll have a look and go on to the

Collectorate.'

There was no real need for anxiety, though he did feel a certain excitement as the jeep sped along. Some skirmishes of this nature were expected and other police contingents were patrolling the town.

The hartal, as far as he could make out, was only a partial success. But as the jeep entered the busier parts of the town, more and more shops were seen either closed or partially shuttered, and groups of people hung around uncertainly, waiting for developments. If there were incidents of intimidation or violence, the news would spread fast and crowds would throng the streets. They made things worse. They were the ones who stuck their necks out and got into the way of the police.

The crowd in front of the shop was not very big and the jeep honked its way in imperiously. People fell back instinctively and Rangaswamy had a first glimpse of the scene.

The glass panes were broken and pieces were strewn all over the pavement. He could see no further evidence of damage as he got down from the jeep. Where were the processions? He could make out from the attitude of the people who hung around that they were mere onlookers, curious but uninvolved. The proprietor himself was standing on the front of the shop and greeted the Inspector with folded hands.

'They are all gone!' that was the first thing he said. 'Look what they have done to my shop...'

'What happened?' Inspector Rangaswamy asked as his eyes took in the scene.

'They asked me to close the shop,' the man was nearly wailing, tears starting from his eyes as he recounted the events to authorities who could find him redress. 'They threatened to ruin the shop ... and pushed me about.' His hand went defensively to his throat.

Rangaswamy looked around. It was a hardware shop

Abhimanyu

and the assailants had obviously not lacked weapons.

'Were they students?'

'Yes, yes . . .' he broke off in the middle, thought for a moment and then added : 'Who knows? There were quite a few youngsters.'

'Were they part of a procession ?'

The man looked blank, then nodded uncertainly.

Involuntarily Rangaswamy's eyes turned back to the road. 'They went away shouting slogans,' a man in the crowd volunteered, waving his hand to indicate the direction they had taken. Then he addressed the proprietor of the shop and said for the benefit of all present, 'You should not have abused them.'

The proprietor's face blanched at this unsolicited comment. 'How dare you say I abused them! I did nothing of the sort. I only . . .'

Rangaswamy said, interrupting him without ceremony. 'We'll look into this later. You leave the things undisturbed— and I suggest you close the shop. You can give a statement at the station.'

The crowd broke into an agitated chatter as the jeep drove away. The proprietor turned angrily to the man who had crossed him a moment ago and started to abuse him at the top of his voice.

Two furlongs down, Rangaswamy saw black smoke billowing up from some point further ahead.

A bus had been set on fire, Rangaswamy saw, as his jeep approached the spot. Oil had spilt on the road and was spreading into a wide, glistening circle. Flames were shooting out from within, consuming and enveloping the seats, and as Rangaswamy watched, a tyre caught fire and burst with a loud hiss, and the vehicle sagged like a stricken animal. A few policemen wielding lathis were keeping the crowd at bay; no attempt was being made to put out the fire. Perhaps it was too late, or really not worth the trouble. As the jeep came nearer, a constable sprinted up to it and saluted him.

Rangaswamy stared silently ahead at the smouldering mass. Flames were licking the roof of the bus tentatively and another tyre exploded, making the crowd step back in panic.

'Someone says they threw a bomb at the bus,' the constable was saying. Rangaswamy looked at him in disbelief.

'What bomb?'

'I—I don't know. This is what a man said.'

Why should anyone throw a bomb at an empty bus? Rangaswamy pursed his lips. Onlookers always exaggerated things. Apparently the bus had been stopped and the passengers asked to clear out ... A can of petrol was all that was needed to set fire to the bus. Anyhow there was no point in wasting time here. There were people to look after that. He could see khaki uniforms among the crowd. His job lay elsewhere, and Rangaswamy decided that the sooner he got there the better...

The procession moved on, a steady stream of people flowing slowly down the street, hemmed in on both sides by tall, cliff-like buildings, gaining intensity as it proceeded. Kesavan, carried forward by the uncontrollable tide, strangely, felt secure all the same among boys he knew so well. Now and then he shifted his grip on the pole he held— a cloth banner with words in red. His hands felt wet and sticky. It must be the heat, he thought. He looked up at the banner as it arched back against the pressure of the wind, and the letters, not quite legible from his position, glowed brightly in the sun, undulating slightly like flames. He had no need to see the words to remember what they said: the banner proclaimed that the students were united and would fight to the finish.

What would be the finish? Kesavan wondered as he

Abhimanyu 221

walked along. He could see Chandran walking a little ahead, his fist clenched and held defiantly over his head, the muscles of his neck taut with the strain of shouting. Slogans came with an admirable facility to him. His voice quivered to the high pitch, loud and inspiring confidence; his zeal and excitement were really infectious. A hundred throats eagerly took up his cry, their faces shining, necks straining, eyes bright with the thrill of it all. Chandran, Kesavan felt, looked like a man in a trance, like the firewalkers he had seen as a little boy during temple festivities. Only, Chandran held a small megaphone and belonged very much to the present. He faced the crowd round now and then, his voice carried along in full blast, creating new eddies and currents of excitement which swept over the procession from its orderly head to the straggling tail. Chandran's red shirt flashed in the sun and Kesavan could see streams of sweat flowing down his face and dropping off the tip of his nose as he moved. He was a leader all right, a leader whom the boys could be proud of.

Chandran had kept his word. There had been no untoward incident, nothing to mar the peaceful nature of the demonstration. The policemen who walked along, watchful that the procession did not block up the traffic, resented the march in the sun perhaps but they showed no signs of it. Occasionally they exchanged jokes with the students. This was the way it should all be. The boys were brimming with excitement and they would spill a little of it on the wayside, pleading a little with shopkeepers who had not responded to the hartal call; well, even abusing a few who ignored the requests. There was no harm in that. The main body of the procession pressed on.

Kesavan felt the sweat running in rivulets down his back, warm except when it reached the base of his spine, where it seemed to touch him as though with a cold finger, sending pleasant vibrations along every nerve in his body. He did not feel tired in the least. He felt he could walk on and on like this for miles before he dropped. The chanting of the slogans, the rhythm of the march and the very presence of so many people thinking of the same thing had a certain hypnotic quality. Was that how people felt in temples and at religious gatherings? What funny notions were entering his head?

He wondered what Nandini would be doing at this moment. Would she be watching the procession from somewhere? It was most unlikely. Her father probably would not let her out of the house today. Kesavan had made one or two desperate attempts to contact her, but each time unfamiliar voices had answered the telephone and he had rung off without a word. She must have expected him to get in touch with her. She might even have waited anxiously. That was thoughtless of him. He should have devised a way and told her about it on the evening that they had spent in the temple. Anyhow, it was a nice feeling that someone like her would be waiting for him. He would be loyal to her for life.

He looked at the policemen walking along the side. Was there an almost imperceptible change in their attitude? They looked less friendly now, some of them even looked grim. Probably the sun was affecting them too. They were the ones who looked fagged out, their caps dark with sweat where they touched the skin of their brows. They seemed resentful now of the quick pace that the procession had been progressively taking. The sound of their boots could be heard distinctly on the hot macadam, alien and vaguely ominous against the swish and patter the students made as they marched along.

'Students unite!'
'We will never give up Parkinsonpet!'
'We are not afraid of police lathis and bullets!'

What was the provocation for that last one? The khaki figures looked harmless enough. Under the students' gaze, they now shifted their grips on their lathis self-consciously

Abhimanyu

trying to compose their faces at the same time into—into what? Kesavan wondered. Neutrality? Even friendliness? The lathis did not appear to him very intimidating. Kesavan looked at them with interest. Just harmless sticks! Held loosely, they seemed to symbolize neither power nor violence. He had never seen a lathi-charge. He had only heard about it or seen pictures in the newspapers. The policemen wielding the lathis always looked clumsy and slightly off balance! Why was that? And the victims in turn looked as though they were submitting to the blows under a trance. Perhaps they were too dazed or afraid to run. Still photographs of action had sometimes that effect of unreality. Even the lathis blurred into nothingness.

'You hardly feel it,' Gopalan had told them once. 'You will, of course, feel scared out of your wits till the first blow falls. That will be the only time when you feel even a small twinge of pain. Thereafter it is nothingness . . . only the white heat of excitement and a hatred for the oppressor. No fear, no pain . . .' He had looked at his own body, chuckling. 'I am speaking from experience . . . You feel the pain only later, when you are calm. Then you know what? You feel you have truly suffered for the cause and nothing else matters.'

All the same, Kesavan thought, at this moment he felt no great eagerness to find out! He looked at the policemen speculatively. They appeared preoccupied and inocuous. It was hard to imagine them in any kind of action, of turning upon the boys in fury. One of them now was actually smiling at a remark made by a student. The picture he presented was one of bored indulgence . . .

'We are there!' the shout came simultaneously from many throats and Kesavan suddenly became alert. He adjusted the pole in his hand and held the banner tightly stretched. Chandran in front turned round and walked backwards, raising his hands over his head and crossing them and uncrossing them as a signal for the procession to slacken its pace.

The stream of people, their forward movement suddenly arrested, began to spread sideways into a restless pool of black heads. Kesavan looked ahead and he could see beyond Chandran the gates of the Collectorate. The posters put up the night before on the pillars and walls were now in bad shape. Some of them had been peeled off and others hung down in tatters. Only those at some height had been left intact. So the police had been active, Kesavan thought. Or was it the Collectorate sepoys? A wall of khaki uniforms hid the gate, and there was a jeep and a police van parked on a side; the officer in charge, he quickly recognized as Rangaswamy.

There was an air of suspense, a sudden stillness. The boys looked at the police posse and Chandran.

'What are we waiting for?' a voice at the back enquired impatiently.

Chandran raised his hand again and watched Inspector Rangaswamy approach. The officer did not seem in the least ruffled. His steps were firm and his face was stern. There was a faint flutter of defiance from the crowd—some desultory slogan-shouting—but the Inspector ignored it and came near and stopped, facing the people.

'You boys had better go home now—quietly,' he said, addressing Chandran. 'The Collector has issued a ban order. Section 144 is in force as from 12 a.m.' He looked briefly at his wrist-watch. 'That means it had been in force from exactly one hour and thirty-seven minutes.' He smiled at the crowd grimly. 'You people have had your fun. Now go home.'

'We have not come here to go home,' Chandran said. 'We want to record our protest . . .'

'That is all right,' the Inspector waved his hand vaguely about. 'You have done it.'

'We have a memorandum to submit. . . '

'Fine. You can hand it over to me.' Rangaswamy held

out his hand. 'After that, I advise you to disband the procession.'

There was a clamour from the crowd and Chandran turned round and shouted an admonition at them. When the noise petered out into a murmur, he again spoke to the Inspector.

'This is a peaceful demonstration. We want to see the Collector.'

The Inspector laughed. He remembered the burning bus. 'I don't think you can see him now. He is busy.'

'We won't budge from here unless we speak to him.'

Inspector Rangaswamy hesitated for a moment. 'All right. I shall tell the Collector that you would like him to address you. I cannot promise anything.'

'By all means! I don't see why not.'

They were again interrupted by shouting from the back of the crowd. Chandran looked annoyed. He waved his hand frantically but this time the clamour did not subside. The crowd was pressing forward and the banner was tattered. Chandran opened his mouth, but no one could hear the words that issued from it.

The crowd, in spite of the best efforts of those in front to hold their ground, inched forward. Kesavan felt elbows and hands pressing against him with a tremendous weight from behind and found himself moving, too confused to notice which way he was going. He was now very close to Chandran and saw the expression on his face. It was a mixture of fury and bafflement.

The Inspector quickly moved a few steps backwards. Oddly, his voice carried over the din made by the people. 'I give you two minutes to disband and leave this place peacefully. Otherwise I'll take your leaders into custody for defying the ban.' He felt instinctively that the point of reasoning had passed. He could interpret the changing mood of the crowd. Strangely, he thought of a bull, pawing the ground, nostrils flared, head lowered . . . Rangaswamy kept his eyes on the people in front.

There was a roar from the back and as though at a cue the crowd surged forward, sweeping Kesavan and Chandran along. The banner swerved wildly like a branch caught in a torrent, fluttered for a moment uncertainly over the heads, and then disappeared from view.

Suddenly there was a cordon of steel-helmeted policemen blocking the path. Kesavan felt himself pressed against one of them, chest to chest, ridiculously close, and he could distinctly see the beads of sweat on the other man's face, his eyes staring into his. He struggled weakly, trying to break free from the stifling pressure all round. The shouts and exclamations were deafening.

'Keep back,' Inspector Rangaswamy's voice came again, over the noise of the crowd. 'this is the last warning. We'll now use force!'

The people still pressed forward.

Then it came. Lathis! Lathis! Kesavan said to himself as he heard cracking sounds from all around him.

This was it! He had a quick glimpse of Chandran grappling with a policeman, both of them holding on desperately to a lathi, both pushing against each other violently. A boy near Kesavan howled and a sharp elbow hit him agonizingly in his ribs, knocking him down. He sensed, rather than saw, things flying over his head, and from somewhere heard the tinkle of falling glass. Inspector Rangaswamy was coming at a trot towards Chandran and Kesavan saw a soda bottle land and splinter into fragments in front of him. There were other sounds, like small explosions, and the air was filled with an acrid smoke that stung his eyes and made the tears flow, blinding him.

Desperately he fought through the haze. He had no aim or direction, just an urgent need to get away from the melee, and he groped and tore at the bodies blocking his way. Suddenly, he realized that he was being pressed past the gates of the Collectorate. The crowd had been gaining ground. The gate swerved forward and back, as though it had a life of its own and had caught the excitement in the air, as people fought against it and spilled into the compound. The pressure behind him suddenly eased and Kesavan found himself inside the gate.

Inspector Rangaswamy, his cap missing and a trickle of blood on his face, had a firm hold on Chandran. The boy clung to his adversary, gripping his uniform and flailing his free hand and kicking wildly. Two constables were near, trying to help the Inspector but apparently not knowing how, and one of them had a lathi raised in hand and would have swung it if a chance came. The other was making a vain attempt to hold on to Chandran's legs. Kesavan watched in fascination. The struggle would be over soon. It would only be a matter of minutes. The tears still partially blinded him, but at that moment there was only one thought in his mind: Chandran was helpless and at the mercy of the police! Kesavan suddenly broke away from the crowd and ran towards his friend.

In that final moment of clarity, he saw Chandran's hand fumbling at the Inspector's waist, closing in on the holster. With a loud curse, Rangaswamy relaxed his hold on the boy and gripped the hand at his waist. Kesavan saw the two hands, fighting each other as though they had a will of their own, and then the dull, black shine of the revolver in the sun.

A sharp report rent the air. He stopped in his stride, feeling as if a gaint fist clutched him from the front, crushing his chest, making him gasp and sputter. The scene before him began to blur, and through a heavy mist closing fast over him, he saw Rangaswamy and Chandran, their hands still loosely on each other, looking towards him—and their eyes were dilated with surprise and horror.

'It is the first blow that hurts,' Kesavan's mind clamoured within, an unrecognizable and strangely impersonal voice, breaking into a sob. 'Thereafter nothing matters...nothing

The voice suddenly rose into a roar, a chant from a thousand throats... Then it receded, like a wave that had spent its force—and it became altogether silent.

Epilogue

THE meeting was an impressive one, solemn, even orderly, Ramdas thought, reporting the event for the *Motherland*. The town hall was packed to capacity and there were crowds at the doors and on the verandahs; some were also perched precariously on the compound walls outside.

The dais was not well lit. The hall, a dilapidated one owned by the municipality, could boast of history and tradition but not of many modern amenities. When the sun was still touching the rooftops of the buildings across the road, inside it was already dark; the electric bulb over the dais, its shade brown with dust and broken, could do little more than drive the darkness into the corners—a temporary truce! Once or twice, when the breeze blew in the light flickered and the people looked at it apprehensively. The occasion not being one of celebration or festivities, no one apparently had thought of additional illumination for the stage.

It was brighter where the audience sat—there were more lights and the fixtures were permanent, as the municipal authorities probably thought that the stage was the responsibility of the people who hired the hall, while the rest of the space with its rows of chairs and benches were part of the contract and therefore its concern. Ramdas looked around with a faint smile of irony. Perhaps it was poetic justice, he thought, that the people assembled here should have been given a better chance to look at not what was going on at the stage but at themselves.

Personally, he was glad that the plan for a funeral procession had been given up. The Collector was hesitant to give it official sanction, and he was saved from having to make a decision by the attitude of the parents. The boy's father, it seemed, had taken a firm stand against it. The police had released the boy early and the cremation was held the next day. To the best of his knowledge, no newspaperman had attended it in his official capacity. The morning editions carried the news item in bold print but tucked away in a corner of the front page. And this again was understood to be in deference to the parents' wishes.

On the dais, as far as he could see, sat the Collector, the Police Commissioner, Raghava Menon and some other political leaders. He mentally made a note that before the meeting was over he should get their names right. In particular, he failed to identify the man who was sitting next to the Collector; could that be the father? Ramdas turned to a man sitting on his left and asked.

'Yes, yes, that's him. The boy's father, poor man. His name is Govindan Nair, I think.'

Ramdas made a note of the name in his book. In the hurry and scurry, he might forget to check that, or fail to mention him altogether in the report. He looked at the man again attentively. His face was in shadow. He sat leaning back in the chair, his hands crossed over his body, chin pressed against his chest. Ramdas felt somehow glad that he could not see the man's face any clearer. He felt no curiosity about the expression on the face of the bereaved.

Suddenly he remembered the Principal. Where was he? Not on the dais and as far as he could see, not in the audience either. Later, he should check on that also, Ramdas decided. Had they forgotten to invite Father Joshe? Or had he refused to attend?

Abhimanyu

One more thing he noticed before the proceedings absorbed his full attention. For obvious reasons, except for the Commissioner, there was not a single policeman in sight.

The Collector stood up and at his request the audience rose with him, standing silent for two minutes—this concession to the dead, ending, as it always did, with a sudden burst of noise, chairs scraping on the floor as people resumed their seats. One must cut these two-minute silences out of all functions, Ramdas thought. They served no purpose, whatever solemnity was built up was usually lost in the scramble for seats that followed. It was an anticlimax—the eagerness to regain the small comfort people had given up a moment ago in honour of the dead! Better make them sit in silence—that was, if you did want silence.

He paid scant attention to the speeches. Only his hands wrote in the book mechanically, unthinkingly, unfeelingly, he would have said. This cliche-ridden sympathy for the dead always struck him as insincere and vulgar. The dead were dead and gone. Only that man there, sitting still with his head bent, felt any genuine or lasting sense of loss. What did those other people want? They were not here to weep, Ramdas was sure of that. In another fifteen minutes, or half an hour, they would forget the whole thing, at least the sensations and the emotions. Later, much later, they would perhaps recall the events in odd moments, gratified at their small role in the making of history, and gropingly reconstruct the past in bits and pieces. They would talk of the crowds, of the speeches and of that man sitting there ...Oh, yes, that would be an image which would stay with them for a long time. It was always hard to forget those whom one had injured. The town's conscience, if it had one, would flutter for a while, exonerating itself slowly of guilt, real or imagined, with each faint convulsion.

There was short lull and Ramdas looked down at his

shorthand notes. Words. Words. Words. Empty, meaningless, hackneyed... why, he could have written the speeches sitting in his chair in the office! There was no real need to sweat it out in this airless place, stuffy with the breath of a thousand people. He could have made an almost accurate guess of what the men on the dais were going to say. 'An irreparable loss... 'My heartfelt sympathies to the parents and to the whole student community ... a horrible accident ... a lesson for us . . .

Ramdas could have laughed at the fatuity of it all. A lesson for whom, he wanted to shout back. For you? For this town? For the country? It was preposterous!

What a costly way to learn a lesson!

The last man to speak was the father. As he was helped to his feet, Ramdas saw the man looking up at the others in helplessness, defensively, holding out his hands as though in supplication or to ward off a blow. There was a sudden hush among the audience. This part of it was at least genuine, Ramdas reflected cynically. People were always subdued at the sight of sorrow. They watched in silence as the man, helped by others, came to the front of the platform and stood near the microphone. He looked now all the more frightened, ready to collapse at the first sign of consent from those august men sitting at the table behind him. He looked round distractedly; he seemed to struggle for words, looking with distrust at the mike—and the people next to Ramdas strained forward to catch his words.

But those were not words that came, grotesquely distorted and magnified by the loudspeakers, but a low wail— or so it sounded to Ramdas—interspersed with grunts and incoherent exclamations. With difficulty Ramdas could make out what the man was trying to say, almost imagining his words or lip-reading.

'There is ... nothing ... for me to say ... I am sorry ... '

They helped him back to his seat. Somebody recited a

prayer in falsetto tones. Then Ramdas wrote viciously at the end of his shorthand notes in deeply etched longhand: end of show.

He came out quickly on the verandah before the meeting began to disperse. There was no longer anyone perched on the walls or gathered at the gates. But he noticed a small group on one side—about ten boys, obviously students. A tall dark youngster was in their middle, and the face with its prominent nose and the thatch of close-cropped hair was faintly familiar.

On an impulse—a quirk of character that had made Ramdas a successful reporter—he walked towards them.

'Are you students?' he asked.

They looked at him coldly, but said nothing.

Ramdas took out his notebook and pencil. 'Would you care to make a statement? You must be friends of the—' He waved his hand vaguely towards the slowly emptying hall. It seemed to him that that was when it struck the tall boy that Ramdas was a newspaperman.

The boy took a step forward and bent close. 'Yes, we have a statement.' He spoke in a very flat, strangely sinister voice. He turned to another boy and jerked his head: 'Show him!'

The one who was addressed hesitated, and then came forward. There was something in his hand, wrapped loosely in a bath towel. He lifted a corner of it gingerly and Ramdas had a brief glimpse of a dark packet, the size of a large melon.

'We had a present here for the condolence committee...' the tall one said. (Quite irrelevantly, Ramdas noticed that his eyes were very red.) 'But...' the boy went on, 'his father was there, so we couldn't deliver it.'

His next words came sharply, chokingly through clenched teeth: 'You go and write that in your bloody paper, friend! Tell them they've seen only the beginning of it!'

In two minutes, the boys had mixed with the crowd and vanished from view. Ramdas slowly replaced the notebook and pencil in his pocket. That thing had shaken him up a bit. He had a feeling that it was a present that the committee would not have appreciated.

Or was this all a bluff? Boys had a taste for melodrama. This whole matter was a terribly stupid accident, of course. This was an ordinary town and everything would be forgotten and it would soon relapse into its state of ennui . . .

Or would it?

When Ramdas stepped out on the road, the breeze suddenly felt chilly.

That was when he realized that his shirt was soaked in sweat.